RELEASE

KAREN MOORE

BLOODHOUND
BOOKS

*To everyone who supported me through lockdown in the writing
of this book.*

CHAPTER ONE

Shielding her eyes against the dazzling sunlight, Hanna shivered as she stepped out into the afternoon heat. Maybe it was the sharp contrast in temperature after the coolness of the cottage. Or was there another reason? Something was bothering her, an uneasy feeling in the pit of her stomach she'd had all day. It was as if the nightmares of the past were lurking in the shadows, threatening to return.

Trying to ignore it, she carried the tray of marinated chicken pieces over to the barbecue where Rhys was busy poking the glowing coals. His tanned face crinkled into a smile.

"Nearly ready now. Only a few more minutes. I'm ravenous. Don't know about you?" Rhys almost had to shout to make himself heard above Eva's shrieks as she tore around the garden after Bryn, his new squeaky doggy toy clamped between his jaws.

Hanna forced a smile. "Me, too."

"How about an aperitif while we wait?"

She nodded and flopped onto a garden lounger. "That'd be great, just what I need."

Rhys wiped the beads of sweat off his forehead with the

back of his arm. "Fine. Won't be a minute…" he said, already making for the back door into the kitchen.

Hanna sat back with a sigh. Cosmo, their adopted cat, stretched out lazily on the patio, basking in the sun, purring contentedly. The heady scent of sweet honeysuckle wafted through the air. The garden was a blaze of colour: swathes of pink and purple mallow, dainty red fuchsias, spectacular blue hydrangeas, giant yellow daisies, and delicate peach roses. *Amazing how they manage to bloom with so little attention*, she thought. There was even a fig tree, although she doubted it would bear fruit in the Welsh climate. The fine weather wouldn't last long.

The warm sun made her drowsy and she was almost nodding off when she heard the chink of ice against glass. Rhys set two tall drinks down on the table, together with a bowl of olives. He collapsed onto the lounger next to her.

"I thought you might like one of these," he said, handing her a glass filled with a sparkling dark-coloured liquid, a twist of blood orange clinging to its rim.

She took a sip, savouring the familiar bittersweet orange flavour that immediately conjured up memories of Sicily. Memories more bitter than sweet. A shudder ran through her as if a dark cloud had passed over the sun. Shrugging it off, she said, "Orange vermouth, my favourite! Wherever did you find it?"

Rhys grinned as he reached for his drink, studying her over the top of his glass. "I saw it the other day in a farm shop and remembered you telling me how much you used to like it."

"It's wonderful, really refreshing. The perfect summer drink," said Hanna, reaching for an olive.

Rhys downed half his drink in one gulp. "Mmm, not bad. I might have to have another one."

Hanna laughed. "You're supposed to sip it slowly and relish its tangy aroma."

"You sound like an advert! No wonder you're in marketing!"

"You'd better get a move on with that chicken. Eva'll be famished after all that running around."

"OK, boss, anything you say." Rhys finished his drink, returned to the barbecue, and started to load the chicken onto the rack.

Hanna took another sip and scanned the garden again. Eva was still charging around after Bryn in a game of hide-and-seek that he seemed to be winning. Peals of laughter and high-pitched squeals from the squeaky toy floated on the air. *Just as well we've no immediate neighbours to disturb*, she thought. Rhys busied himself at the barbecue, deftly wielding a pair of tongs, humming softly to himself.

So much had happened since Sicily and her daughter's kidnapping two years earlier. By some miracle Eva had emerged remarkably unscathed, and as her fifth birthday approached, she was growing into a chirpy and inquisitive little girl. She seemed happy in their new home, an old stone cottage in the little village of Abergarron, slightly set back from the North Wales coast, and had settled in well at the school she had been attending for the past few months.

But for Hanna it hadn't been so easy, and she still bore the scars of her Sicilian husband's betrayal and deceit. What hurt the most was the apparent ease with which he had shunned both his wife and daughter in favour of the noxious family business. But at least that was all behind her now, and Luciano was paying the price: a fourteen-year jail sentence in Palermo's Pagliarelli maximum-security prison.

Trying to dismiss her feeling of foreboding, Hanna reminded herself she had much to be thankful for. Eva no longer asked about Luciano and her Sicilian grandparents, and had accepted Rhys without too many questions. Hanna's own relationship with Rhys was warm and loving, a bond that had developed naturally without any great effort on either part.

"OK, folks, grub up!" came a shout from across the garden, startling Hanna from her reverie.

"Oh, heck, I've not set the table!" she cried, jumping up.

"No rush, I'll give you a hand," said Rhys, coming towards her, heading for the kitchen.

Raising her voice, Hanna yelled, "Eva, food's ready! Stop fooling around with Bryn and come and get something to eat!"

A muffled cry of "Coming!" could be heard from behind the fuchsia hedge and a tousled and breathless Eva appeared, grinning, her face smudged with dirt. *"Eccomi!"*

Hanna frowned. Eva rarely resorted to Italian these days, but some words and phrases still came out naturally in that language. The same thing happened to her from time to time. She couldn't very well criticise her daughter for something that she too was guilty of. Instead, Eva's comical appearance made her chuckle.

"Go and wash your face and hands first. You look a right mess!"

"OK," said Eva grudgingly, dragging her feet towards the back door.

"Hey, watch where you're going!" Rhys cried, jerking sideways to avoid her as he emerged from the kitchen clutching glasses and a bottle of chilled white wine.

Eva giggled and ran off to the bathroom.

Hanna followed Eva into the cottage, quickly collecting cutlery and plates, the bowl of mixed salad she'd prepared earlier, and a fresh *ciabatta* bought from the local deli. Loading everything onto a tray, she stepped out into the garden again just as her mobile phone started to ring. Rhys rushed over and took the tray from her. Hanna fished the phone out of the pocket of her shorts and looked at the screen.

"It's your sister," she said before responding.

"Hanna, it's me, Ceri."

"Hi, what's up? Is everything OK?"

"Something's happened. I thought you should know straight away..." Ceri's voice trailed off.

Hanna was worried by her friend's serious tone. "What is it? Are you and Sergio okay?"

"Yes, we're fine. It's not about us. I don't quite know how to tell you this... It's Luciano. He's... err... he's been released from prison."

CHAPTER TWO

"Released? But… but… how's that possible?" Hanna sank into the nearest chair.

The day suddenly darkened, the sun disappearing behind a cloud. A chill spread through her body, as if the blood flowing through her veins was turning to ice.

"Sergio heard about it from one of his sources. That's all we know at the moment. We don't have any more details."

Hanna felt dizzy, her head pounding as she tried to take in the devastating news.

"I just don't believe it. Christ, he's only served, what, not even a couple of years of a fourteen-year sentence. What could have happened to quash that? Surely it must be a mistake?"

"Probably some technicality drummed up by his lawyer. It all seems to have been done on the quiet. Sergio's doing some digging as his newspaper's interested, but he's not hopeful. No one seems to know anything much. Even Sergio's dad – and he's in the police – has only just heard."

"Are you sure he's been released for good? It's not a temporary reprieve of some sort?"

"The informant reckons it's permanent."

Hanna felt goosebumps prick on her arms. "This has come as a hell of a shock. I wasn't expecting him to get out for years, even if he didn't serve his full term. I thought Eva and I were safe, but now, who knows? And great timing, too, what with your wedding coming up..."

"Hope it won't change your mind about coming over," said Ceri hesitantly.

"No, no, it'll be fine. Once I get my head around it."

"Well, see how you feel. I wouldn't want anything else to happen. You and Eva have both been through enough already."

"If you hear there's any possible threat..."

"I'll let you know straight away if there's any further news. Try not to worry too much. I'll call again in a day or so, or sooner if there's anything urgent. Take care, and give our love to Rhys and Eva."

"Will do. Love to Sergio too. Speak soon. *Ciao.*"

Hanna ended the call, her mind in a whirl. How could Luciano have been set free with all the overwhelming evidence against him? God knows what lengths his family lawyer and associates had gone to in order to secure his release. Probably pulled strings in high places, called in a favour or two, or brought pressure – or even blackmail – to bear on those with influence. She was aware of Rhys hovering close by, his face drawn into a deep frown, his gaze an unspoken question.

"It had to happen one day," he said gently, leaning down and wrapping his arms around her.

"Yes, but I never imagined it would be so soon." She rested her head briefly on his shoulder, then suddenly pushed him away, hunching over as she struggled for air, on the verge of a panic attack.

"Are you OK?" asked Rhys in concern, bending over her as she wheezed and tried to catch her breath.

"I'll be f...f...fine. Just give me a minute..."

"Try to take deep breaths."

She followed his advice. As she gradually calmed down, her breathing returned to normal.

"Feeling better?"

Hanna nodded.

"Try not to worry. It'll be fine, you'll see. After all, you've not heard from Luciano or his family one way or another since he went inside," Rhys pointed out reasonably. "There's nothing to say that things will change now, or that you've any reason to fear…"

She looked at him, a flicker of anger in her eyes. "But his father and brother were also sentenced, remember? Pretty difficult for any of them to act from inside prison. Now Luciano's free, he could well try to get Eva back. I always thought it was strange that he gave her up so easily."

"But didn't he agree to leave you alone as long as you didn't grass on him to the authorities?"

"Yes, but he doesn't play things by the rules. And the fact he was arrested so soon after Eva's release might have made him suspect that I had something to do with it. He might come after me wanting revenge."

"Really? Isn't that pretty unlikely now, in the circumstances?"

Hanna sighed. "Rhys, anything is possible with Luciano." As she said the words, she realised yet again how little she had known of Luciano's true character during their time together. So many sides, so many personalities: exciting lover, caring family man, and at the same time a heartless and hard-nosed criminal, married to his family's business interests.

Rhys took hold of both her hands, fixing her with his steady gaze. "You and Eva have a new life here, far away from Sicily, with me to protect you. You should both be safe enough now."

"Yes, you're right," said Hanna with a faint smile, more to

appease him than out of any real conviction. After all, she remembered only too well that it was here in North Wales that Eva had been kidnapped by one of Luciano's rivals, trying to muscle in on her husband's lucrative illegal business interests back in Sicily.

If it had happened once, it could happen again.

The news had done little to dent Rhys' hunger. He tucked into the barbecued chicken with gusto, as did Eva, having worked up an appetite running around the garden after Bryn. Hanna struggled to keep pace, chewing mechanically, the food like soggy cardboard in her mouth. She soon gave up, resorting to wine which slipped down much more easily. Much too easily.

The sun had reappeared, bathing the garden in warmth. Rhys was entertaining Eva with his jokes, resulting in peals of childish laughter alternating with groans. Hanna made an effort to join in. She could feel Rhys' eyes on her from time to time.

"Penny for them?" asked Rhys, interrupting her thoughts.

"Sorry," she mumbled. "I was miles away."

Rhys gave her a sympathetic look. "I know. Have you finished? Can I start clearing the plates?"

Hanna pushed her plate of half-eaten food towards him. "My appetite seems to have disappeared."

"Not really surprising after hearing that. More wine?"

She nodded and he refilled her glass. As she went to take a sip, she noticed Eva slip a chicken thigh off her plate, clearly intended for Bryn waiting patiently under the table.

"Stop that, Eva, please!" she said, more sharply than she'd intended. "Chicken bones are bad for him."

A wounded expression flitted across Eva's face. "But you give him bones from the butcher..."

"That's different. He can have raw bones but not cooked ones."

Eva looked puzzled but Hanna's usual patience had deserted her, and she couldn't be bothered to explain. She stood up and started to help Rhys gather the dishes. Eva sat back in her chair and folded her arms tightly across her chest, her bottom lip protruding. Bryn whined at her side, no doubt wondering where his promised chicken thigh had disappeared to.

"Never mind!" said Rhys. "Why don't you give him one of his favourite chicken chews instead? Then we can all go down to the beach for a walk."

Eva's face lit up and she scrambled down from the chair and rushed off into the kitchen, returning with a chew clasped triumphantly in one hand. Bryn went berserk, running around her in circles, jumping up, trying to snatch it from her grasp. Eva giggled and ran away, making it into a game. Hanna laughed at their antics, cross with herself that she'd been so offhand with her little girl.

Rhys finished clearing the table. "C'mon, gang, let's get going before the sun goes in," he said, rattling his car keys.

Hanna was glad of the distraction; on the other hand, she needed some time to herself to come to terms with the situation. Rhys had never met Luciano, and would never be able to understand how cold and calculating the man was. Ruthless, and capable of anything he set his mind on. And distance was no barrier.

CHAPTER THREE

Rays of sunlight streamed through the bedroom curtains. Hanna lay in bed, watching them sway gently in the light breeze coming through the open window. By her side, Rhys snored softly, his back towards her. She glanced at the clock on the bedside table: 6.53. She might as well get up; there'd be no more sleep for her. Not that she'd managed to get much. Try as she might, she hadn't been able to shake off the thought that Luciano might come back into their lives to seek revenge.

A sudden crash from Eva's room startled her. She jumped out of bed and rushed across the landing to investigate, only to find her daughter still tucked up in bed. A guilty-looking Cosmo stood on the windowsill, looking down at the lamp he'd knocked over.

"What was that noise?" Eva turned over, rubbing her eyes sleepily.

"It's only Cosmo up to his usual tricks," Hanna replied, picking up the lamp and returning it to its place on the windowsill.

Cosmo leapt onto the bed, nuzzling Eva for a cuddle. The bedroom door creaked open a notch and Bryn appeared, wagging his tail frantically, not wanting to be left out if there were cuddles to be had. The little bed groaned as both animals vied for the youngster's attention. Eva sat up, squealing in delight as Bryn smothered her face in sloppy kisses, while Cosmo waltzed across the pillow and settled across her shoulders.

Rhys popped his head round the door. "The noise woke me up. Is everything OK?"

"Everything's just fine." Hanna smiled. Life was good. She wouldn't let Luciano do anything to jeopardise their happiness.

Feeling tired after her restless night, Hanna dragged herself into the kitchen, closely followed by Eva and the two animals. It was Eva's job to feed them, a task she took seriously, although Hanna had to keep an eye on her to make sure she didn't overdo it. She watched her daughter take two packets of dry pet food out of the kitchen cupboard and fill their respective bowls to the brim.

"Eva, how many times must I tell you? That's way too much. You'll make them so fat they won't be able to move," she said patiently.

Eva giggled. "OK, sorry, I keep forgetting." She emptied half the contents back into the packets and laid the bowls on the slate floor. Both animals began to devour the food.

Hanna smiled. "You can give me a hand setting the table if you want."

Eva groaned slightly. Hanna handed her a tub of Greek yoghurt, a packet of granola, and a bowl of fruit. "You'll need bowls and cutlery, too. There's a tray in the corner to put everything on."

Hanna watched as her daughter carefully balanced the items on the tray, her face screwed up in concentration. She carried everything over to the table, weaving precariously around the pets who were still noisily tucking into their breakfast.

She was a good kid; no real problems at home or at school. The kidnapping hadn't left any lasting effect on her, just that spell of bad dreams. That had passed, thank God, and now she was just like any normal child of her age. Perhaps a little precocious at times, but nothing they couldn't handle. And Eva adored Rhys as if he were her own father.

Still deep in thought, Hanna went about her morning routine as if on autopilot, making coffee and popping some croissants in the oven. She took the coffee pot and two mugs over to the table, returning for the butter dish and a pot of homemade apricot jam. Rhys appeared in a dressing gown just as she was about to call him, his hair still wet and tousled from the shower, his face flushed and glowing.

"Great timing," he grinned, taking a seat at the table next to Eva who was already helping herself to a generous portion of granola.

"What have I just told you?" said Hanna. "Don't fill bowls to the brim. You'll never eat all that."

"But I will 'cos I'm hungry," complained Eva.

"You won't have room for croissants and jam afterwards."

"OK, OK," said Eva reluctantly, poised to empty half the bowl back into the packet.

"Here, give me that," said Rhys, pouring it into a spare bowl instead. "Share a banana with me?"

Eva nodded and smiled.

I'm always the baddy telling her off, Hanna thought, *while Rhys always gets to play the good guy.*

After breakfast, they all piled into Hanna's Citroën Cactus, Bryn included, barking excitedly, for the short journey across to Anglesey.

It was late July and the first week of the school holidays. Keeping Eva amused during the long break was going to be challenging. Rhys had arranged to have the week off work so they could spend some time together. Today was the first of their planned days out, a trip to Puffin Island that Eva had been clamouring for, ever since she'd learnt at school that the puffins had returned, if only for the breeding season. That was nearly over now, and Rhys had checked the likelihood of seeing them before booking the tickets.

What a perfect day for our trip, thought Hanna, relaxing in the passenger seat as Rhys drove off. It was already warm, with a light breeze and a few wispy clouds in an otherwise flawless sky.

In the back of the car, Eva chattered away merrily to Bryn who was lapping up the attention. Rhys glanced over at Hanna and grinned, taking his hand momentarily off the steering wheel to squeeze hers. She grinned back, and they drove on in companionable silence apart from the incessant monologue and occasional bark from the back seat.

The traffic on the A55 was light as they'd managed to miss the rush hour, such as it ever was, although the road could get busy with ferry traffic at times. The next ferry for Ireland wasn't due to depart from Holyhead until the afternoon. As they crossed the Menai Straits, Hanna gazed in awe at the spectacular view. On a fine day like today, it reminded her of Sicily: yachts bobbing on the shimmering water against an azure sky and verdant coastline, the lofty peaks of Snowdonia towering in the distance away to the east. Her thoughts turned momentarily to Luciano again, but she tried to push him to the back of her mind, determined not to let him spoil their day.

"You know, before I came to live here, I never imagined that Wales could be so beautiful," she mused.

Rhys glanced at her and gave a wry smile. "Why do you think I've never left?"

"I really can't blame you on a day like today. Mind you, it's not so beautiful when it's pouring with rain and blowing a gale and you can't see anything beyond your own nose."

"Bad weather just adds to its mystery and drama, and makes you appreciate the fine weather even more."

She punched him playfully in the ribs. "You've always got an answer for everything! Well, at least we're in luck today. It's perfect for the boat trip."

"A boat? Are we going on a boat?" piped up a voice from the back seat.

"You know we are, poppet. We're going to see the puffins on Puffin Island, remember?"

"Yippee!" Eva started to bounce up and down with excitement, kicking her feet against the front seat. Bryn joined in, barking loudly.

"OK, OK!" said Hanna, trying not to laugh. "Let's have a bit of calm in the back seat! We're nearly there now." She glanced at her watch. Just after 10.30am, plenty of time to get to Beaumaris for the 11 o'clock cruise. "How about a game of I-Spy?"

"I'll start!" shouted Eva. "I spy with my little eye something beginning with W."

By the time they reached the pretty little coastal town, they still hadn't come up with the correct answer despite numerous attempts. "OK, we give up," said Hanna. "What's the word?"

"Whale!!" said Eva triumphantly, at which they all fell about laughing.

"If you've seen a whale in the Menai Straits, I'll eat my hat!" said Rhys.

"You haven't got a hat," Eva pointed out, "and Ms Jones says that there **are** whales off Anglesey."

Ms Jones was Eva's class teacher and seemingly the fount of all wisdom.

"Yes, she's right, but you don't see them very often," Rhys replied, driving past the elegant Georgian terraces on the seafront into the main car park.

It was peak season, and fine weather always attracted a crowd of day trippers. He drove around for several minutes before spotting a parking space. They left the car and made for the pier where a queue of people waited to buy tickets for the boat trip.

"Sorry, folks, the morning cruise is fully booked now," said a weather-beaten chap who appeared to be the skipper. "You'll have to wait for the afternoon one."

A collective groan rose from the queue. *Thank God we booked our tickets online, otherwise we'd never have got on,* thought Hanna. She rooted them out of her backpack and handed them over to the skipper, who smiled and ushered them towards the boat. His mate held out his arm to steady each of them in turn as they stepped on board, Hanna gripping Eva's hand and Rhys keeping Bryn on a tight lead.

"C'mon, you two! Look, we can sit right at the front!" Eva cried, wriggling free and pushing past people to reach the bow of the boat.

Hanna and Rhys followed in her wake, smiling apologetically at their fellow-passengers. As soon as everyone was aboard, the skipper started up the engine and pulled slowly away from the pier. He launched into an amusing commentary, peppered with anecdotes about the places of interest along the way.

Away from shore, the wind picked up, whipping Hanna's hair into her eyes. She cursed and pulled her hood up, wishing she'd had the foresight to tie it back, and fastened her jacket against the brisk breeze. Cormorants and gulls circled over their heads, before diving down and settling on the surface of the sea. The skipper pointed to another flock of white birds with a distinctive shape and markings: gannets. With their long, pointed beaks, yellow heads and black wingtips, they glided low over the water before rising into the air, then plunging spectacularly into the water.

He also mentioned possible sightings of dolphins and porpoises. Eva avidly scoured the waters for any signs, but her face fell with disappointment when none appeared. They wouldn't be able to land on Puffin Island, he explained, as it was a bird sanctuary. And, as it was near the end of the breeding season, they might not see any puffins at all. Eva scowled at hearing this and looked if she might burst into tears.

A few moments later the uninhabited island came into view and a small, stocky bird flew by. Eva leapt to her feet, pointing upwards. "Mummy, Mummy! Look over there, it's a puffin!" she shouted excitedly. "And there goes another one..."

As they drew nearer to the island, the distinctive comical-looking birds could clearly be seen, strutting along the cliffs, swimming in the shallows, and skimming through the air. Grey seals basked on the rocks in the sunshine. Eva jumped up and down, beside herself with excitement. Hanna caught Rhys' eye and grinned.

The grin faded as she felt her mobile vibrate. She snatched it out of her pocket and stared at the screen, fearing more bad news from Ceri. But it was only Nerys, her old neighbour from when she'd first arrived in Wales.

"Hanna? Hi, it's Nerys. Hope I haven't caught you... bad time ..."

"No, it's fine but the signal's not too good."

"I'll be quick then. There seem to be... strange people at

your old cottage. As it belongs... National Park, I thought Rhys should know... wondered if he... pop over and take a look?"

"I'm sure he could. What seems to be the problem?"

Rhys stared at her questioningly.

Nerys' response was masked by static.

"You're breaking up," said Hanna, her voice rising. "Look, we'll call you later and arrange something."

"Fine," said Nerys, before the line cut out altogether.

"What was all that about?" Rhys asked.

"It was Nerys. Something about dodgy goings-on at my old cottage. Asking if you could go over and check it out."

CHAPTER FOUR

Back on dry land, they bought fish and chips for lunch and ate them sitting on a bench along the seafront. Eva tried to feed her leftovers to the gulls that were milling around in anticipation, but Rhys stood up and shooed them away.

"Hey, what are you doing?" Eva shouted angrily. "Don't chase them. I'm feeding them."

"Sorry, poppet, it's not allowed. The birds can get a bit nasty, and they've hurt people in the past," Rhys explained gently. "You don't want them to hurt you, do you?"

"They wouldn't do that, they're my friends," said the youngster, defiantly.

"Yes," Hanna cut in to head off any potential argument, "but if they start fighting each other for food, they could peck you accidentally if you get in the way. We don't want that, do we? That's why it's forbidden." She pointed to a sign that confirmed this.

Eva shook her head, defeated. Bryn whined, as if sensing the food might come his way instead. She held the food tray down to the dog who guzzled it up before anyone could object. Hanna suppressed a smile.

"What are we doing now?" asked Eva.

"I thought we might go and see the old Victorian gaol," Hanna said.

"Oooh, yes!" said Eva, her face breaking into a smile. "We've been learning about that at school."

"I think I'll give Nerys a quick ring first." Rhys fumbled in his pocket for his phone. "See what she wants."

Hanna nodded. "Fine, we'll make a start towards the gaol. You can catch us up."

The gaol was only a few streets away, and Hanna and Eva had nearly arrived when Rhys appeared behind them, panting and looking slightly anxious.

"Everything OK?" Hanna asked.

Rhys glanced around him before responding in a low voice. "She reckons there've been a lot of comings and goings on the road up to your old cottage. Vans arriving at all hours, sometimes ending up at her place by mistake. Not delivery drivers, either. She's seen several young girls there, too. Too many for just one family."

Hanna frowned. "Really? That **is** weird. Isn't it supposed to be a holiday let?"

Rhys nodded. "All our cottages are. I told Nerys I'd check out the rental agreement just to be sure and find out who took it out. And I promised to go over there and take a look."

"Maybe we can all go. I've not seen Nerys for a week or two, and you know how Eva loves going up there and seeing all the animals."

"Good idea. How about the day after tomorrow?"

Before she could answer, Hanna felt Eva tugging at her arm.

"Stop talking and come on, both of you," complained Eva. "I want to see the ghost. Ms Jones says there's a ghost..."

I'll have to have a word with this Ms Jones, thought Hanna.

Eva's imagination was active enough without it being fuelled by lurid stories of ghosts.

Much to Eva's disappointment, the ghost didn't put in an appearance. But the promise of an ice-cream and a treasure hunt around the town brought a smile back to her face. The sun was starting to go down by the time they finally returned to the car. Hanna's face was tingling from the sun and her feet were starting to ache. It had been a long day. Eva fell asleep straight away in the back seat, with Bryn lying across her lap. She didn't wake even when they arrived home. Rhys carried her into the cottage and put her to bed.

"Fancy some supper?" Hanna asked, going into the kitchen.

"Could do with a little something. How about you?"

"I'm a bit peckish too but it's a bit late to start cooking. I'll rustle something up."

"Great," said Rhys, taking a bottle of South African Pinot Noir out of the wine rack. He popped the cork, poured two generous glasses, and handed one to Hanna.

"And it was a great day. Thanks for suggesting it. Eva had a lot of fun."

"Not just Eva, we all did!" Rhys grinned as Hanna hastily laid the table with an assortment of local cheeses and cold cuts, crusty bread, and a spicy tomato chutney.

"Will this be enough?"

"Perfect!" said Rhys replied, planting a playful kiss on her cheek.

An image of Luciano flashed through her head. Hanna realised it was the first time that she'd thought of her ex-husband all day. A grim thought occurred to her: while he might be an ex in her head, she reminded herself that legally they were still married.

Hanna arranged for them to go up to Nerys' for lunch on Tuesday. She was looking forward to it, a chance for a catch-up. Eva could see all the animals again, and Rhys would be able to check out the cottage. They'd decided to make the trip in Rhys' National Park pick-up truck, the back of which was open to the elements.

"Can I sit in the back with Bryn? Please, please? Can I, can I?" Eva persisted.

Hanna frowned. "I've told you before, no. Maybe later when we're off the road. You can navigate instead, if you remember the way, that is."

"OK, I'll try my best." Eva grinned, temporarily appeased.

Thank God for that, thought Hanna. Keeping her amused was difficult enough at the best of times, but the school holidays were already proving pretty exhausting.

They all piled into the double-cab pick-up, Hanna and Rhys in the front, Bryn tethered alongside Eva in the back. After about twenty minutes, they reached the track that led up to the little settlement of Heulog. A fine drizzle masked the hills, becoming more persistent the higher they climbed. This was where Hanna and Eva had come to live when they first arrived in Wales after leaving Sicily. It made her think back to how Rhys, Ceri's brother but a virtual stranger, had helped them out. Over time their friendship had blossomed and developed into something more. Hanna remembered how Rhys' draughty old Land Rover, a real bone-rattler, used to jolt its way up this track over rocks and potholes, making sure any passengers felt every single one. The new pick-up took the track in its stride, gliding smoothly over the rough surface.

Hanna felt a kick to the back of her seat. She turned round to find Eva wriggling with excitement at the thought of seeing Nerys and her growing collection of animals again. "Tell me again about the hip people," she asked.

"The hippies who used to live in the hills, you mean?" Rhys smiled. "There are still New Age travellers living in these parts..."

Eva's eyes grew wide in wonder as Rhys launched into one of his many stories. Hanna's thoughts turned to Nerys, and wondered yet again how she managed to look after her menagerie and run her pottery business. Lars couldn't be much help; he was either busy painting in his studio or away touring with one of his exhibitions. The animals were clearly Nerys' domain.

The familiar landscape made her thoughts turn back to those early days when they'd just arrived, and, inevitably, back to Luciano and their reason for being there in the first place. And all that had happened since – Eva being kidnapped, having to go back to Sicily to rescue her from her captives...

"So, is that okay with you?" Rhys glanced at her, his voice cutting through her thoughts.

"What? Sorry, I was miles away..."

"I'll drop you off at Nerys', then I'll pop over to the cottage to see what's going on. Shouldn't be too long and I'll be back in plenty of time for lunch. OK?"

"Fine," Hanna said. "That'll give us a chance to get around all the animals first, won't it, munchkin?"

Eva beamed and bounced up and down on the seat, clapping her hands in delight. "Great! Are we nearly there yet?"

"Yep. Just a few more minutes." Rhys drove on, past the turning to her old cottage. As they rounded the bend, Nerys' place came into view, darkly silhouetted in splendid isolation against the distant hills.

The drizzle had stopped now, and the sun was starting to fight its way through the thinning clouds. Hanna opened her window a crack. A faint sweet smell wafted through, along with the melodious strains of birdsong. The hedgerows were peppered with summer colour, and the slopes glistened after the rain. A kestrel hovered overhead, stalking its prey. A place of such beauty and inspiration, thought Hanna. It was easy to see its attraction for a creative couple like Nerys and Lars, especially after living in London.

Her mind drifted back to Luciano. There'd been no more news from Ceri. She wasn't sure if that was a good – or bad – sign.

CHAPTER FIVE

Rhys parked the truck in the yard next to the outbuilding that Nerys had converted into a pottery studio. As Brady, her chocolate Labrador, ambled up, Bryn started barking. Rhys let him out of the truck, and he bounded over to the other dog. Brady watched placidly as if indulging a puppy, while Bryn raced around him. Eva was about to join in the melée when Nerys appeared in a long, baggy dress in a vivid tropical print, her unruly hair tied back by a matching scarf.

"Lovely to see you all again!" she said, hugging each of them in turn. "And thanks for coming so quickly. Come on in. I've just made a pot of coffee."

Hanna smiled. Nerys never changed. She was always chatty, so chatty that at times it was hard to get a word in. Maybe it was overcompensation for all the time spent on her own. They followed her into the cottage while Eva stayed in the garden, playing with the dogs. Nerys led them into the kitchen where the aroma of fresh coffee filled the air.

"Sit yourselves down." She started to pour coffee from a cafetière into heavy earthenware mugs. "There you go. And help yourself to Welsh cakes. Still warm, straight out of the oven." She pointed to a plate on the kitchen table.

Rhys' eyes lit up. "Yum, my favourite! Don't mind if I do," he said, helping himself.

"So, what's all this about the cottage?" said Hanna, keeping an eye on Eva through the window. "You sounded worried."

"Well, maybe I'm overreacting, but there's been a lot of traffic on the road up here of late. As you know, it only leads to the turn-off to your old cottage and then on to our place. They're certainly not coming here, although some of them have overshot the turning and ended up at ours by mistake."

"When you say 'they', who or what do you mean?" asked Rhys, between mouthfuls of Welsh cake.

"We've seen a dirty white transit van a couple of times. No markings on the side. Difficult to tell if it's the same one or not. And when we've been walking Brady over that way, we've seen fleeting glimpses of several young black women at the cottage. No more than girls really. But not in a family-type situation; no men with them. It seems strange in this neck of the woods, out of place somehow..."

"I'll go over there now and take a look," said Rhys, finishing his coffee. "You two stay here. I won't be long. Back for lunch."

Armed with his car keys, he made for the front door before anyone could protest, waving a cheery goodbye. Hanna heard him rev up the Isuzu truck and accelerate off down the track.

Turning to Nerys, Hanna said, "So, how are things with you? How's the pottery going, and what's the latest animal count?"

Her friend smiled. "The pottery's going well. I've found some new outlets, one in Conwy, another in Caernarfon, plus one on Anglesey. Lars has a couple of commissions on the go, with pressing deadlines. He's in the studio working at the minute, but he'll join us for lunch. As for animals, they just seem to increase..."

Hanna laughed. "Not on their own, they don't! This place is becoming more of an animal sanctuary than a home! Come on, tell me about the latest additions. Eva will want to see them, for sure, as well as all the other residents."

"Well, we've got two new cats in addition to Tabitha, our tabby. They'd been living outside and were quite feral, but slowly they started venturing into my studio and soon after into the cottage. They still like to hunt though, so you might not see them today. But there's a new star attraction. C'mon, I'll show you. Eva will love them." Nerys stood up and beckoned Hanna to follow her out of the back door.

"Let me get Eva. She won't want to miss this." Hanna opened the kitchen window and called her daughter. Eva ran over immediately, eager to see the new members of the household. Together, they crossed the back garden down to the pond, home to a variety of ducks and geese that quacked and honked in a flurry of activity as they passed. Hanna could tell that Eva was tempted to stop but her curiosity spurred her on. Past the chicken coops and pig pens, they were heading for a field that at first glance looked empty. As they approached, Hanna could see two furry animals, one chestnut brown, the other fawn, grazing contentedly.

Eva whooped with joy. "Ooh, they're so cute! What are they? Can I pat them? Are they friendly?"

Nerys laughed. "They're alpacas, Eva. They **are** friendly, but they have to get to know you first and learn to trust you. Once this happens, we can put them on a halter and take them for a walk, if you'd like?"

"Could we, really? That would be awesome!" Eva jumped up and down in delight.

Hanna frowned, unsure of this idea and at the same time,

wondering where her daughter had learned the word 'awesome'. Not from either Rhys or herself, that was certain. Instead of pursuing the issue, she heard herself asking, "Why on earth are you keeping alpacas, Nerys?"

"Because, as Eva says, they're cute and cuddly and have great personalities. I can sell the wool too. It's much in demand. Aren't they lovely?"

Eva was easily persuaded, Hanna less so.

"What are they called, Auntie Nerys?" asked Eva.

"The brown one is Eric and the lighter coloured one is Lulu. Here, you can feed them these if you like." Nerys handed Eva a plastic bag full of carrot sticks. "Shake the bag to get their attention."

Eric and Lulu stopped grazing and pricked up their ears at the sound. It must have been something they were used to, for they began to make their way cautiously across the field. Hanna had to admit they were cute, and couldn't resist joining in.

"Put a couple of sticks on your hand and hold it out flat for them," said Nerys, shooting Hanna a reassuring glance. "They won't bite, they'll just nuzzle your hand as they're eating."

Eva did as she was told, with a serious face. The alpacas approached and nibbled the titbits, making her dissolve into giggles. "Oooh, that tickles!"

Nerys put a finger to her mouth. "Careful, Eva, you don't want to make a noise that might scare them."

"Sorry," said Eva, the serious face returning.

Lulu came over to Hanna and daintily picked at the morsels in her hand. Hanna couldn't resist gently stroking its neck. The animal readily accepted the caress as if it were the most natural thing in the world.

"You've done this before," said Nerys, watching her.

"I went on a llama trek some time ago. I must have remembered from then," Hanna answered.

The alpacas quickly finished off the last of the carrot sticks and trotted back into the middle of the field. Eva reluctantly waved goodbye and went off to find the dogs, who were still romping around in the front garden. Nerys and Hanna turned back towards the cottage.

"Eva must meet Rufus before you go," said Nerys.

"Rufus?"

"He's a lionhead rabbit. And so adorable, she'll want to take him home."

"Might be better not to show him to her, then," said Hanna. "That'll be the next thing on her wish list, and we've already got a boisterous dog and a cantankerous cat. She'll be thinking that your place is the norm, and we're the poor relations with only two animals."

Hanna glanced at her watch. Rhys had been gone for a little over an hour. Maybe he'd found something of interest after all. Eva was calmer now she'd seen all the animals, except for the two new cats which were nowhere to be seen. Hanna was helping to set the table for lunch. Nerys carried a large, brightly-coloured ceramic bowl over to the table.

"Smoked mackerel and beetroot salad for lunch, followed by summer berries and ice-cream. Hope that's okay for everyone?"

"Sounds delicious," said Hanna. She looked at her watch again. "I'm wondering where Rhys has got to. He should be back by now..."

At that moment the back door opened, and a voice called out, but it was only Lars. He came into the kitchen, dressed in shorts and a polo shirt so spattered with paint that it was difficult to make out their original colour.

"Great to see you, Hanna," he said, grinning and giving her a hug. "Where's the rest of the gang?"

"Rhys has gone over to the cottage to take a look around, and Eva…"

As if on cue, laughter rose from the garden where Eva was still playing with the dogs.

"Still as obsessed with animals as ever?" he asked.

Hanna smiled. "Absolutely, she's always nagging us to be more like you two and get more pets. You're a hard act to follow."

"Well, she's always welcome to come and visit any time, you know that. She can give Nerys a hand cleaning them out and feeding. That might put her off a bit. Let me go and get cleaned up before lunch." Lars turned and made for the stairs.

"You know, I'm really grateful to you for offering to look after Eva and the animals while we're over in Sicily for the wedding," said Hanna. "Are you sure they won't be too much trouble?"

Nerys smiled. "'Course not. It'll be fun! Eva loves being here, what with all the animals and dabbling with the clay in the pottery. We're looking forward to it. Don't worry, we'll take good care of her."

"I'm a bit concerned after what happened before."

"Don't be. It's all in the past. You go and enjoy yourselves…"

The sound of tyres crunching over gravel could be heard outside. Hanna looked out of the kitchen window as Rhys pulled up in the yard and jumped out of the pick-up. "Here's Rhys now," she said, opening the back door.

"How did you get on?"

Rhys frowned. "Nothing, no sign of anyone. The place looks deserted and there weren't any fresh tyre marks on the track. I waited for a bit, but still nothing. I even parked up some distance away and went back on foot. Maybe it was the wrong time of day to go. Perhaps I need to go in the evening or at the weekend."

Nerys looked disappointed. "Sorry, I've brought you up here on a wild goose chase. You've had a wasted journey. I was so sure you'd see something. We'll keep track of the times of any future sightings and keep you posted."

"No worries. Any excuse for a visit and to sample your hospitality," said Rhys, planting a kiss on Nerys' cheek. "It's such a lovely part of the world."

"You'd say that about anywhere in Wales," Hanna pointed out.

Rhys nodded, putting his arm around her shoulders. "Yes, *cariad,* you're right, I probably would. So, where's this lunch you promised us, Nerys? I'm starving!"

It was late afternoon by the time they left. After a good lunch and a walk across the hills with the dogs, they were all feeling quite tired. Eva curled up with Bryn in the back of the truck. Hanna's eyelids soon started to droop but flew open when Rhys swerved sharply to avoid a white transit van approaching them at some pace in the middle of the road. The jolt threw her to one side, her seatbelt restraining her and preventing any real damage. Their pick-up ground to a halt as the van thundered past.

"What the hell...? That bloody van driver nearly had us off the road." muttered Rhys, looking over in concern. "Are you OK?"

"I'm fine, just a bit shaken." Hanna's first thought was Eva. There was no sound coming from the back seat. She turned around, conscious of the twinging pain down one side as she did so. Eva and Bryn had been flung into a corner and both seemed a bit dazed but otherwise unharmed. The little girl whimpered and looked as if she was about to burst into tears. Hanna unfastened her seatbelt and slowly got out of the car and went to join them in the back seat. She hugged Eva tightly to her chest and stroked her hair, trying to reassure her.

"Is she okay?" asked Rhys, watching in the rear-view mirror.

"She'll be fine. A bit shocked, that's all."

"That must have been what Nerys was talking about," said Rhys grimly. "I only got a quick glimpse, but the van driver looked vaguely familiar. And sitting next to him were two young black girls. I could see them quite clearly."

CHAPTER SIX

They continued their journey home in silence. Something strange might be going on at the cottage, but Hanna was more concerned that she hadn't heard from Ceri. She slipped into the kitchen as soon as they got home to call her.

"Ceri, it's me. Any news about Luciano?"

"Not really. But Sergio's informant reckons that his younger brother, Giulio, was released even earlier than he was. Not sure about his father. You're not having second thoughts about coming over for the wedding, are you?"

Hanna hesitated. "I'm in two minds, to be honest. I was nervous enough about returning to Sicily before Luciano got out of prison, but now... Difficult to know if he poses a threat or not. Rhys and I are still planning to come, but I can't risk bringing Eva. She's been through enough already. She's going to stay here with my friend Nerys. If Luciano **has** got it in for me and hears about you getting married, he'll guess that I'll come back for the wedding. I don't want to endanger you or make any of your guests a target."

"Don't worry about that. Sergio's dad is organising a covert police presence at the wedding and the reception as a precaution."

Hanna fell silent. She remembered when they'd gone to collect Eva from the kidnappers: the police presence in the quarry hadn't managed to prevent Sergio's estranged brother, Pino, being killed. She shuddered. A police presence offered little reassurance.

"In the meantime, both Sergio and his dad are trying to get some intel on Luciano and what he's up to. We should have some more information in the next few days."

"Let's hope so," said Hanna, feeling unconvinced. She could sense Ceri take a sharp intake of breath. "What's up? How are the wedding arrangements going?"

"Fine, it's not that."

"What is it, then?"

A slight pause. "I'm a bit worried about Sergio's job, that's all. You know that he's always chasing down stories of corruption and organised crime. He makes light of the risks and danger he might be facing, but it's a constant source of worry for me. He's been offered a job on the mainland, but he's not keen to go. He seems to have got the bit between his teeth on a story he's working on and wants to see it through to the end. You know what he's like..."

Hanna did. She wondered privately why he was so attached to Sicily. Did he enjoy being a big fish in a small pond? If he went to work on a newspaper in Rome or Milan, he'd be the new boy and would have to make a name for himself all over again. Maybe Sicily offered more of an adrenaline rush and he enjoyed the excitement, the thrill of the chase. Or was it something more personal, wanting pay-back for his brother's death? Pino had got himself involved in organised crime and was a member of the clan that had kidnapped Eva. Luciano and his associates had also been caught up in Pino's murder. Maybe Sergio wouldn't rest easy until he felt he'd got retribution.

"I suppose you both need to think about the future, not only about his career but also whether you feel comfortable staying in Sicily, especially if you want to start a family," said Hanna, trying to choose her words carefully so as not to add to Ceri's distress. "It's possible, but you may always be looking over your shoulder, wherever you are."

"I know," replied Ceri glumly. "But there's no easy solution. Sergio loves his job; it's like an addiction for him. Whether he'd feel quite the same away from Sicily, I don't know."

"You need to talk things through with him before you get married. Otherwise, it could cause all sorts of problems later..." Hanna's words trailed away. She was loath to voice the thoughts running through her head.

"Yes, you're right." Ceri sighed. "I'll try and find some time to talk to him in the next day or so. He's usually home so late, especially now as he sometimes calls in to see his mum on the way home."

"How's she doing?"

"She's had a series of falls; no real damage, but she's getting quite forgetful. Fortunately, Sergio's sister Lina lives nearby and pops in during the day to make sure she's okay and get her some lunch. Sergio's father is worried that he may have to reduce his hours, although the police have got their hands full with the continuing migrant situation."

"And what do you want?"

"With everything going on, I'd prefer to move away, but I don't want to pressurise Sergio in doing it just for me. It has to be a joint decision."

"Good luck with that one."

Ceri sighed again. "The whole thing is taking the edge off the wedding preparations, but we do need to talk about it."

"I'll let you go. Get in touch if there's any more news."

"Don't worry, I will." Ceri rang off.

Hanna didn't envy their situation. She could see how difficult it would be for Sergio to move away, although mainland Italy wasn't that far. Whatever they decided, there would always be downsides. She felt something brushing against her leg and heard a pitiful whine. A pair of imploring eyes looked up at her. Feeding time again.

Shortly before 8 o'clock the following morning, Eva wandered into the kitchen dressed in her hedgehog pyjamas, rubbing her eyes sleepily. "Where's Daddy gone?"

Hanna stared at her, startled. Eva had always called Rhys by his first name, but a few times lately she had referred to him as Daddy. Was she finally starting to accept him in that role? Hanna hoped so.

She smiled and said: "He's had to pop into work this morning. So we're going shopping today, just the two of us. I want to go to the market in Llangefni and see if we can get you some new shoes for school. We need to have breakfast and get going. Can you feed the boys please?"

"Okay."

Bryn and Cosmo circled Eva's legs eagerly, almost knocking her over, in their anticipation of breakfast. She mechanically filled their respective bowls with pellets of dried pet food and put them down on the floor to a rapturous reception. The bowls clattered on the slate tiles as the animals gobbled up every last morsel.

"How come Bryn's still here?" Eva asked.

"Daddy had a few meetings in the office today and thought he'd be better staying here."

The little girl seemed satisfied with this response. "I'll go and get dressed now," she announced, marching out of the kitchen. Hanna watched her go in disbelief.

It came as no surprise that Eva's attempt at dressing herself wasn't entirely successful. She'd managed to put on a pair of shorts and even zip them up, but the polo shirt was inside out and the buckles on her sandals had proved too difficult. Still, it was progress, Hanna noted, marvelling at how quickly she was growing up. After taking Bryn for a quick run, they left him in the cottage looking sad at being left behind.

"You'll be fine. We won't be long," Hanna assured him. He watched glumly from the window as they got into the car and drove off. Hanna pulled the visor down to shield her eyes from the bright light, despite the sky being more overcast than it had been of late. The temperature had dipped several degrees.

She glanced sideways at Eva who was looking out of the window at the passing countryside and humming to herself. "Are you okay? Missing school?"

Eva contemplated the question as if she'd just been asked about world peace or climate change.

"Not really," she replied finally. "It's great being here with you and Bryn and Cosmo. But I miss seeing all my friends. It'll be nice to see them again. And Ms Jones."

That teacher of Eva's again! She'd certainly made an impression on the youngster, which could only be a good thing. Hanna remembered from her own schooldays how she'd flourished whenever she'd developed a special affinity with a particular teacher.

"Apart from new shoes, is there anything else you need for school?" Eva's old school shoes were too small; she was growing so quickly.

"A new schoolbag," replied Eva without hesitation, as if

she'd been expecting the question. "I'd like one with those furry animals on, those with the funny name that Auntie Nerys keeps in her garden."

"Alpacas?"

"Yes, them," Eva confirmed, nodding her head firmly. She must have given the issue some thought.

"Well, we can look but I don't know if we'll find one. Anything else?"

"I'd like some of those glittery pens, too."

Hanna laughed. "I think the budget will probably run to that. And possibly an ice-cream later?"

Eva's eyes lit up at the mention of her favourite treat. "Oooh, awesome!" she said, clapping her hands together.

For the umpteenth time, Hanna recalled Rhys' suggestion about them having a child together. She had to admit that she was sorely tempted. If she left it much longer, there'd be too much of an age gap between the siblings. Should she, or shouldn't she? She'd have to decide soon; Rhys was waiting for an answer.

The trip to Llangefni turned out to be surprisingly successful, providing everything they wanted. At the market, Hanna bought a piece of salmon for dinner, along with fresh bread, some local cheese, sausages, and a range of fruit and vegetables. She even managed to get a pair of school shoes for Eva. Laden with bags, they were about to leave the market when she heard a squeal of joy.

"Mummy, look! Look over there!" Eva pointed at a stall selling bags of all shapes and sizes. "That's just what I want!"

Hanna followed her gaze to a small, duck-egg blue rucksack printed with white llamas or alpacas. She had to admit that it was seriously cute. "Try it on and see how it feels."

The stallholder, a stout middle-aged woman who was serving another customer, nodded her approval. Hanna put down her bags and helped Eva slip her arms through the straps.

"I love it!" the little girl declared. "Can I have it, Mummy? Please?"

The price tag was marked £8.50. A snip: she'd have paid twice as much for something similar elsewhere. "We'll have it!" she said to the stallholder, holding out a £10 note.

"Shall I wrap it for you, dearie?" the stallholder asked.

Eva scowled as if she didn't want to be parted from her new find.

"Better not. It might end in tears!" Hanna replied, smiling, and taking her change.

"You can put some of the shopping in my new bag," Eva suggested, pointing to her back.

"OK."

Hanna started to rummage through the bags to find some lighter items that would be suitable, then she caught a snatch of conversation from a small group of women gathered at the neighbouring stall. From the mixture of Welsh and English, she could just make out something about young black girls roaming the streets of Holyhead late at night. The conversation soon ended, and the women drifted off as if they sensed they were being overheard. *Curious*, thought Hanna, wondering if they might have anything to do with the people staying at her old cottage?

CHAPTER SEVEN

Bryn's ears twitched and he started to whine, a sure sign that Rhys was in the vicinity. Eva ran to the window in expectation. Hanna looked up from the sofa and in the twilight saw the faint glow of the porch light reflected through the window. No sound of a car engine or footsteps on the path. But Bryn knew better. A few minutes later she heard the key in the lock and Rhys appeared in the doorway. The dog leapt to his feet, barking and jumping up to welcome his master home.

"Whoa, there, Bryn! Let me at least get in the house!" He staggered in, laden with a carrier bag in each hand. "Sorry I'm late. Stopped off for a drink after work at Aled's leaving do. Did you get my message?

"Yes, sorry, didn't I reply?" Without waiting for an answer, Hanna pointed to the bags. "What's that you've got there?"

"Remember we were talking about your next writing project and I mentioned we had some information in the archives that you might be interested in? Well, this is it. Personal stories about Snowdonia and its past that people have given us over the years. Stuff about the castles, the princes of Gwynedd, the slate industry. There seems to be loads about witches and witchcraft passed down from generation to generation. You've not got long with it, mind. There's a team from Bangor University coming in next month to sift through it all and archive anything important."

"Fancy you remembering!" Hanna rose, threw her arms around him and planted a kiss on his cheek. "Rhys Morgan, you're a marvel! I'll put it all out of harm's way."

She picked up the bags and disappeared upstairs into the spare room she used as an office. Taking a quick peep into one of them, she pulled out several slim volumes filled with spidery faded handwriting. Clearly some sort of journal containing not only text, in a mixture of Welsh and English, but symbols and sketches too. She longed to explore further, but it would have to wait for now. Her fascination with local folklore had flourished to such an extent that she'd decided to pen her own novel, one that would be steeped in these legends. This would make perfect research material and help her develop the outline idea she had for the book. She put the journals back and placed both bags next to the desk, ready for her to start work on them.

Back in the lounge, Bryn was still bouncing around Rhys in excitement, barking loudly.

"Bryn, that's enough now. Down!"

The dog obeyed his master's command and sheepishly retreated to the rug in front of the fireplace. Eva bounded over and threw her arms around Rhys' legs in a big hug.

"Hi, munchkin! What have you two girls been up to today?" He tousled her hair before picking her up and putting her across his shoulders. Eva squealed in delight. She was getting a bit too big for that now, Hanna thought.

"Mummy bought me a new bag for school, and it's got alla ... appa ... What are they called, Mummy?"

"Alpacas," Hanna confirmed.

"It's got them on it," said Eva, triumphantly, wriggling to get down now, in her eagerness to show him the bag.

"I don't suppose you've had time to look up the rental agreement on my old cottage?" asked Hanna, as Eva scurried across the room to retrieve her new bag.

"Actually, I did. Funny thing is, I looked everywhere but there was no sign of an agreement. No hard copy, no computer record, nothing. It's as though the cottage is empty and hasn't been let out to anyone."

Hanna frowned. "That's really weird. You don't think they could be squatters, do you?"

"Who knows? Something strange is going on, that's for sure. I'll have to look into it further and find out exactly what."

The following morning, Rhys took Eva and Bryn off for a walk to give Hanna a chance to get some work done. She had a pressing deadline for the forthcoming Anglesey Show, and was sitting at her laptop in the spare room, trying to finish off the press packs, when her mobile rang. She glanced at the screen.

"Hi, Ceri, what's up?"

"Just checking in. All quiet here. Not heard anything else about Luciano or his family. In fact, Sergio's informant seems to have gone to ground."

"Is that a cause for concern?"

Ceri sighed. "Who knows? But maybe no news is good news."

"You may be right. But I can't help but worry, now that Luciano's on the loose again."

"I'd do the same in your place. Hope you haven't changed your mind about coming over for the wedding? It's not far off now, only a month away, and I'm counting on Rhys to give me away."

"Well, everything's arranged but I've still got my doubts. I'd hate to miss it, but I wouldn't want my being there to jeopardise the whole thing."

"Sergio's dad can look into getting you police cover while you're here if you're still worried." Ceri's retort was prompt, as if she'd been expecting this response.

"I'd just like some reassurance that Luciano will leave us alone. Preferably before we come. What are the chances of that, d'you think? Surely there's a possibility, either through Sergio or his father?"

A moment of hesitation. "We can try, but it'll be tricky; you know that. I'll speak to Sergio about it."

"Thanks, Ceri, appreciate it. Everything OK, otherwise?"

"Oh, meant to tell you. I've started doing some voluntary work helping out at the local refugee centre."

"That can't be easy."

"It's not. You hear such harrowing stories: people who've been tortured, or whose families have disappeared without trace, young girls who've been trafficked. But at least I feel I'm doing my bit to support them."

Hanna heard Sergio calling Ceri's name in the background.

"Sorry, gotta go."

"Let me know how you get on."

"Will do. I'll call you as soon as there's any news." Ceri hung up.

Hanna didn't know how worried she should be about returning to Sicily. The wedding would be a perfect opportunity for Luciano to take action if he was intent on retaliation. Would police protection be enough? She'd be on tenterhooks the whole time, not only for herself and Rhys, but also for Ceri and Sergio, their family and all the guests. Was she being selfish even thinking about attending the big event?

The sound of voices drifted up the stairs of the cottage.

Rhys and Eva must have returned from their walk. The stairs creaked and Rhys appeared in the doorway, his face flushed.

"We took the truck up near your old cottage and saw a small group – seven or eight – young black girls, maybe early teens but dressed way beyond their years, in the back garden," he blurted out. "And you'll never guess who was with them!"

"Go on," Hanna prompted impatiently as he paused for breath.

"It was the van driver we saw the other day. Remember I said his face was familiar? Well, I recognised him from school. He picks up his little boy sometimes. Can't remember his name but it's unusual. You'd know. I think he's Italian."

Hanna stared at him. "D'you mean Ottavio's father? The little boy who used to be at nursery school with Eva?"

Rhys nodded. "Yes, that's him!"

Hanna gulped. Ottavio's family was from Sicily.

CHAPTER EIGHT

———————————

Try as she might, Hanna struggled to switch off and get to sleep, despite the fact she could hardly keep her eyes open after dinner and had been fighting back yawns. She was plagued by fears of a possible connection between the quiet Welsh community where she lived and her previous home in Sicily. What was going on? And would it affect her and her family in any way?

Hanna's thoughts turned back to Sicily and Luciano's release from prison. Memories came flooding back of the death threat delivered to her home – the three silver bullets, one for each of them. And then it suddenly hit her: the sickening realisation that it wasn't only Luciano she needed to worry about.

She awoke bleary-eyed and alone. The bedside alarm clock told her it was 8.23am. Rhys must have crept out of bed and gone off to work again without waking her. So much for the week off. But she could hear noises coming from the kitchen. She flung the duvet off and padded across the bedroom floor to investigate.

A soft sing-song monologue drifted through the cottage. Hanna popped her head around the kitchen door to find Eva attempting to feed Cosmo, who was, for once, waiting patiently. The kibble she was trying to pour into a bowl scattered across the kitchen floor, much to Cosmo's delight. He chased after the food and gobbled it up. The scene was so comical that Hanna had to suppress a desire to laugh.

"Hi, pumpkin. D'you need a hand?" she asked instead.

"No, Mummy, I'm fine," replied Eva, struggling with the bags of pet food.

Hanna smiled and took them off her. "Breakfast?"

Eva nodded. "Remember I'm going out with Megan today?"

"'Course I do. Let me check what time they're picking you up."

Hanna reached for her mobile phone and scrolled through her messages. 9.30am. Enough time to get ready and have breakfast. Hanna was staying behind. She had to finish off and send out the press packs for the Anglesey Show while Eva and her best friend Megan were going out for the day. Megan's mum was taking them to the Welsh Mountain Zoo in Colwyn Bay. Eva had never been before and was beside herself with excitement.

Hanna popped some bread into the toaster and poured out two bowls of cereal, passing one to Eva sitting at the kitchen table.

"Did I tell you they've got red pandas?" Eva asked, banging her spoon against the bowl. Red pandas were her favourite animal.

"Yes, only about a thousand times!" Hanna replied with a grin. "Let's hope you get to see them – they're really cute. You'll have a great day. Now eat up or you'll be late."

Eva started shovelling cereal into her mouth. "And snow

leopards," she said, with her mouth crammed full. "And meerkats."

"They're not like the ones on the TV adverts, you know. They don't talk," said Hanna.

A brief scowl flitted across Eva's face. "Of course I know. I'm not a baby."

"Here, have a piece of toast and marmalade. Then you need to get dressed. They'll be here soon."

Polishing off the toast in a couple of mouthfuls, Eva rushed off. Hanna had laid out her clothes the previous evening so all she had to do was brush her teeth, have a quick wash, and put them on. Hanna decided to leave her to it.

Hanna looked at the time on the computer screen. 11.42am. She'd managed to get a lot done; it was so much easier to work when there were no distractions. She rose from her desk and went downstairs into the kitchen to make some coffee.

Returning up the wooden stairs to her desk, she placed the steaming mug on the mat by the side of her laptop and started to browse news items on Sicily. Sergio's by-line appeared frequently, mostly articles he'd written for his own newspaper, *La Gazzetta della Sicilia,* but also the occasional magazine piece.

One particular story caught her eye: a recent report in a major Italian broadsheet on the Italian government clamp-down on boats bringing migrants across the Mediterranean from North Africa over the last year. Although it had resulted in fewer migrants travelling to Sicily (the usual first port of call), rescue ships had continued to operate until Italy closed its ports to them the previous month. The suggestion was that the clamp-down was resulting in traffickers resorting to ever more desperate efforts to ply their illicit trade.

Hanna wondered whether Luciano would still be involved in people-trafficking despite the changed environment and his years in prison, or would he have been forced to turn elsewhere? Were there still fatalities, people drowning and forced to travel in squalid, cramped conditions? And were unscrupulous Sicilians, Luciano included, still profiting from their misery? She hated to think how likely this was.

Her previous attempt to help had only resulted in a temporary reprieve. What else could be done? The situation seemed hopeless. *Don't get involved,* she told herself, *it's too dangerous. It's up to the authorities to take action, not you.*

The beep of a text alert on Hanna's mobile phone broke her train of thought. A photo of Eva and Megan, standing by one of the zoo enclosures, with broad grins on their faces, a red panda in the background. They must be having a great day. Shame I couldn't be there too, she thought wistfully, as she turned back to the computer screen.

Rhys arrived home shortly after 7pm to the sultry strains of a samba floating through the stone cottage. Bryn bounded in by his side, heading straight for his bowl in the kitchen.

"That dog, he's always hungry!" He kissed Hanna by way of greeting. "Where's Eva?"

"She's staying over at Megan's tonight after their trip to the zoo. I'm going over there in the morning to pick her up. Good day?"

"Yes, fine, thanks. We've been out repairing stiles and way-markers most of the day. Hot, sweaty work in this weather. What about you?"

Hanna smiled ruefully. "Well, I've been stuck inside all day, but at least I've got everything sorted for the show now."

"That's great! Think I'll go and have a quick shower," said Rhys, disappearing upstairs into the bathroom.

"Don't be long. Dinner's nearly ready," Hanna shouted after him. The sound of the jets being turned on masked his response.

She went back into the kitchen to check the food in the oven, then uncorked a bottle of Nero d'Avola and poured out two glasses. No time to let it breathe. She took a sip as she prepared a salad, humming along to the Latin American beat. As she was carrying it over to the table, she spotted Rhys at the top of the stairs emerging from the bathroom, a towel wrapped around his waist. His face was pink and glowing from the steam, and damp locks clung to his cheeks and forehead.

"Don't worry, I'll throw some clothes on first!" He grinned and vanished, reappearing a few minutes later in a t-shirt and jeans.

Hanna carried a steaming dish of pasta over to the table.

"Wow, that looks so good! I'm famished!" He greedily eyed up the food.

Hanna laughed. "You're just like Bryn!"

"Must be all the fresh air and hard work that does it. What's in it?"

"It's a pea, pesto and sausage lasagne. I got it out of the freezer this morning, completely forgetting that Eva wouldn't be here. There'll probably be loads left over without her here to eat it."

"I wouldn't bank on it!" Rhys said as he dished out two generous portions, handing one to Hanna. "By the way, I popped into the office to check the computer. I've managed to track down the rental agreement on your old cottage."

"Oh? I thought you couldn't find it?"

"It'd been saved in the wrong folder. In last year's rentals rather than this year's. Easy mistake to make." He levered a forkful of pasta into his mouth.

"And?" she asked, impatient to hear more.

"Well, it's a holiday let made out to a Gareth Jones for a period of four months, which is quite unusual in itself. Normally, the longest rental allowed is three months. The address he's given is in Llanberis, so he's a local."

Hanna chewed a mouthful of food thoughtfully. "So, where do all the young girls fit in?"

"No idea. It all seems a bit bizarre."

"So, what now?"

"Well, I've got a hunch that I'd like to follow up, but it'll have to wait until the weekend when I can go up there again."

CHAPTER NINE

Hanna left the cottage just after 9.30 the next morning, eager to get out after being cooped up inside the day before. It was a beautiful day, already warm, with a clear blue sky and light breeze. She was in no hurry, having met her deadline for the press packs the day before. The prospect of a leisurely drive through the scenic Conwy valley to the pretty hamlet where Megan's family lived was appealing.

She started up the car and switched on the radio which responded with a harsh-sounding rap. She replaced it with an easy-listening channel and soon joined the sparse traffic heading east on the A55. At a whim, she turned off before Conwy to take the Fairy Glen road through the Sychnant Pass. It was one of her favourite routes and a place she often visited with Eva, the two of them making up their own fairy stories whenever they went up there.

Shortly after the Fairy Glen Hotel, as the road started its ascent through the pass, her phone rang. As Ceri's name and number flashed up on the display, Hanna touched the screen to respond. "Any news?"

"Yes, can you talk?"

"I'm driving on hands-free but I'm pulling over now." Hanna steered the car into a small lay-by, just before the road narrowed. "What's going on?"

"Well, the original informant has completely disappeared. Sergio's heard from another source that Luciano's business kept going while he and his father and brother were in prison. It was being run by two of his cousins, apparently, despite the recent crackdown on letting migrant ships through."

Hanna remembered the recent newspaper article she'd read. "Really? So, nothing has changed. Not even a temporary lull in their activities. We've not achieved anything." Her heart felt like a lead weight in her chest.

"Apart from escaping a death threat and rescuing Eva, you mean? That was pretty major. Bringing Luciano to justice was always secondary, wasn't it?" said Ceri.

"Yes, you're right," Hanna sighed, still feeling downhearted. "But I'd hoped he might have been stopped in his tracks, at least for a while."

"The important thing is that you're both safe now. Trying to fight organised crime is like trying to struggle against an incoming tide, you know that. You're lucky to be well away from all that now."

"But am I? Any news about whether Luciano's likely to come after us?"

"Nothing, I'm afraid. We're not even sure where he is at the moment, so it's going to be difficult to get any more information on him for now."

Hanna sighed again, her eyes misting over. The spectre of her past was ever-present, lurking in the background. Would it never leave her?

"There's more news," Ceri continued. "The police have

uncovered a massive Mafia fraud of EU funding destined for Sicilian farmers. There'll be loads of arrests in the next couple of days. Sergio's really excited – he's had exclusive access to a lot of information through his contacts, so his story will be pretty much a scoop. He's hoping that the foreign media will pick it up. Great for his career prospects."

Hanna didn't know what to say. It seemed wrong somehow to advance your career on getting insider information on Mafia activities. Wrong, and dangerous too, she thought, distractedly weaving an elastic band round her fingers. "Has he thought any more about that job offer on the mainland?" she asked.

"He's still considering it. He may even end up with more offers once this story is published; who knows?" Ceri sounded thrilled at the prospect.

No doubt it was easy to be swept up by Sergio's journalistic ambitions, but this was no impartial media environment he was working in. This was one where influence could be bought, and opponents easily disposed of. Was Ceri forgetting this?

"Just be careful, Ceri. Both of you. All this proves that the Mafia still has a stronghold on the island, and we know they don't treat their enemies too kindly. Or even opposing clans. Look what happened to Pino."

Ceri fell silent, then said, "You're right. I was getting carried away, what with the wedding and all."

"How's it going? Any last-minute nerves or change of mind?"

Ceri laughed nervously. "No, of course not! You **are** still coming, aren't you?"

"You ask me this every time we speak," said Hanna. "Yes, as long as nothing else happens..."

"I'll let you know if it does. And keep your eye out for news on the arrests over the next few days."

"Will do."

Hanna ended the call, feeling uneasy, and unsure as to whether she had anything to fear from Luciano or his rivals. The prosecutors and the police posed more of a risk to him than she did. But what if he still wanted revenge, or tried to get Eva back?

CHAPTER TEN

As Ceri had predicted, an article appeared in *The Daily Herald* on Saturday morning about the Mafia EU farming sting in Sicily and a massive police raid at dawn that had resulted in over 70 arrests. The operation had involved more than 500 paramilitary *carabinieri* and financial police. Among the arrests were the heads of two clans, several public officials who helped farmers apply for EU aid, a local mayor, and an accountant. The media story was dubbed as exclusive, and attributed to Sergio.

Hanna read through the article quickly as she gobbled down her breakfast, an icy shiver running through her body. She remembered hearing the story of three sisters whose farm near Corleone was being terrorised by the Mafia, their crops systematically ruined, their animals killed. They had refused to bow to the pressure and pay the protection deal on offer. Instead, they had complained to the authorities, which hadn't gone down well with the local community. Whether the sisters had managed to win their battle, she wasn't sure. If the Mafia could do that to their fellow-Sicilians...

"My God, that's quite some raid," said Rhys, reading over

her shoulder. "Is that a new side-line for organised crime in Sicily?"

She shrugged. "There's big money involved. Sergio reckons it's been going on for a while. It must have, given the scale of the operation. Proving it, though, is something else. And making the charges stick is quite another."

Rhys rattled his car keys. "Shall we make a move?"

Hanna nodded and swallowed her last mouthful of coffee. "We can drop Eva and Bryn off with Nerys. That way, they won't disturb us at the cottage."

"Good idea. It may still all come to nothing..."

"You've not told me what your hunch is yet."

Rhys smiled apologetically. "I'll explain on the way up there."

Hanna went into the kitchen and called out to Eva who was playing in the back garden with Bryn. She picked up a flask of coffee and stuffed a sweater into Eva's new rucksack in case it turned chilly. Although the bag had been bought for school, her daughter insisted on using it straight away. Eva came running in.

"Right, we're off. You and Bryn can spend an hour or so with Auntie Nerys and the animals, OK?"

The little girl's face lit up. "Great! Maybe I can take the alcapas for a walk?"

Hanna laughed at her mispronunciation and ruffled her hair. "Yes, maybe you can. Come on, gang, let's hit the road!"

Hanna pulled a light fleece over her head, then poured some coffee into the cup from the thermos flask. "Want some?" she asked, proffering it to Rhys.

"Thanks," he said, taking the cup from her and setting the high-powered binoculars down on the grassy bank beside him.

A cool breeze had arisen in the forty or so minutes they'd been there, and the chill was starting to get to them.

From this track high above the cottage, they had a clear view of the stone building and the surrounding land. But up to now, there were no signs of life: no people, no vans, no animals. The place looked deserted and neglected, as if no one were living there, the curtains drawn and the garden overgrown. Hanna was getting restless; perhaps she should have stayed with Eva and Nerys.

"You don't think they've moved on, do you?" she asked tentatively.

"What, from a few days ago? Don't think so."

"Only asking," she said, shifting uncomfortably from her prone position on the bank.

Rhys sipped his coffee, then picked up the binoculars again, glancing at his watch as he did so. The low growl of a loaded transit van came into earshot, growing louder as it drew nearer, struggling to negotiate the climb.

"There you are!" Rhys whispered triumphantly. "Just as I thought!"

Hanna looked at him quizzically. He still hadn't explained his theory. The van progressed slowly along the rough track towards the cottage. Rhys altered the focus of the binoculars. Eventually the van ground to a halt and two men emerged from the front, disappearing around the vehicle to open the back doors. Even without binoculars, Hanna could make out a group of about eight or ten young black girls, looking no older than thirteen or fourteen, carrying small holdalls. Some were dressed in sombre clothes, while others wore brightly-coloured wax prints that Hanna thought looked to be of African origin. They looked so out of place in the Welsh hills. The men quickly ushered them into the house.

"So, what was it you were thinking?" she asked.

Rhys lowered the binoculars and looked at his watch again.

"Given the time, I think the van may have picked these girls up from the Dublin ferry at Holyhead."

"Really? What gave you that idea?"

"I could be wrong, but it was something you said about the voluntary work that Ceri's doing. I think there could be a connection..."

Before Hanna had a chance to reply, one of the men emerged from the cottage and marched towards the van. He looked vaguely familiar. She snatched the binoculars from Rhys and raised them to her eyes. She could see the face of the man clearly now. Her heart started to pound, and her breath grew increasingly shallow.

"Oh my God, I don't believe it! It can't be..." She took another look. "Christ, it **is** him! That's Angelo, one of Luciano's cousins. What the hell's he doing here?"

CHAPTER ELEVEN

Hanna and Rhys observed the cottage for another hour or so in silence, each wrapped in their own thoughts. Hanna's head was pounding, an acrid taste in her mouth. Nagging fears gripped her, almost sending her into a panic. Could Angelo be one of the cousins who had been running the family business while Luciano was in prison?

Stay calm, she remonstrated, *there could be a perfectly reasonable explanation.* But what, she didn't know. Whatever it was, she felt Angelo's presence so near to home presented a real threat to their safety, their lives. Her head churned as she tried to grapple with her thoughts and come up with a plausible explanation.

She became conscious of Rhys stirring beside her. He stretched and stood up.

"It's all gone quiet at the cottage for the minute. The girls and one of the men are inside. The other one you say is Luciano's cousin has gone off in the van. It doesn't look as if he's coming back anytime soon. I think we should call it a day. You coming?" He gently nudged her arm with his foot.

"Sorry I was miles away."

"Now we've confirmed something fishy is going on, we just have to find out exactly what. Let's go back to Nerys' and think what to do next."

Hanna found Eva standing in Nerys' kitchen, looking bedraggled. Her clothes were splattered in mud, her hands grubby, and she had a dirty splodge on one cheek. By her side, Bryn wagged his tail. The kitchen floor was covered with muddy pawprints.

"What the heck have you two been up to?" she asked.

"We've been out with the alcapas!" Eva replied with a grin. "We had great fun! But Eric got a bit excited, and I fell over."

Nerys smiled apologetically. "Hanna, I'm really sorry," she said, drying her hands on a tea towel. "I meant to get her all cleaned up before you got back. We took the alpacas out for a walk and Eric became pretty lively and tried to bolt. Strange for him as he's usually quite docile. Must have been the wind that made him frisky. Anyway, Eva was holding his lead and he pulled her over. No harm done, though; just a grazed knee as far as I can see."

"No worries, these things happen," Hanna replied, knowing instinctively from Eva's reaction and the lack of histrionics that it was only a minor scrape. Bending down to examine the little girl's knee more closely, she could see a few spots of dried blood where the skin had been broken.

"Nothing serious, you'll live!" she declared, ruffling Eva's messy hair, vowing to take her for a haircut in the coming week before it became totally unmanageable. "But we **will** need to clean it up."

"Go ahead," said Nerys, waving her arm in the direction of the bathroom. "You'll find antiseptic cream and dressings in the bathroom cabinet."

Hanna was steering Eva towards the door before she could object when Rhys came in. He raised his eyebrows in an unspoken question, having presumably caught the last bit of conversation.

"Only a grazed knee," Hanna explained, disappearing through the door with Eva.

A few moments later they were back, with Eva sporting a criss-cross zebra-striped plaster on her knee and a wide grin as if showing off a trophy.

"Look what I did!" she said proudly, pointing to it.

"What happened?" asked Rhys, prompting Eva to repeat the tale of Eric the alpaca, this time with a few embellishments for dramatic effect. She was a good mimic, and her imitation of Eric, making a lowing noise punctuated with high-pitched squeals, made them all fall about laughing.

Lars appeared at the kitchen door and looked surprised to find them all in such high spirits. "Hi, everyone! What's going on?" he asked, joining them at the table where Nerys was laying out a tray of wraps.

"Thought you'd be hungry, so I've made us a spot of lunch – falafel and salad wraps, with homemade elderflower cordial," she explained. "Hope that's OK for everyone?"

They all nodded and began to help themselves to the food. As they ate, Nerys related the tale of the eventful alpaca walk and Eva repeated her impersonation of Eric, to yet more laughter.

Hanna ate little. The thought of Luciano's cousin being so close left her feeling nauseous. She pushed her plate away, her wrap only half-eaten.

"Can I go out and play?" Eva asked as soon as she'd finished eating.

"Yes, but don't wander off. Stay in the garden," Hanna said.

"OK." Eva wriggled from her chair and ran into the garden, followed by the dogs.

"So, how did you get on at the cottage?" Nerys asked when Eva was out of earshot. There was no disguising the curiosity in her voice.

Rhys swallowed a mouthful of falafel. "Well, the place was empty when we got there, but after a while a white van turned up. Two men and several young black girls – young teenagers, as far as we could see – got out with small bags and went into the house. Bit of a strange set-up. God knows what's going on."

"What's even stranger and more worrying," Hanna cut in, in a subdued tone, "is that I recognised one of the men. Not a local. One of Luciano's cousins."

"What?" said Nerys, her eyes widening in disbelief. "But how... What does that mean?"

Hanna shrugged, trying to appear nonchalant, but struggling to overcome the knot of fear rising within her. Her mouth felt like sandpaper, and she took a gulp from her glass of cordial.

"It's bizarre," said Rhys, taking control of the conversation again. "Given the timing, I'd hazard a guess that the van had just picked the girls up from the Dublin ferry at Holyhead. For what purpose, who knows? We need to keep an eye on what's going on over there. We could do with having a continual watch on the place."

Lars wiped his mouth with a paper napkin. "And how would we do that?"

"If we could set up a surveillance camera outside, we'd be able to capture all the comings and goings. That would give us a better idea," Rhys replied.

"Wouldn't it need wiring up?" Lars asked.

"I'm no expert, but you can get battery-operated cameras that work outdoors and save the footage to the Cloud. That way you'd have easy, real-time access to the footage," said Rhys. "I'm sure there'll be someone at work who can advise. After all, it **is** a Park property that we're talking about."

Nerys frowned. "Shouldn't we just call the police and let them investigate?"

"I doubt they'd take us seriously without any real evidence," Rhys replied. "If we can get CCTV footage of the place, we can monitor what's going on and decide whether we need to involve the police or not. I'll check out a suitable system and get hold of it from somewhere. Agreed?"

Nods all round.

"Fine, that's settled then."

It was nearly mid-afternoon by the time they left. The atmosphere in the car on the way home was subdued. Bryn snored gently in the back of the pick-up, Eva by his side, quiet and drowsy after the morning's excitement.

Hanna mulled over what they had seen at the cottage and the disquieting presence of Luciano's cousin. Was it just a coincidence, or was there more to it? Either way, she didn't want Angelo anywhere near her family. Was there a plausible explanation for him being there? Her gut feeling told her otherwise. A chill crept over her. She glanced at Rhys who seemed lost in his own thoughts, a faraway look in his eyes. He didn't seem to fully appreciate the potential risk. She needed to talk it through with Ceri, and get her views.

She dug her mobile out of her pocket and checked the screen. As she thought, the signal there was intermittent. The call would have to wait.

As soon as they got home, Hanna disappeared into the garden to call Ceri. "I think we may have a slight problem here," she said, and went on to explain about Angelo being at the cottage with the group of young girls.

Ceri seemed to be listening attentively, interrupting occasionally to ask the odd question. When she had finished explaining, Hanna paused for breath, then asked, "So, what do you think?"

But there was no answer. The line had gone dead.

CHAPTER TWELVE

Hanna called her straight back and Ceri picked up immediately. "Sorry, don't know what happened there," she said.

"No problem," said Hanna, though impatient to hear her friend's reaction.

"You know what it sounds like, don't you?" said Ceri.

"I know. That would explain Luciano's cousin's presence. But here in Wales?"

"It seems odd. You need more information before you can do anything, but I can't see it being anything legit. Sounds way too fishy for that."

"Rhys is going to set up a surveillance camera outside the cottage so we can get a better idea of what's going on."

"Good idea. Meanwhile, you'll need to be extra careful with Angelo around."

"You don't need to tell me that..." muttered Hanna grimly.

"I'll tell Sergio and see what he reckons. Let me know how it goes."

"I will," said Hanna. "Any news about Luciano?"

"Nothing as yet. Did you see the story on the EU farming

scam? It was picked up by several of the major European nationals with Sergio's by-line on it. Great for his career!"

But not great for his safety, thought Hanna with concern, *or of those around him.* Aloud she said, "You look after yourselves. And get Sergio to think seriously about that job on the mainland."

"Who knows, maybe things might be quietening down here now?" Ceri said.

Hanna could hear the wistfulness in her friend's voice.

"Wishful thinking on your part. We both know that the Mafia is so entrenched into Sicilian culture, it's unlikely to ever disappear. It'll just morph with the times as it always has done."

Ceri sighed. "Yes, you're probably right, even with all the backlash here against organised crime."

A whoop of joy rose from the kitchen and Rhys appeared in the doorway, both hands in a thumbs-up gesture. "Got the camera!" he mouthed, his eyes shining with excitement.

"Gotta go, Ceri. I'll give you a ring as soon as there's any more news."

"Same here. Take care. *Ciao.*"

Hanna pocketed the mobile and turned to Rhys, who was slipping a light fleece over his head.

"I've spoken to Owain at work. He reckons there's a camera in the office that would be perfect for monitoring the situation. I'm going over there now to pick it up. With a bit of luck, we might be able to fit it tomorrow if the coast is clear."

"Shall I call Nerys and see if they can let us know when the place is empty?"

"Good idea! Maybe we could go up there tomorrow afternoon if there's no one about. Right, I'm off! See you later; won't be long," said Rhys, pecking her on the cheek as he made for the front door. Bryn followed expectantly, wagging his tail.

"Correction, **we** won't be long!" he said, opening the door for the dog.

Rhys had obviously underestimated the time needed to pick up the camera. He was gone for a couple of hours, and it was starting to get dark by the time he arrived home. Eva had refused an early dinner, insisting on waiting so they could all eat together. Hanna relented, making it clear that she was only making an exception because it was school holidays.

She heard the key in the front door, then a whirlwind rush of fur as Bryn burst into the cottage, leapt onto the sofa, and started smothering Eva in sloppy kisses. The little girl tried to fend him off, giggling relentlessly as she did so. Rhys struggled through the door, laden with several boxes, an apologetic smile on his face.

"Sorry, I've been a while," he said, kicking the door closed. "Owain was showing me how to install it and view the footage. Think I've got it now. How did you get on with Nerys?" He set the boxes down on the coffee table.

"Oh, fine. Lars has volunteered to go over there tomorrow and keep watch. If the cottage is empty, he'll give you a hand fitting it."

"Great, it shouldn't take long. The camera's battery-powered so it doesn't need to be hooked up to the mains or anything complicated."

"Can we eat now?" asked Eva, bouncing up and down impatiently.

Hanna frowned. "Can you not do that, please, poppet? And it was you who wanted to wait, remember?"

"I know but I'm hungry now. My tummy's rumbling."

Rhys laughed. "Mine, too. You go and feed Bryn and I'll give your mum a hand."

Eva's face broke into a broad grin as she slipped off the sofa. "Deal!"

All three of them converged on the kitchen at the same time, ending up in a squash in the doorway and a fit of giggles. Rhys disentangled himself and went over to the cooker, lifting the lid on the pan simmering on the burner.

"Mmm, cawl, one of my favourites. That smells so good," he said.

"It's not really a summery dish, but I know how much you like it," Hanna said.

Rhys came over, threw his arms around her and nuzzled her hair. "I've never been so well fed, thanks to your wonderful cooking. I am so blessed."

What a curious expression, thought Hanna. She looked up at him and their eyes met in a look charged with emotion.

"Watch out!" yelled Eva from behind them, breaking the spell. They turned to see kibble scattered across the kitchen floor and Bryn looking sheepish. "It was Bryn. He nudged my elbow and made a mess!"

Hanna laughed and wriggled free from Rhys' grasp. "Don't worry, we'll soon get it cleaned up," she said, getting a dustpan and brush out of the cupboard.

"Bowls or plates?" asked Rhys.

"Bowls would be better." Hanna smiled to herself. Back to reality.

Cosmo had appeared from nowhere, rubbing against their legs, waiting for food and adding to the confusion in the compact kitchen. They danced around each other in a kind of awkward ballet as Eva refilled the animals' dishes with kibble and Rhys rifled through cupboards and drawers in search of bowls and cutlery. It took him a couple of minutes to find them. Hanna wondered why he could never remember which cupboards contained what. She said nothing and ladled out the steaming lamb stew into the waiting bowls. Rhys helped her carry them over to the table.

A few moments of uncustomary silence fell as they settled down to eat. Hanna felt a warm glow, a fleeting sense of serenity and contentment, a feeling of sheer contentment that came from just being together. She recalled Rhys' words. *We are all blessed,* she thought as she tucked into her bowl of stew. *We've come too far to let anyone, or anything, ruin our lives now.*

CHAPTER THIRTEEN

Rhys spent Sunday morning scouring the internet for information on surveillance cameras. His colleague Owain had given him detailed instructions on how to install the camera and monitor the footage, but he wanted to be thorough. After all, as he said, he wasn't in the business of tracking people's movements. Animals, on occasions, yes, but this was a whole new ball game for him.

Hanna left him to it and wandered out into the garden where Eva and Bryn were playing on the grass. She moved a lounger into the sun, put on her sunglasses, and settled down with the Sunday paper. Half-way through an interesting feature on the work of the anti-Mafia organisation *Libera*, Hanna heard Rhys shout from inside the cottage. Shortly afterwards, he dashed out of the back door towards her, the camera boxes in his arms.

"That was Lars on the phone," he said, his voice animated. "They've gone, all of them! Left the cottage and gone off in the van, with bags in their hands. He's just seen them as he was walking Brady over that way. Looks as if they'll be away a while.

I'm going to scoot over there and fix up the camera while they're out."

"Fine," said Hanna, standing up and tucking the newspaper under her arm. "But leave Bryn here. He'll only get in your way otherwise. Eva and I'll take him out for a run while you're out."

"Don't forget to take your mobile with you," Rhys said, rooting in the pocket of his jeans for his car keys.

"Will do. Sure you'll be okay?"

"Should be fine. Lars will give me a hand, and I can always call Owain if I get stuck."

Hanna was happy to stay behind, convinced she'd be more hindrance than help. "OK, see you later. Take care." She kissed him lightly and watched him disappear around the side of the house, then heard the sound of the pick-up truck starting up.

She turned and shouted over to Eva: "C'mon, you two, let's go down to the beach and work off some of that energy!"

Along the coast, a light breeze was blowing, the air soft and gentle against her face. It had a curious relaxing quality that Hanna had come across nowhere else, not even in Sicily which she had once loved so much. She tried to push any thoughts of her former home to the back of her mind.

Oystercatchers wheeled over the calm water, the air shrill with their staccato cry. Bryn chased after the few birds that had dared to venture onto the beach, followed by Eva running behind, delighting in the game. Against the azure sky, the Menai Straits stretched out towards the horizon, with Penmon lighthouse in the distance.

On the other side of the beach, the verdant slopes of the hills rose steeply reaching for the sky. Although it was Sunday, few people were about. Such a beautiful peaceful place, thought Hanna, only to have this thought dashed a moment later by a shriek from Eva who was now frolicking in the shallows with Bryn. Hanna walked on at a brisk pace, relishing the opportunity to stretch her legs. She was almost lost in her own little world when her mobile rang. Thinking it would be Rhys, she glanced at the screen and was surprised to see it was Ceri.

"Sorry, it's me again." Ceri sounded agitated.

"What's up? Has something happened?"

"They've only gone and firebombed the *Gazzetta* offices last night..."

Hanna gasped. "Oh my God, that's terrible! Has Sergio been injured? Or anyone else?"

"No, no, he's fine. Fortunately, he was at home at the time. It happened in the early hours so only a few staff were around. A couple had superficial burns and smoke inhalation but no major injuries. The Fire Brigade managed to get there pretty quickly and put the fire out so there's no serious damage to the building. But I'm worried sick. Just as I thought things might be settling down..." Her voice trailed off as she started to sob.

Hanna felt helpless, thinking nothing she could say would comfort her friend.

"And how's Sergio feeling? Has he had a chance to speak to his dad about it?"

"He's not said much. We've not really discussed it in any detail. You know how he is, pretty sanguine at the best of times. He's playing it down, but I'm really concerned. And the timing, straight after the *Gazzetta* broke the Mafia fraud scam story that ran with Sergio's by-line. It can't be a coincidence. And then the story got all that wider coverage around Europe. It's a warning, Hanna. What if they come after him next?" Ceri started to sob.

"I'm sure it won't come to that," Hanna replied, although she was less than convinced. "The police will be on to it straight away. He needs to discuss it with his dad."

The sobbing subsided. "Yes, you're right. I'm sure he will.

It's only just happened, and I'm obviously still upset. What with the wedding and everything. This won't put you off coming, will it?"

"As long as nothing else happens," said Hanna, instantly regretting her words.

"What d'you mean? What else could happen?" Ceri replied, a touch of hysteria in her voice.

"Nothing, I'm sure," said Hanna soothingly, trying to reassure her. "It'll be fine, just a one-off."

"That may be," said Ceri bitterly. "Nevertheless, it's a show of strength, a demonstration that despite everything, organised crime means business and isn't going away."

Hanna's was struggling to speak, her mouth dry. With some effort, she managed to piece together a few reassuring phrases to try and pacify her friend. By the time she hung up, Ceri seemed a little calmer. Privately, Hanna thought that if Sergio continued his relentless anti-mafia pursuit, it could only be a matter of time before he too became a target.

CHAPTER FOURTEEN

Hanna woke the following morning to the sound of rain battering against the bedroom window and the wind howling round the cottage. She instinctively reached out for Rhys, but the space next to her was empty and cold. Although the bedside alarm confirmed it was 8.21am, the room was still dark, a sure sign of the gloomy conditions outside.

She lay in bed, listening to the birdsong. Even that was subdued. Other than that, the cottage was quiet. No sound or sign of life from Eva or Bryn. But Rhys would have taken Bryn to work as he usually did. She yawned and stretched, hoping that the sudden change in the weather didn't indicate that summer had come to an end. Slowly, she swung her legs out of bed, shivered, and reached for her fleecy dressing gown.

She padded over to Eva's bedroom but found it empty. A demanding miaow rose from the kitchen. She went downstairs to investigate, and found Cosmo pacing up and down on the worktop keeping a close watch on Eva who was struggling to fill his bowl from a new bag of kibble. Hanna suppressed a giggle.

"Here, let me help," she said.

The determined frown on Eva's face softened. "I thought I could do it, but it's a bit..."

"Heavy? Awkward?"

"Yeah." Eva looked relieved as Hanna took over the task.

No protest for once. For a little girl she could be notoriously stubborn at times. *I wonder where she gets that from*, thought Hanna. She filled the bowl and gave it to Cosmo who attacked the food as if he hadn't eaten for days.

"So, what do you fancy doing today? It's not very nice outside."

"Not sure." Eva shook her head and yawned.

Hanna picked up on the cue. "Did you sleep okay?"

"No, not much. The tree kept banging on my window. I kept thinking someone was outside."

Hanna looked at her closely. Eva didn't seem unduly worried, but there was still a nervousness there, left over from the kidnapping. It was probably only to be expected. Hanna wondered whether the trauma had left any deep-seated damage that would come out in later years. The child psychologist she'd consulted in the aftermath had warned her that this might happen. She didn't want to overreact and make a fuss which could only make matters worse. She vowed to keep an eye on her, as she had ever since it happened. And she'd need to trim that damn tree back.

"So, do you want to go back to bed?"

Eva shook her head again.

"Maybe curl up on the sofa and watch a film?"

Eva's eyes lit up. "Oooh, yes! That'd be great!"

"Anything in particular you'd like to see?"

The little girl pondered for a few minutes before answering, "How about the one about the rat in the restaurant, or the other one about the sheep?"

Hanna instantly understood what she meant. She'd been

clamouring for ages to see both *Ratatouille* and the *Shaun the Sheep* movie.

"I'll see if I can find them. Let's have breakfast and get dressed first. I'll light a fire in the lounge so it's nice and snug. Then we can go out somewhere later if the weather improves."

Eva beamed and threw her arms around Hanna's legs in a hug. Hanna bent down to pick her up and tossed her into the air.

"My, you're getting a bit big for this!" she said, catching the little girl and putting her down again.

"More, more!" insisted the youngster.

"Breakfast!" said Hanna firmly, looking Eva straight in the eye.

"Okay." A reluctant reply as her daughter started to assemble the breakfast things without being asked.

Hanna smiled. Eva was a real joy. But did she really want another child?

Eva was still glued to the antics of Remy the rat, giggling from time to time as the *Ratatouille* story unfolded on the TV screen. Sitting next to Eva on the sofa, Hanna had her laptop open on her knee. She was idly browsing local history and legends, looking for inspiration for the book she was so keen to write. There was no end of material, from tales of piracy and shipwrecks to endless battles and grisly deaths, and umpteen ghost stories. She hadn't yet made a start on all the material that Rhys had brought home. She jotted down a few ideas before turning to contemporary news items.

One report in particular caught her eye. It concerned Italy's struggle to deal with people-trafficking, using the example of the shipwreck off the Sicilian island of Lampedusa where, in 2013, 368 people had died. A handful of arrests were made but no sentences were ever passed down, despite the arrested men languishing in prison for years awaiting trial. The problem wasn't just confined to Italy. Authorities across Europe had declared war on the people responsible for such tragedies at sea. Their aim was to dismantle the criminal networks behind this human misery and capture the smugglers responsible. But they seemed to be making little progress, and the trafficking continued unabated.

Hanna wondered if Luciano and his family might have been involved in the Lampedusa incident. It was perfectly feasible. Just thinking about her and Eva's lucky escape from that world made her feel queasy. There'd been a temporary reprieve, for them at least, while he was inside. But now he was free again, who knew what might happen? The fire-bombing of the newspaper offices was a warning, a sign that the underworld still posed a threat. What she didn't know was whether Luciano posed a threat for her and Eva.

A spasm convulsed through her. She gasped and breathed deeply waiting for it to subside, then stumbled upstairs to the bathroom to splash cold water on her face, resting it against the cool tiles. For the umpteenth time, she wondered if she was doing the right thing by going back to Sicily for the wedding and whether she was putting herself and Rhys in any danger. And what was going on here on her own doorstep? She had a feeling that things were about to unravel.

The weather that afternoon showed no sign of abating, growing worse as the day progressed. It was so dark it was as though the day had never properly dawned. The log fire sapped any desire to move away from its comforting warmth.

After lunch, Eva settled down on the sofa again to watch film number two, *Shaun the Sheep*. Hanna didn't have the heart to tell her otherwise and cuddled up next to her, the flames from the fire lighting their cheeks in an orange glow. Cosmo leapt onto the sofa, sensing a warm spot. Eva curled up in the crook of her mum's arm and together they started to watch the antics of Shaun the Sheep. But Hanna couldn't concentrate, and her mind kept wandering. At some point she must have dozed off, waking halfway through the film with a thumping head and the vague recollection of a jumbled dream, a montage of the past and present, all mixed up with her fears for the future. Eva was still wrapped up in the film, a smile on her face.

Hanna wriggled free and went into the kitchen. The digital clock on the cooker indicated 4.28pm. She started to comb through the cupboards and fridge to see what she could rustle up for dinner. With her back was to the window, she had the strange sensation that she was being watched. Goosebumps appeared on her arms, and she could feel the hair at the nape of her neck stand on end.

Whirling around, she fully expected to see a figure outside looking in on her. But all she could make out were the shadows of the bushes framing the window in the fading light. Gathering her courage, she unlocked the kitchen door and stepped outside, triggering the security light as she did so. She couldn't see anyone or anything. The garden seemed empty. It must have been her imagination.

She breathed a sigh of relief and turned to go back inside. Then she noticed an imprint in the muddy flower bed under the window.

The clear outline of a large boot print.

CHAPTER FIFTEEN

"So, how was your day?" asked Hanna, setting down a large bowl of steaming pasta on the table as Rhys sat down.

Before he had chance to answer, Eva butted in, eyeing up the food. "Mmm, that smells good! What's in the sauce, Mummy?"

Hanna frowned at her; she knew better than to interrupt. "It's your favourite, tuna," she replied, ladling out portions into smaller bowls.

Eva grabbed a fork and started to shovel food into her mouth, tuna sauce dribbling down her chin and onto her sweatshirt in her haste.

Rhys smiled. "Hey, take it easy, young lady! You're almost dropping more than you're getting in your mouth! "

Eva mumbled something and wiped her mouth with the back of her hand.

"Here, try this instead," Hanna admonished, handing her a paper serviette. Eva accepted it sheepishly.

Bryn sauntered over to the table, sniffing the floor and hovering in the hope that some titbit might fall his way.

Hanna turned to Rhys again. "So, how was work?"

"Pretty full-on as usual. I've been more in the office today than out and about. Meetings about the new Partnership Plan that's due out for consultation next year."

"Did you get a chance to check the surveillance camera at the cottage?"

Rhys nodded, his mouth full of pasta. He chewed and swallowed before responding. "I did. The only visitor was a middle-aged woman who arrived with a load of shopping bags from Aldi. She stayed an hour or so and then drove off. No sign of the men or the young girls."

"A local woman, d'you think?"

"Depends what you mean. She's obviously not living there. She looked as if she could have been one of the girls' mothers..."

"You mean she was black?"

Rhys nodded again. "I don't know what's going on, but it's certainly not a holiday let. Let's see what else the footage throws up before we decide what action to take. What did you two get up to today? Did you brave the atrocious weather?"

Eva launched into an explanation of their lazy day, told in excited bursts between mouthfuls of pasta. Rhys listened patiently. Hanna marvelled at the way the little girl could recall the plot of both films in such detail. She was dying to tell Rhys about the intruder, but she'd have to wait until Eva was in bed.

"Did you actually see someone?" Rhys asked, when she'd finished.

"Well, no, not really. But I felt as though I was being watched, and I thought I saw a shadow at the window."

"Could it just have been your imagination?"

"What about the boot print? Surely that's proof enough that someone was out there watching us through the window?"

"A hiker who'd strayed off the path, maybe?" suggested

Rhys. A public footpath ran down one side of their garden, and more than once they'd found the odd stranger who'd strayed even after they'd put up a low boundary fence.

Hanna shrugged. It was a plausible explanation. Perhaps she'd simply overreacted. "Maybe."

"I'll go and take a look to try and put your mind at ease." Rhys opened the kitchen door to a blast of cold wind and disappeared into the back garden. There had been no let-up in the weather all day.

Hanna could see him clearly through the kitchen window thanks to the security light. The thought suddenly struck her that if someone really had been there, why hadn't the light activated?

He reappeared a few minutes later. "Looks like the print of a walking boot to me. Must have been a passing hiker. I don't think it's anything to worry about. I'll check the fence tomorrow, when I get chance, in case there's a gap."

"Thanks, I just feel a bit on edge…"

"That's understandable," he said, coming over and taking her in his arms

"With everything that's going on…"

"Maybe you need a distraction," he murmured, nuzzling her hair. He turned her face towards him and kissed her, gently at first, then more insistently, his hands working their way under her sweatshirt.

Hanna felt a surge of passion flood through her body and they both collapsed onto the sofa, all thoughts of a possible intruder forgotten for the moment.

The following morning, Hanna awoke with a groggy head as if she had a hangover. It was a hangover, of sorts. Rhys was already up. She could hear the pulsating jets of the shower coming from the bathroom. An image of Rhys' muscular body flashed through her mind, and her body trembled in response. She tried to summon the energy to get up but failed. Instead, she snuggled up under the duvet for another few minutes. She had almost dozed off again when Rhys appeared with Bryn, tail wagging, at his side. He set a cup of coffee down on the bedside table next to her.

"Sleep well?" he asked, bending down to kiss her, a cheeky grin on his face.

"You bet!" she smiled.

"I'm off in few minutes. Anything you want to confess before I go?"

"Such as?"

"Oh, you know, some wild fantasy or other."

"I think we worked some of those out last night."

"Plenty more where that came from!" Another lascivious grin.

"Get away with you! What we do need to talk about is Eva's birthday trip to Dublin. We haven't booked the ferry or any attractions yet, what with the cottage and events in Sicily, and it's only a few days away."

"You're the tour guide. What have you got in mind?"

"Ex-tour guide," Hanna reminded him, sitting up and reaching for her coffee. "And remember I don't know Dublin at all."

"No, but you'll probably have it all worked out."

"Not really, but we did promise we'd take Eva to the zoo to see the red panda cubs and she's quite sold on the idea of the ghost bus."

"Well, why don't you book tickets for those and we can talk about other ideas tonight?"

"OK, will do. I'd better get up."

"Stay there and enjoy your coffee. Eva's still fast asleep. I'll leave Bryn with you as I'll be in and out of meetings most of the day."

With a final kiss, he disappeared out of the door. Hanna listened to him starting up the pick-up and driving away, the sound gradually fading.

Later that morning, Hanna watched Eva in the garden from the kitchen window. The little girl's face screwed up in concentration as she scoured the lawn in search of daisies to make a chain, Bryn by her side. The day was glorious, a light blue sky speckled with the occasional fluffy cloud, and the sun was warm, drying up the damp from the day before. It was if there had been a change of seasons from one day to the next.

Hanna felt cheerful and upbeat, unsure whether it was caused by the weather or the events of the previous evening. She smiled to herself, relishing the inner glow that flowed through her body. As she approached the table to switch on her laptop, ready to book the events in Dublin, her mobile rang.

"More girls have arrived at the cottage!" blurted out an excited Rhys.

CHAPTER SIXTEEN

"What? Different girls, or the same ones?" Hanna asked.

"I'm pretty sure these girls are new. It's the same van, with the two men and that woman I saw the other day. It's difficult to tell much from the footage as it only gives you a limited view. I'm going to swing over there later if I get a chance. It might have to wait until I finish work, whatever time that is."

"Be careful, don't let yourself be seen," warned Hanna, feeling slightly alarmed. "If there are any connections with Luciano, there's no telling—"

"Don't worry, I will. Just thought I'd let you know. Whatever's going on, the cottage seems to have a pivotal role."

"And something that may be best left to the authorities to investigate."

"That's not what you said before..."

"I know, but that was different. It was personal, I couldn't risk anything happening to Eva. Don't get involved. Please tell me you'll hand it over if there's anything suspicious."

A slight pause. Hanna could sense he was reluctant to agree with her.

"OK, OK. Don't worry, will do," said Rhys. "But actually, I

have every right to intervene on behalf of the Park Authority if they're in breach of the rental agreement."

"Fine, but just be careful, that's all. We've been through enough already. We don't want any reprisals."

"I won't do anything that will compromise our situation, I promise. See you later."

With a final "Take care", Hanna rang off. She could still see Eva from the kitchen window and was thinking about her old cottage when her mobile rang again. This time it was Ceri.

"Hi, how are things? Has something else happened?" Hanna asked.

"No, thank God. Everything's gone quiet, but there's a strange atmosphere in Palermo. Tense, like the calm before the storm, as if there's something brewing..."

"That must be unnerving."

"It is, especially with the wedding only three weeks away. Just as well we're getting married outside the city. You're both still coming, aren't you?"

Hanna sighed; she was getting tired of being asked this. "Yes, all being well. Any news of Luciano?"

"None. He seems to be keeping a low profile. That doesn't mean he's not up to something, but nothing that's attracting any attention. How are things with you?"

"Well, the surveillance footage is showing that there's still movement at the cottage. Rhys is going over there later today to see if we can find out anything further."

"He's not thinking of confronting them, is he?"

"I've warned him to be careful and to notify the authorities rather than getting involved directly."

"Quite right, too. I talked to Sergio about it, and he was all for coming over in person to investigate. He's convinced that this is all part of a network for trafficking women from Africa into Europe via Sicily. If so, it would make a great case study for the story he's working on."

"Christ, Ceri, that could be bloody dangerous! I can't help thinking it's too much of a coincidence that Luciano's cousin seems to be involved..."

"I know, you're still scared for Eva and yourself."

"For all of us, Ceri. This time, it has to be the authorities that run the risks, not us."

A deep sigh down the phone. "Tell that to Sergio. He wouldn't have got the EU farming fraud story without taking chances."

Hanna felt her heart plummet. "But the stakes are so high. You're about to get married and have an opportunity to make a new life for yourselves on the mainland."

"But he'll always want to hunt down stories and perpetrators of injustice. It's just the way he is. Even if we did move away, there'd be some peril or other lurking on the horizon."

Hanna laughed nervously. "Well, I'm fortunate to be well away from that. I swapped life in a Mafia family for a tranquil existence in the Welsh hills."

"Or did you? What's going on at the cottage seems to be far from tranquil."

"Thanks for reminding me. But it's not affecting any of us directly. Yet."

"Long may that continue. Well, I'd better be going. Got my stint to do at the refugee centre this afternoon."

"How's it going?"

"Good. I'm beginning to find my feet now. A lot of the work is to do with sorting out health checks and papers. It takes time to win over the women's trust. They've obviously been through such hardship just surviving the journey, let alone what they went through in the countries they've come from and what they've suffered and seen en route. We try to give them practical advice and support and help them overcome some of the official hurdles."

"Do they ever open up about what they've been through?"

"Rarely. Maybe with time..."

"I don't know how you do it."

"At least, I'm trying to help make a difference."

"Good for you. I'm sure it's appreciated," said Hanna, feeling a twinge of guilt as she remembered the past. She had turned her back on the migrant situation to focus solely on Eva, trying to forget, and distance herself from that world. Had she been selfish? Or was it a normal reaction for a mother with a small daughter who'd once been kidnapped? Yes, she took an interest in the plight of the migrants coming through Sicily, but it was detached and at arm's length now, rather than anything personal.

A curt text from Rhys later that afternoon alerted Hanna to the fact that he was 'onto something'. No further explanation. Hanna wondered if he'd gone up to the cottage on his own or had taken one of his colleagues with him. Knowing Rhys, he'd be on his own.

Eva was engrossed in watching a TV programme about African wild cats, Bryn curled up asleep at her feet. Hanna turned to her laptop to pick up on the research she was doing for her book. But her heart wasn't in it. She stared at the contents on the screen, but her mind kept wandering back to Rhys.

As soon as the programme finished, Eva started clamouring for food. Hanna checked her mobile. No further message from Rhys. She shut down her laptop and went into the kitchen to prepare dinner. She'd promised Eva bangers and mash, with onion gravy, another of her daughter's favourite dishes. She made a start on peeling the potatoes.

"Can I help cook the sausages, Mummy? Please?" pleaded Eva, who'd crept up behind her.

"OK," said Hanna, retrieving the pack from the fridge and setting it on the worktop. "You'll need to cut the links between them and then prick each of them with a fork a couple of times. Carefully."

Eva clambered onto the stool she used to reach the worktop. "Why do I need to prick them?"

"Because that way, they'll lose some of their fat and be healthier for us."

"Oh, alright," said Eva solemnly as she began to separate the sausages. "Will they take long to cook? I'm starving!"

"No, we'll pop them under the grill, and they'll be ready in next to no time."

Eva grinned as she brandished a fork and started to stab the sausages.

Hanna glanced at the kitchen clock. Ten past six and still no word or sign from Rhys. Should she text him to see if he'd make it for dinner? *No,* she thought, *I can always cook some more sausages when he gets back.*

"Can we have baked beans, too?" Eva asked.

"'Course we can, poppet," Hanna replied, getting plates out of the cupboard.

It was only when they sat down to eat that Eva noticed Rhys was missing.

"Where's Daddy? Why isn't he home for dinner?" she asked, dangling a chunk of sausage from her fork.

"He's working, sweetheart. He'll be back soon."

"Will he be back before I go to bed so I can say goodnight?"

"Yes, I'm sure he will be. Now, eat up your sausages."

Eva didn't need much encouragement and soon polished off

the lot, leaving smudges of tomato sauce around her mouth. She got down from the table and went off to play with Cosmo in the lounge.

By her bedtime, there had still been no word from Rhys. Hanna was getting really agitated now, sure that something had happened. It wasn't like him; he was usually so eager to keep in touch, so dependable. It took all her strength to console Eva and reassure her that everything was fine. By now, she'd tried ringing and texting him several times but hadn't been able to reach him or get any response.

Her mobile rang shortly after 11pm. She snatched the phone from the sofa and stared at the unknown number on the screen.

"Hello, who is this?" she demanded.

"Is that Hanna Sullivan, partner of Rhys Morgan?" asked a gentle female voice with a pronounced accent.

"Yes. Who's this? What's happened? Is he OK?"

"This is Staff Nurse Agnes Wysocki from the Accident and Emergency Department at Gwynedd Hospital in Bangor. Rhys has had a bit of an accident. Nothing too serious, just a few stitches and some bruising. He's been treated and is ready to be discharged. Are you able to come and collect him?"

A cold chill spread through Hanna's body. "Yes, yes, of course," she stammered, her mouth so dry she could hardly respond. "I'll come straight away. Can I speak to him?"

"We've checked him over and he's well enough to go home but he's still a little bit – how do you say? – woozy? He's having a lie down at the minute."

"OK, I'll leave straight away. I'm only in Abergarron, so it won't take me long."

"Thank you. We'll see you shortly, then."

Hanna ended the call. She could feel her head hammering and her heart thumping as she gathered her car keys from the coffee table. What the hell had happened, and why hadn't he called her himself? At least it wasn't anything serious. What about Eva? She couldn't leave her on her own; she'd have to take her along. She opened the bedroom door quietly. Eva was sleeping peacefully, but not for long. Hanna bundled her up in the duvet and carried her out to the car.

The little girl slowly opened her eyes. "What's going on? Where are we going?"

Hanna gritted her teeth. Memories of the day they'd fled Italy came flooding back. "It's fine, go back to sleep. I'll explain later."

CHAPTER SEVENTEEN

"So, are you going to tell me what happened?" asked Hanna, stealing a sideways glance at Rhys from behind the steering wheel. Livid bruising covered the right-hand side of his face, with several ugly black stitches over one eye.

He winced as he shifted uncomfortably in the passenger seat next to her, trying to turn his head to check on Eva.

"Don't worry about her," said Hanna, looking in the rear-view mirror. "She's dropped off to sleep."

"Think I took a few kicks in the ribs, too," said Rhys, trying to find a more comfortable position. He let out a faint groan. "The painkillers are starting to wear off."

"We'll be home soon. You can explain later if you don't feel up to it now."

"No, it's OK. At least I'm alive to tell the tale."

His half-hearted attempt at humour didn't fool Hanna. She could tell he was in quite some discomfort but was trying to put on a brave face.

"Well, I went up to the cottage after work and the white van was parked outside but no one was about. After about half an hour or so, the same two men came out carrying a number of small boxes which they loaded into the van. Then that woman I'd seen up there before came out with a group of girls. She was shouting at them and waving her arms, but I couldn't understand anything; it was all in some guttural, foreign language. The girls were obviously reluctant to get in the van. I ran back to the pick-up and decided to follow them to see what they were up to." He paused as if speaking was an effort. "Not the wisest move, as it turned out."

Hanna shot him a sympathetic smile. "Tell me later, it'll keep."

"No, it's fine," he insisted, picking up the thread again. "I followed the van onto the A55 towards Holyhead. By now, it was getting dark. I should have called you, but I didn't want to lose them. The van pulled up near the freight terminal and some of the girls got out, together with the older woman and one of the men. The other guy drove off with the rest of the girls. It seemed such a strange place to leave the girls. There was hardly anyone about at that time of night.

"I left the pick-up behind a lorry and got out to get a closer look. I could see the girls huddled together under a streetlight. But as I watched, figures appeared from the shadows and approached them. There appeared to be some negotiation with the woman, then the girls would sidle off with the punters behind the containers. It's obviously an established arrangement."

"Oh my God," said Hanna in disbelief. "How old would you say these girls were?"

"Hard to say, but maybe thirteen or fourteen. Fifteen at the most."

Hanna felt sick, a knot forming in the pit of her stomach.

"I was trying to capture it on my phone when, next minute, I felt a thump on the back of my head. I remember falling, then nothing more. I must have blacked out. Next thing I know, I'm in a taxi being taken to A&E. The driver found me in the street."

Hanna sighed and shook her head in exasperation, thankful that nothing more serious had happened. "I told you not to get involved. Did you tell the hospital staff you'd been hit on the head?"

"No, I know the drill all too well. They'd have insisted on keeping me in for observation. I've had worse. And if they knew I'd been attacked, they'd have made me report it to the local police. I said I'd fallen in the street, and they seemed a bit sceptical but didn't question me further. My damn phone seems to have disappeared, so I couldn't call and let you know what had happened, and no photos either."

"There's still time to report it," said Hanna, stealing another glance at him. His face was contorted with pain, but he kept on talking.

"I know, but there's no real harm done," Rhys replied as if he'd already made his mind up. "Better not to involve the local plods at this stage. Is Sergio serious about coming over to investigate?"

"I wouldn't have thought so."

Hanna pulled up outside the cottage. Rhys opened the car door and clambered out slowly, moving with difficulty.

"The only problem is that now they know someone's on to them," he said. "And what's worse, they know that someone is me."

The following morning, Rhys tried to get out of bed, but the effort was etched on his face. He begrudgingly admitted that his ribs were sore, and he was still feeling light-headed. Hanna made him stay him in bed to rest up, and called the Park Authority to tell them he wouldn't be coming into work.

He staggered into the kitchen late morning, clutching his head.

Hanna frowned. "How are you feeling?"

"As if I've got a bad hangover," he said, slumping into the nearest chair.

"Here, take two of these," she replied, putting a pack of paracetamol and a glass of water on the table in front of him. "I'll make some coffee."

He popped two tablets out of the blister pack straight into his mouth, washing them down with a swig of water. Shouts rang from the garden where Eva and Bryn were playing. He grimaced.

"I'll be fine in a bit," he said in answer to Hanna's unspoken question.

She said nothing, knowing her concerned face spoke volumes. She carried the cafetière over to the table with two mugs.

"So," she said softly, pouring the coffee and handing a mug to Rhys, "it looks like we have a child prostitution ring on our hands. What do you think was in the boxes?"

"Who knows? Drugs, probably," said Rhys, taking a sip and recoiling as the drink scalded his tongue.

"Christ, this is serious," said Hanna. "If Luciano's cousin, Angelo, is involved, there **must** be a Sicilian connection. With Luciano too, no doubt. I need to speak to Ceri and Sergio first before we even think about reporting it to the police. If we're going to, that is. There's no real proof at the moment. But they'd only have to put a watch on the cottage and track the girls' movements in Holyhead to get the evidence. That's if they've got the resources..."

Rhys rubbed his head and took a slurp of coffee.

"Still sore?"

"A bit, but nothing to worry about. If only I had my phone,

we'd have some evidence. I must have dropped it when I was attacked."

An hour or so later, Hanna's mobile rang. Another unknown number.

"Hello?" she answered, wondering who the caller might be.

"Hello, is that Hanna Sullivan?"

"Yes," she confirmed. "Who is this?"

"It's Staff Nurse Wysocki from the Accident and Emergency Department at Gwynedd Hospital."

Hanna's heart sank, anticipating a problem relating to Rhys' injuries. "Yes, what is it? Is anything wrong?" she asked tersely.

"Nothing to worry about. I'm ringing to let you know that the taxi driver from last night found your partner's mobile in his cab and handed it over to us. If you want to pop over and pick it up sometime?"

"Oh, great, I'll come over straight away," said Hanna, feeling relieved. "If that's okay with you?"

"Yes, I'll be here – just ask for me when you arrive."

"Fine, see you in about half an hour then. And thanks for letting me know." Hanna rang off.

Rhys looked at Hanna, questioningly.

"That was the staff nurse from last night. The taxi driver found your phone in his cab and handed it in. I'll pop over to the hospital now and pick it up."

"I wonder if it's still working."

"She didn't say."

Rhys smiled. "If it is, we might have some evidence after all."

CHAPTER EIGHTEEN

Hanna and Rhys drove first to the hospital to pick up the phone, with a reluctant Eva in the back seat with Bryn. After checking that Rhys would be fit enough to drive, Hanna drove on to the freight terminal in Holyhead to collect the pick-up that he'd left there the night before. This gave Rhys a chance to examine his phone. The screen was smashed, but it still seemed to be in working order. He gave a triumphant whoop of joy when he found the photos of the previous evening's activities. Hanna pulled in at the side of the road.

His joy was short-lived. "Damn!" he said, looking disappointed. "These don't prove a thing." He handed the phone to Hanna. "Back to square one."

The images were hazy, the figures blurred under the streetlight.

"Never mind," she said. "There'll be other opportunities. I'm beginning to think we should turn the whole thing over to the police and not get involved any further. Didn't you have a friend in the force?"

"Yes, but he's moved down to Aberystwyth. He could

always give us advice though, and he's still got all his old contacts up here."

"I think it's unlikely that your attackers could identity you. From what you've said, it was pretty dark, and everything happened so quickly. They didn't get hold of your phone either, so I think we're safe for the moment."

Rhys gave her a strange look, as if to question whether she would ever feel truly safe. "You reckon?"

"Not really. It's just with Angelo being involved, it seems to make it more personal somehow. You think I'm being a bit paranoid, don't you?" asked Hanna, with a slight nervous laugh.

"Not after everything you and Eva have been through." Rhys paused. "Weren't you going to call Ceri?"

"Yes, I... Let's talk about it later." Hanna didn't want to discuss it further in the car, conscious that Eva might be listening.

She drove on, and talk turned to their plans for the trip to Dublin that weekend. Half an hour later, they reached the freight terminal at Holyhead. Fortunately, the lorry Rhys had parked behind was still in the same place and he managed to recognise it easily enough. They returned home separately, Bryn insisting on going with Rhys while Eva stayed with her mum, telling silly jokes all the way home.

Once back at the cottage, Hanna heard a thud coming from Eva's bedroom. She popped her head round the door and found the little girl looking forlorn, her alpaca bag and its contents strewn across the floor.

"What's going on?" she asked.

"I was packing my stuff for our trip to Dublin. The bag fell off the bed and everything's gone everywhere," the youngster wailed, her words tumbling out breathlessly.

"Never mind. Nothing's broken, has it?" Hanna said, going over to help her daughter to pick up the items.

"Don't think so. We **are** still going, aren't we?" asked the little girl anxiously. "Daddy will be well enough, won't he?"

"I'm sure he'll be just fine," said Hanna firmly, putting the refilled bag back on the bed. "We don't want you to miss out on your birthday treat, do we?"

"And who's going to feed Cosmo?"

"I've arranged for a lady in the village to do that."

Eva's face broke into a beaming smile. "We *are* still going to see the red pandas, aren't we?"

Hanna hugged her tightly. "Of course, we are, poppet. Can't wait!"

Hanna hovered in the doorway, watching Rhys toss some clothes into a weekend bag. "Feeling better?"

"Yes, much. A few days away will do us good. What did Ceri say?"

She sighed. "More what did Sergio say. He's convinced that this is all part of Luciano's operation, and he definitely wants to come over and investigate further. Apparently, he's uncovered similar operations in other parts of Europe – Germany, France, the Netherlands, but none as yet with a direct link back to Luciano. He's got his sights on nailing this story. It could be the breakthrough he's looking for. It'll stand him in good stead for that job offer on the mainland."

"But when? The wedding's only a few weeks away, and we're not here for the next few days."

Hanna shrugged. "You know what he's like when he's onto a story. He's talking of coming over for a few days when we get back. Just him, not Ceri."

Rhys looked thoughtful. "Well, I suppose if he's got the

time. It may be a way to put paid to the whole thing, once and for all. What d'you reckon?"

"And at least that way, we won't be involving ourselves directly."

He nodded. "OK, seems like a plan."

"And no sleuthing when we're away. This trip's a chance to forget all about it for a few days."

Hanna had always wanted to go to Dublin, but the thought of the ferry crossing put her off. It had taken some time before Rhys finally managed to persuade her that the Irish Sea wouldn't be as rough as she'd imagined, not during the calmer summer months. And when Eva heard about the red panda cubs at Dublin Zoo, it seemed like the perfect opportunity.

Hanna's last ferry journey had been a nightmare. She'd caught the overnight boat from Naples to Palermo when a gale-force wind had appeared out of nowhere. The usually calm Mediterranean Sea became a mass of angry waves that buffeted the ship for several hours until it was eventually able to dock. She clearly remembered passengers wailing, and the pervasive stench of vomit. Not an experience she was keen to repeat any time soon.

But this time was different, with a relatively calm sea, and only a slight breeze. They were able to venture on deck in the hazy sunshine to get some air. Eva was as excited as if they'd taken her on a first-class cruise ship, running from one side of the ship to the other, and Bryn couldn't stop barking.

And the excitement didn't stop there. Their accommodation, an apartment in an old converted woollen mill close to the city centre, was more than they could have hoped for. Exposed brickwork and beams, floor-length windows, squidgy grey velour sofas, Hanna couldn't believe their luck, particularly with having Bryn in tow. Not many places accepted dogs.

Their break in Dublin promised to be a welcome distraction from recent events.

And it was. Each day was a whirlwind of trips: to the zoo, bus and ghost tours, exploring Grafton Street and walking along the River Liffey, even enough time for Rhys to sneak off to the Guinness factory. And lots of traditional Irish fare to savour: slow-cooked lamb stew, succulent sausages and colcannon, mouth-watering burgers, soda bread and bannock. Not forgetting a special birthday tea for Eva – fish and chips for her, steamed mussels for them, followed by ice-cream sundaes. The only reminder of home and events of the previous few days was a text from Sergio to confirm his arrival the day after they got back.

Before they knew it, their long weekend was over, and it was time to come home.

They boarded the ferry for the return crossing and had just settled down on deck when Rhys jumped up, as if startled.

"Are you OK? What is it?" asked Hanna, standing up and trying to follow his line of vision.

Rhys strained his neck, trying to see through the throng of people.

"I... I can't see her now. For a moment, I thought I saw that woman from the cottage..."

Hanna scanned the crowd of summer visitors but failed to see anyone who might fit that description.

"Perhaps it was my imagination," he said apologetically.

Eva tugged at Hanna's sleeve, pointing out to sea. "Look, look over there! I can see fins!" Hanna turned her head and looked out to sea.

"Where? I can't see anything."

"Over there, there!" Eva jumped up and down with excitement, continuing to point in the same direction. All Hanna could see was the endless swell which was starting to make her feel a little queasy, when a dolphin surfaced briefly before disappearing again into the waves.

"Oh, wow! How great to see a dolphin!" Hanna said.

They scoured the surface for any more sightings, but the dolphin had vanished. Eva's face fell.

"He must have got separated from his family and friends in the pod and is searching for them," said Rhys.

Eva's face fell even further.

"But he'll be fine," added Rhys quickly, "It's quite common for this to happen, but they usually find their way back okay. We've been very lucky to have seen him at all. You did well to spot him."

A faint smile from Eva.

The rest of the crossing proved uneventful, although the wind was getting up and they had to seek shelter inside. Hanna was thankful she'd taken her seasickness medication which seemed to be keeping her on a more-or-less even keel.

It was only when they returned to the car shortly before arriving back at Holyhead that Hanna noticed Rhys staring intently out of the windscreen.

"Have you spotted that woman again?" she asked.

Rhys nodded and pointed at the vehicle several cars in front. A white van, with the back doors open, where a stout, middle-aged black woman was ushering a group of young black teenage girls into the back. The sight brought them back to reality with a sickening jolt.

CHAPTER NINETEEN

Up ahead, the driver of the white van started the engine and pulled slowly off the ferry car deck and headed away from the terminal towards Holyhead town centre. Rhys and Hanna's Cactus joined the convoy, all moving in the same direction towards the A55.

"I know what you're thinking," said Hanna, glancing sideways at Rhys who was focusing on the van in front, almost hidden now by an HGV with an Irish number plate. "You're tempted to follow the van back up to the cottage."

Rhys smiled ruefully. "Is it that obvious? You know me too well."

A mournful wail sounded from the backseat, echoed by a soft canine whine. "Are we nearly home yet?" asked Eva, rubbing her eyes. She was tired now and growing ever more fractious.

"We will be soon, munchkin. Not long to go now," said Hanna soothingly.

"What if I drop you off at home and go up there on my own?" said Rhys.

"And achieve what exactly?" asked Hanna, feeling slightly

irritated. Whatever was going on at the cottage, she didn't want them getting involved any more than they had to. "We've got a rough idea now what they're up to. Sergio's coming over tomorrow, and he'll have all the time in the world to follow it up properly without us having to get more involved."

"Yes, you're right," Rhys agreed reluctantly. "I'll check the surveillance camera footage when we get home and catch up with the past couple of days."

They continued in silence, following the rest of the ferry traffic until they reached the A55 which linked the town and the island of Anglesey with the North Wales mainland.

"That's strange," said Rhys, as the traffic began to disperse. "The white van's disappeared. There's no sign of it. We didn't see it turn off anywhere. Where the hell's it gone? Maybe they're not heading straight for the cottage after all."

At Eva's suggestion, they picked up takeaway pizzas for supper on the way home. It was a good idea as they were all hungry and tired. Hanna was glad she didn't have to start cooking when they got home. They ate the pizzas straight out of the box, sitting cross-legged on the lounge floor. Eva started yawning halfway through hers but managed to polish off most of it. She announced she was off to bed almost immediately afterwards and disappeared into her room. Rhys looked at Hanna with raised eyebrows; she usually wanted to stay up as late as possible, especially during the school holidays.

Hanna laughed. "All the excitement of the last few days must have proved too much. Must say I feel pretty whacked, too. Don't think I'll be far behind her."

"I'll just make a start on the surveillance footage," said Rhys, opening his laptop. "What time did Sergio say he's arriving?"

"His flight gets into Manchester late afternoon. He should

be here for dinner, by the time he clears customs, collects his hire car and drives down."

"Right, I need to get a move on then. I won't have much time tomorrow as I'll be back at work."

Hanna frowned. "But aren't you tired? You did all the driving, after all."

"Don't worry about me, *cariad*," Rhys grinned, catching her arm as she passed by. "I still have loads of energy!" As if to demonstrate, he drew her closer to him and they exchanged a brief passionate kiss before he pulled away again. "Away, now! Don't distract a man from his work!"

"Fine, I'll clear up and leave you to it," replied Hanna with a smile as she began to pick up the pizza boxes from the floor.

After tidying up, Hanna settled down on the sofa to read a little more of the novel she was halfway through. Rhys was glued to his laptop, scrolling through the footage.

"Found anything of interest?" she asked.

"Not as yet," he mumbled, his eyes not leaving the screen. "There's still a bit to go through."

Hanna tried to focus on her book, but she ended up reading the same passage several times without taking in the words. After an hour or so, she couldn't contain her curiosity any longer and asked again.

"Well," he said, turning to her, "I've not watched it all, but there's a definite pattern emerging. The older woman seems to be staying at the cottage now with the girls. Every now and again, she ventures out with one of the men in the van to do food shopping. The girls are there during the day, but leave in the van at about the same time every evening and return late on. It's quite difficult to make out what's going on properly once it gets dark, as the camera doesn't have decent night vision. You can just about make out the headlights of the van and blurry figures. It looks as if the same number of people return, but I can't be sure."

Hanna mulled this over before replying, "What I don't get is that if a new group of girls arrived from Ireland, what happened to the previous ones? There's not enough room in the cottage for one group, let alone two. Where do they sleep? There aren't enough beds for all of them."

"That's one for Sergio to look into. I've had enough for one day. Time to turn in," Rhys said, switching off the laptop and closing the lid. He stood up, stretched, and yawned almost in the same movement. "Hopefully, he'll be able to get to the bottom of what's really going on and provide us with some answers."

CHAPTER TWENTY

Hanna was up early the next morning, early enough to have a coffee with Rhys before he left for work. She had a busy day ahead, preparing for Sergio's arrival that evening. He'd only visited them once before in their new home, not long after they'd moved in. Ceri had come over on her own a couple of times since then, as Sergio was always pursuing some story or other he couldn't tear himself away from. Hanna wanted to prepare a traditional Welsh dinner to welcome him, so the first task was a quick dash to Tesco after breakfast to stock up on food for the next few days.

"But I don't want to go shopping," said Eva, sitting at the table, still in her pyjamas, and playing with her cereal. "I want to stay here and play in the garden."

"We need something nice for dinner tonight when Uncle Sergio arrives. You can't stay here on your own. We won't be long, and you can help me choose the menu. You can have a quick look around the toys too, if we have time," cajoled Hanna.

Eva's face lit up at the mention of Sergio, who she'd taken a real shine to during his last visit. "Is Auntie Ceri coming too?"

"Not this time, sweetheart. And Uncle Sergio will be busy working most days. He's not come for a holiday."

The little girl's face fell again.

"But he'll be here for a couple of days so you will see him," said Hanna hastily before Eva became difficult again. "Now, go and get dressed and we'll be off."

The quick dash to Tesco wasn't quite as quick as Hanna would have liked. Dragging a reluctant youngster round the aisles was no joy. Not even the toys held any appeal for Eva that day. Boring, boring, she declared, until she spotted boxes of brightly-coloured pansies.

"Mummy, Mummy, look at those flowers with the smiley faces!" she said, tugging at Hanna's sleeve with excitement. "They look so happy, just like people! Can I have some to put in my garden? Can we get some, pleeease?"

Hanna laughed. She'd always liked pansies herself; they reminded her of growing up in a small Lancashire village in the hills. Pots of pansies waving in the breeze, either side of the front door to their little terraced house. Happy flowers, happy times.

"Aren't they lovely?" she replied. "Yes, of course we can get some. Which colours do you like?"

Eva deliberated for ages, weighing up the various colour combinations. Finally, she picked her favourites: one, a vivid yellow and apricot mix, the other, a deep pink with paler faces. A school project earlier in the year had sparked her interest in gardening. Hanna had cleared a small patch in the garden just for her. After sowing a few seeds and forgetting to water them, the attraction had quickly waned. Eva's attention seemed to flit from one project to another at alarming speed these days. Hanna reminded herself that this was probably the sign of an enquiring mind, a positive rather than a negative. Perhaps she'd grow up to be a starter, not a finisher, more of an ideas person. Anyway, Hanna was happy to see her enthusiasm rekindled.

The food shopping finished, they loaded up the car, Eva insisting on putting the boxes of pansies on her lap for the journey home. She then addressed them as if they were new pets, launching into an explanation of where they were going and what their new home would be like.

"You'll have to look after them you know, just like Bryn and Cosmo," Hanna said, trying to keep a straight face. "They'll need water, and food every so often."

"Food?" asked Eva. "How do they eat? They don't have mouths."

Hanna had to laugh this time and proceeded to explain to her wide-eyed daughter how you fed plants.

"We'll have some lunch, then I'll show you how to plant them," Hanna promised. "You can do that while I get the spare room ready for Uncle Sergio."

"Deal!" said Eva, a broad smile lighting up her face.

Hanna hastily prepared a lunch of houmous, served with warm pitta breads, a tomato salad, and a pitcher of homemade lemonade. She piled everything onto a tray and took it into the garden where the hazy sunshine had warmed the air enough to eat outside. Eva bolted her food down, smearing houmous across her face and all over her fingers. She was restless and fidgety, keen to make a start on planting her precious pansies. Hanna made her wash her face and hands while she rummaged through the shed for a trowel. Eva's 'garden' was simply a patch of bare soil, dotted with the odd piece of slate and some shells and pebbles that Eva had brought back from the beach.

"You'll have to clear away all the stones and shells first to make room," Hanna said, kneeling down next to her daughter. "Then, you'll have to dig holes for each pansy to go in, like so..." She demonstrated. "You need to be very careful with each pansy, so you don't damage the roots. When they're planted, you'll need to get the watering can and water them in. That way they'll feel at home."

Eva nodded. "OK. Let me do it now."

"Right. Shout if you get stuck."

"I'll be okay," her daughter answered, brandishing the trowel in a determined fashion.

Hanna smiled. As she cleared away the lunch plates, she wondered for the umpteenth time whether she wanted another baby. Would it be good for Eva? There would be a bit of an age gap. Would it be good for Rhys and her? Rhys was really keen, and she was tempted. Perhaps if it were a little boy this time?

After washing the dishes, she made a start on the spare room, clearing her work papers away from the desk and moving her laptop into the bedroom, before making up the spare bed. She vacuumed the rug and left a pile of clean towels on the chair next to the bed, before attacking the lounge and bathroom, while keeping an eye on Eva. Each time she checked, she found her little daughter absorbed and talking to her new 'friends'.

By mid-afternoon, the cottage was sparkling clean and tidy. Hanna looked round in satisfaction. As a finishing touch, she went into the garden and picked a bunch of brightly-coloured phlox to put in a vase on the mantelpiece. Perfect.

Time for a coffee. As she switched the kettle on, her mobile beeped. A text from Sergio to say there was a slight delay with the departure of the flight, but he hoped to be with them for about 7.30pm. A quick break, then she'd make a start on dinner.

CHAPTER TWENTY-ONE

Later that day, Eva was listening to a CBeebies bedtime story about a dancing cat when Bryn uttered a low growl. He padded over to the porch, his growl intensifying into a sharp bark. A car door slammed. Eva jumped up and ran to the front door.

"Sounds like Sergio's arrived," Hanna called up the stairs. Rhys was getting changed, having not long returned from work. She rose from the sofa where she'd been idly flipping through a magazine. Through the window, she could see Sergio getting a small case out of the boot of his hire car. She reached over Eva to open the front door, Bryn barking frantically at her heels. Rhys thundered down the stairs.

"*Salve*, Hanna," said Sergio, a beaming smile on his face, He threw his arms round her in a bear hug, and kissed her on both cheeks, nodding to Rhys and Eva behind her. "Lovely to see you all again."

"And you," said Hanna, as he turned to embrace Rhys and then scooped Eva up into his arms, much to her delight. She immediately dissolved into a fit of giggles.

"Come on in. How was the journey?" Rhys asked.

"Fine. We ran into a tailwind, so the flight made up time. I only had cabin baggage, so I passed straight through passport control to pick up the hire car. A bit of traffic on the roads, but nothing major."

He balanced Eva in his arms and followed them into the lounge, bending down to pat Bryn at the same time. "Mmm, what's that delicious smell? I could eat a horse!"

Hanna smiled, remembering his legendary voracious appetite. "I thought you'd be hungry, so I've prepared a little Welsh lamb supper to welcome you. Should be ready in about ten minutes or so."

"Time for an aperitif, then. G&T?" asked Rhys.

"*Perfetto*, just what I need!" Sergio set Eva down and collapsed onto the squishy sofa with a smile. He seemed pleased that Rhys had remembered his favourite tipple.

"Even the gin is Welsh. It comes from a distillery a few miles away," said Rhys, as he fetched glasses and started to prepare the drinks. "They do quite a range now. You may want to take some home with you."

"*Magari*! If only," said Sergio. "But I don't think bottles of gin in my hand luggage would go down too well with airport security. Shame, though, especially now that Ceri's taken a liking to it, too."

Hanna seemed to remember that gin had always been a favourite tipple of Ceri's. Had she gone off it at some point that Hanna couldn't remember? She felt a sudden pang that the distance between them could be affecting their close friendship. A noise distracted her. Eva was trying to drag the suitcase across the floor.

"Eva, leave that, please!" said Hanna, "Here, let me take it up to Sergio's room out of the way."

"I was only trying to help," said Eva, looking crestfallen.

"I know, poppet, but it's a bit heavy for you." Hanna took

the case off her and disappeared momentarily upstairs. Rhys handed her a tumbler as she returned to the lounge.

"*Cin, cin!*" said Sergio, raising his glass in a toast. "Here's to a successful conclusion of this affair, whatever that may be."

"Absolutely," said Hanna at the same time Rhys said, "We'll all drink to that."

"Can we eat now?" Eva whined. "I'm starving!"

Hanna laughed. "'Course, we can, sweet pea! I think we all are. Come and give me a hand in the kitchen."

Dinner was a noisy affair that reminded Hanna of her former life in Sicily. The happy days before she'd discovered the truth about Luciano. It was a chance to catch up with the wedding preparations and discuss Rhys' speech. Little was said about the real reason for Sergio's visit.

After they'd finished the smoked mackerel pâté starter, Hanna brought over the *pièce de résistance*: a platter bearing a leg of roast lamb, still sizzling from the oven, surrounded by crisp roast potatoes, all cooked in garlic and rosemary.

Eva clapped her hands in delight. "Yummy, yummy! My favourite!"

Another of her favourites, thought Hanna with a smile.

"*Meraviglioso!*" said Sergio, grinning. "If you're going to feed me like this, I'll have to go on a diet when I get home, otherwise I won't fit into my wedding suit!"

"Get away with you!" replied Hanna, setting the platter on the table. "It's not only in Sicily where you can eat well, you know. I thought you might appreciate some Welsh lamb."

"Obviously!" said Sergio, almost salivating as he watched Rhys set about carving the joint. "But I see that you've kept the wine Italian." He pointed to the bottle of Barbera, opened earlier and left to breathe. "Shall I do the honours?"

Hanna nodded and went to fetch the vegetables and gravy. Sergio poured the wine and they each helped themselves to the plentiful food. Once their plates were piled high, Rhys raised his glass.

"A toast," he said, "to the coming nuptials. May you and Ceri have a fabulous day and a long and happy life together."

"I'll drink to that!" said Sergio, taking a sip of the robust red wine.

"Hear, hear!" said Hanna, almost simultaneously, while Eva giggled and slurped her apple juice.

Bryn barked and lurked by the side of the table, hoping for titbits.

"No," said Rhys sternly. "You're not to beg at the table. Go and lie down."

The dog slunk off and did what he was told but kept a mindful eye out for any scraps falling to the floor.

Talk turned again to the big day, the conversation growing louder with each glass of wine. By the time they'd cleared their plates, Eva was starting to get fidgety, a sure sign she was tired.

"Still got room for pud?" Hanna asked her.

Eva nodded slowly. "I think so."

Rhys gave Hanna a hand to clear the plates, while Sergio chatted to Eva about what she'd been doing in the school holidays. Eva seemed to perk up when the attention was focused on her.

Pud was Welsh rhubarb cake, served with dollops of cream.

"This is wonderful!" said Sergio, patting his stomach appreciatively when he'd wolfed his second helping. "Rhubarb is not something we eat very often at home."

Hanna couldn't help noticing that despite a few extra kilos, Sergio seemed to look much the same as when she'd first met him. He must have a great metabolism, she thought, given the amount of food he could put away. But his job probably kept him pretty active, much like Rhys.

"Coffee, or would you prefer something else?" she asked.

"I have the perfect solution," he said, vanishing upstairs and reappearing from his room holding several bags. From one, which bore the logo of the airport shop, he pulled out a bottle. "An *amaro*, I think. What do you say?"

Hanna hugged him. "You're a treasure, you remembered! I've always loved Averna and it's so difficult to find here. Make yourself comfortable in the lounge while I get some glasses."

A clatter of chairs sounded against the stone floor as they left the dining table and headed for the lounge.

"I brought you each a little *regalo*," Sergio said, smiling, handing each of them a bag.

Eva's eyes lit up, her tiredness disappearing in a flash. Diving into her bag, she pulled out an exquisitely-wrapped present. She tore off the wrapping paper to reveal a box and whooped with joy when she opened it and saw what was inside.

"Oooh, alcapas! Awesome! *Grazie tante, zio Sergio!*" she said, climbing onto the sofa and giving him a massive hug. "Thanks so much, Uncle Sergio!"

"*Prego, signorina!*" said Sergio, laughing, almost smothered by the little girl's embrace.

Hanna's heart gave a jolt; it was strange hearing Eva speak Italian after so long. Clearly, she hadn't forgotten it.

Eva got down and waved her present in the air. "Look, look what Uncle Sergio got me! An alcapa watch! I just love it! It's the best thing ever! I'll be able to wear it to the wedding!"

Hanna shot Sergio a warning glance not to say anything. She'd have to pick the right time to talk to Eva, once it was certain they'd be going without her. She bent down and took a closer look at the pretty blue and pink watch, the strap adorned with llamas in various poses. "Here, let me help you with it," she said, fastening it around her daughter's wrist. "There, doesn't that look good?"

Eva was so excited by the present that it took some time before she reluctantly agreed to go to bed. Even then, she refused to take off the treasured gift.

"Well, Sergio, that certainly went down well," said Hanna, once Eva was safely tucked up. "How did you know she liked alpacas or llamas?"

"It was Ceri's idea," Sergio replied. "You told her about how besotted Eva had become after seeing Nerys'. She saw the watch in a shop and thought it would make an ideal present." He nodded towards the other bags. "You'd better take a look at your own presents."

Hanna delved into hers and pulled out a small box wrapped in gold paper with an elaborate black and gold bow almost bigger than the box itself. She opened it carefully and squealed with delight when she saw the contents: a filigree silver bracelet with a single sea urchin charm.

"That's amazing, really beautiful!" she said, slipping it on and holding her arm out to admire it

"Another of Ceri's brainwaves!" Sergio smiled wryly.

Rhys tore into his oddly-shaped present to find a joint of Nebrodi cured ham, one of his favourite Sicilian delicacies. "Wonderful, we'll really enjoy this! Thanks again, Sergio!"

"You're very welcome," said Sergio. "And now before it gets too late, we need to get down to the serious stuff and the real reason for me being here. Tell me all you know so I don't waste any time and can get on to it first thing tomorrow."

The atmosphere in the cottage changed in an instant. It was as if the temperature had fallen several degrees.

"Yes, you're right," said Rhys, a little reluctantly, having been mellowed by the food and wine. He levered himself up from the sofa. "I'll get the footage so we can make a start."

CHAPTER TWENTY-TWO

Hanna and Rhys saw little of Sergio over the next few days. He would get up early, even before Rhys, and return late, sometimes in the early hours of the morning. One night he didn't come back at all. He'd warned Hanna this might happen and not to worry. When they did see him, he was usually tired out, hungry, and monosyllabic. Hanna wondered if he usually worked like this and how Ceri coped, especially in light of the risks he might be facing. She must be used to it by now, Hanna thought, grateful that her own life was much more settled than before.

He had promised a full update before he left, whenever that would be. Hanna and Rhys were both bursting with curiosity to know what was going on, but decided to leave him to it; he'd tell them soon enough when he was ready. The hardest part was dealing with Eva's constant questions. She couldn't understand why Uncle Sergio was staying but not spending any time with them.

"He'd love to, sweet pea, but he's working," Hanna explained patiently. "He's not on holiday like you."

"But what does he do?" the little girl persisted.

"He's a journalist and writes articles for a newspaper in Sicily," explained Hanna.

"What's he doing here in Wales, then?"

"He's working on a story. I don't know the details," Hanna said, keen to avoid any further explanation.

Eva looked puzzled. "But..." she began, only to be interrupted by Hanna's mobile ringing.

It was Ceri, full of news about the wedding, especially the wonderful place out in the countryside they'd booked for the reception where she'd been that day to finalise the arrangements.

Hanna waited for a lull in her excited chatter, then asked, "And how are things after all the arrests for that agricultural fraud?"

"Pretty quiet at the moment," Ceri responded. "It'll be some time before the case comes to court. Still no news about Luciano. How's Sergio getting on? Has he said how long he'll be staying?"

"Not sure. We've not seen much of him, actually," Hanna replied, surprised that Ceri seemed to have no idea when he'd be returning home.

"These things take their own course," said Ceri philosophically. She was evidently used to him disappearing for days at a time, with very little contact.

"But the wedding is only a couple of weeks away..." said Hanna.

"I know, I know," said Ceri, "but all the arrangements are in place and it's better that he's not here. He'd only try to interfere, otherwise. This way, he can focus fully on getting all the evidence he needs for the story. It'll be a massive scoop and will make his name as an investigative journalist."

Hanna could hear the pride in her voice as she spoke of him.

Proud, but pragmatic too. They'd obviously developed a close understanding over the years.

"Don't worry, Sergio'll let us both know soon enough what he's up to," was the last thing Ceri said before hanging up.

Sure enough, on the Saturday morning Hanna found a note on the dining room table:

"Sorry I've been so busy, and you've not seen much of me. I'm on to something – just need the weekend to see things through. Can we talk Monday? Planning to fly back Tuesday morning. Hope that's OK with you? Sergio xx"

She wondered what he'd discovered. Not long to wait to find out, she thought.

Sergio was gone all weekend. He'd left the cottage early that morning and hadn't returned by the time they went to bed on Sunday night. He must have got back at some point during the night, and was still in bed when Hanna got up on Monday morning. Rhys was home too, having worked over the weekend. Summer was a busy time for wardens, with the increased number of visitors to the National Park.

Hanna was clearing up the breakfast dishes when Sergio wandered into the kitchen, heavy-eyed, his dark hair tousled, looking as if he'd just woken up.

"Sorry," he said with his customary shrug, "I had a bit of a late night, or rather an early morning."

Hanna smiled. "I'll make you some coffee. Anything to eat? An almond croissant?"

"That would be great, thanks."

"I'll bring it out into the garden," said Hanna. She glanced at him expectantly, dying to question him further, but he still looked half-asleep. It would take a few coffees to revive him, especially if he'd had little sleep. She'd have to curb her curiosity a little while longer.

Sergio wandered out into the garden, his laptop under his arm. Another warm and sunny morning. Through the kitchen window, Hanna could see him strike up a conversation with Rhys but couldn't make out the words. Further down the garden, she could see a giggling Eva wrapped up in a tug-of-war with Bryn, one that the dog seemed to be winning.

After popping a couple of croissants in the microwave, she put several heaped spoonfuls of ground coffee in the cafetière, added hot water, then frothed up a jug of milk, enough for three *cappuccinos*. She carried everything out on a tray to where Sergio and Rhys were deep in conversation, their voices muted, heads lowered and close together, as if sharing a secret. They sprang apart as she approached.

She set the tray on the table, sat down, and handed round the coffees. Sergio's face lit up. He looked more awake now, a far cry from a few minutes ago. He smiled, took a sip of his coffee and bit into a croissant.

"So, Sergio, are you going to tell us what you've been able to find out?" Hanna asked, unable to restrain her curiosity any longer.

"Well," he said, swallowing a mouthful of pastry. "I can't say for certain that there's a definite pattern after only a few days, but it fits with what I've seen in other places, and there's no doubt that it all stems from Sicily."

He paused for another sip of coffee and a bite of croissant. Hanna swivelled round to check that Eva was out of earshot.

"Go on," Hanna urged. Rhys shot her a glance, warning her to be patient.

"A bit of background first," said Sergio. "You probably know that people-trafficking from Africa across the Mediterranean continues to be a problem. You hear less about it in the news, but that doesn't mean it's gone away.

"The infamous trafficking route through Libya and then on by boat can cost each migrant somewhere in the region of 35,000 euros. Migrants pay a fee upfront and agree to pay off the rest by working in their country of destination. Thousands of African women are lured to Europe by the promise of jobs as domestic assistants, nannies, even hairdressers. But all that's waiting for them at the other end is prostitution and/or drug trafficking."

"But why don't they escape and go to the police?" said Hanna, sensing the answer even as she asked the question.

"They're too scared. Many of them are forced to undergo a juju ritual before they leave and take an oath to repay their debt. If they fail, they believe they will die."

Hanna went pale. "Oh my God! Can't the authorities do anything to stop it?"

"They do their best, but it's hard to crack these trafficking rings. Often, it's African gangs working with the local Mafia. From time to time, arrests are made but they're usually the *pesci piccoli* – the little fish, the small fry – and the trade continues unabated."

Rhys continued to listen intently while a fidgety Hanna sat on the edge of her chair, clearly agitated. "Go on!" she urged again.

"*Eh, pazienza*, Hanna! I'm getting there. There's a growing demand now for underage girls, not only in Sicily and on the mainland, but also in the rest of Europe. That's what I've been investigating, the links between Sicily and Europe. I've already got evidence from Germany and France."

"And now you think Wales is involved too?" asked Rhys.

Sergio nodded.

"*Esatto*. Increasingly, the trafficking rings have been looking for new markets, quieter routes, smaller cities. That's what I think we have here."

Hanna was dying to ask whether he thought Luciano might be involved. Rhys must have sensed her growing impatience and shot her another warning glance. Sergio was talking quickly now, warming to his subject, his voice animated. Hanna looked at him expectantly, hoping to spur him on.

"Just let me finish my breakfast and I'll tell you what I've discovered," he said, reaching for a second croissant.

CHAPTER TWENTY-THREE

Sergio wiped the last crumbs from his mouth, drained his coffee cup, and launched into his account of the last few days.

"*Allora*, it was Tuesday when I got here. You saw the white transit van coming over from Dublin the day before, with a group of young black girls and the older woman on board. You didn't see them leave Holyhead, but they must have headed for Hanna's old cottage at some point. I can only assume these girls had only just arrived in the country. By the time I turned up there on Wednesday morning, there was no sign of the van or the men, but I could see the woman and the girls quite clearly through the windows. Every now and again the girls would venture outside, but this seemed to annoy the older women who would chase them in again.

"The girls seemed very young, no more than fourteen, fifteen at most. Difficult to say precisely how many of them there were – my guess would be between eight and ten.

"The van returned early evening, with the two men. I managed to get some shots of them," he said, turning to his laptop and angling it so that Hanna and Rhys could see. "You might recognise them."

Hanna and Rhys peered at the photos on the screen.

"That's definitely Angelo, Luciano's cousin," said Hanna, with a shiver, pointing to a man with an olive complexion and dark hair, cropped short and peppered with grey. "And the other one is Ottavio's father."

Rhys nodded. "I've definitely seen them on previous footage from the surveillance camera. And they were both there the night I followed them into Holyhead."

Sergio nodded and continued. "At about half seven, they all piled into the van: the two guys, the woman and the girls, hardly recognisable now, all dressed up, their faces plastered with makeup, like dolls or mannequins. No prizes for guessing where they were heading."

"The docks at Holyhead," said Rhys, grimly. "Just like the other night."

"*Esatto.* The van pulled up by the container terminal and the woman and most of the girls got out. It was pretty deserted at that hour. Then it drove away. That first night I stayed with the main group. I parked up and managed to get quite close to them but stayed out of sight. Once it got dark, there was a steady flow of male visitors, some arriving on foot, others by car. Some of them seemed to be lorry drivers.

"The girls were obviously being made to offer sex, but I could tell from the expressions on their faces that they weren't happy about it. The woman was doing all the negotiating, obviously acting as the madam. From what I could tell, the transactions were carried out behind the containers. All very sleazy. This carried on until the early hours, when the van returned to pick them up and take them home.

"The second night, I followed the van into the town centre. It parked up and four of the girls got out, two with each guy. The guys seemed to be showing the girls the ropes. This time, it was pushing drugs, not themselves. Some of the business was done on the street, sometimes they'd disappear into a pub or club for a while. It all seemed to be a well-rehearsed ritual."

Hanna's eyes widened with astonishment. "Oh my God! Was no one bothered that they were so young? How can they get away with this? Were there no police around?"

Sergio smiled sadly at her naïvety. "Unfortunately, it's a specialist market with growing demand. The appeal is that the girls are underage, I'm afraid. It's happening all over Europe. As I said before, the problem is nailing the big boys and trying to stop it happening. If I can get enough evidence – and I'm sure I can – that the roots are in Sicily, we'll be able to get the bastards behind it once and for all."

"But why North Wales?" asked Rhys, with a puzzled expression.

"*Aspetta*, hang on, I'll explain," replied Sergio. "So, the same thing happened the following day and the day after. The girls stayed at the cottage during the day, then ventured into Holyhead at night to do business.

"But on the Saturday, the pattern was different. The van arrived at lunchtime and they all piled in, this time carrying bags. I wondered if they were leaving for good. Again, I followed them and ended up in a scruffy backstreet in Manchester. The van parked up and they all disappeared into a shabby terrace. Hours later, it became apparent why. Again, a constant stream of men passed through the house from early evening onwards. It only quietened off towards early Sunday morning. Same thing happened again on Sunday night, although things didn't go on quite so late. Then they got into the van and came back to the cottage."

Tears sprang to Hanna's eyes. "Those poor girls. Can't we do anything to help them?"

Sergio shrugged. "If we do anything rash, we might help this group of girls but there'll be plenty of others. We need to... *dobbiamo stoncarlo sul nascere* once and for all."

Rhys looked mystified.

"Nip it in the bud," Hanna translated mechanically.

"Get those running the trafficking network," Sergio concluded, pausing for breath.

"So, where do you think Wales fits in?" asked Rhys.

"As I said earlier, the traffickers seem to be using less well-known routes to escape detection. Coming into the UK via Ireland is a new one to me. North Wales could be a testing or training ground for new girls. Once they're 'trained', they're moved on to cities where there's a bigger market and more money to be made. Then new girls arrive..."

Hanna shuddered at the thought, wondering how many young girls were caught up in this plight across Europe.

"And how can you be sure that it all stems back to Sicily?" she asked.

"Well, we know that Luciano's cousin, Angelo, is involved. But there's one important thing I've not told you." Sergio hesitated for a moment. "A third man turned up on Saturday morning and accompanied the group to Manchester but didn't return with them. Proof without doubt of the Sicilian connection."

Hanna felt her stomach lurch, anticipating Sergio's answer.

"Luciano."

CHAPTER TWENTY-FOUR

Hanna felt sick. Her head began to spin. She tried to speak but nothing came out. An increasing feeling of nausea and light-headedness washed over her, and she grabbed the arms of the chair to steady herself

Rhys hurried over and put a tentative arm around her shoulders. "Are you okay, *cariad?*"

She nodded, but the slight movement made her feel worse. She jumped up and dashed inside to the bathroom where she retched into the basin. A few minutes later, Rhys appeared in the doorway.

"Better?"

Hanna nodded again, almost imperceptibly. She straightened up and let him help her into the lounge where she sank heavily onto the sofa. Sergio brought a glass of water in from the kitchen. She sipped at it slowly at first, then gulped down the rest. The two men watched her in concern, obviously at a loss to know what to say.

Gradually, the dizziness passed, and she began to feel a little better. Thoughts whirled through her mind. She shook her head. "I just knew he'd have something to do with it," she said eventually. "But what was he doing **here**? D'you think he was trying to track us down?"

Rhys and Sergio looked thoughtful, as if considering the question and how best to respond. Rhys was first to break the silence.

"Well, there's no evidence that Luciano ever knew you'd come here when you left Sicily. When Eva was kidnapped, he wasn't responsible, it was the rival clan. But the fact that Ottavio's father is involved in this trafficking could potentially lead Luciano back to you."

"Problem is we don't know Luciano's state of mind, whether he's harbouring a grudge thinking you turned him into the authorities, or whether he's moved on," said Sergio.

Rhys frowned and turned to face Hanna. "But why would he come after you now? You're no longer a threat to him and his operations."

Hanna sighed. "We've talked about this before. As Sergio said, he might be trying to get his own back on me if he thinks I gave him in to the police."

"Even after all this time?" Rhys looked sceptical.

"Unfortunately, time doesn't matter when it comes to payback for these people," said Sergio. "But I get the feeling that this is purely business, that for some reason he's come over here not to get back at you, but to check up on this part of the set-up."

Hanna stared at Sergio, wondering whether he was serious or merely trying to reassure her. He returned her gaze, looking her straight in the eyes. He seemed sincere enough, and she'd known him long enough to know that he wouldn't try to fob her off with empty words.

"But how can we be sure?" she asked.

Sergio shook his head and shrugged. "We can't be. But the fact that he hasn't returned suggests that he was only here temporarily and has probably gone back to Sicily."

Hanna wondered whether Luciano's fleeting presence was no more than that, a business transaction, a mere coincidence that all this was happening so close to home. Was this too much to hope for?

"And there's no evidence that he's tried to track you down or get in touch, is there?" Sergio continued.

Hanna thought back to the boot print outside the kitchen window. Had that simply been a lost hiker, or could it have been Luciano trying to see Eva with him being so nearby?

Rhys looked at Hanna questioningly.

"No, not really," she said, hesitantly.

"Are you sure?" Sergio scoured her face for a reaction.

"A few days ago, Hanna felt she was being watched through the kitchen window," explained Rhys, as if reading her mind. "We found a footprint, but I'm pretty sure it was someone who'd strayed off the right of way and nothing more. Nothing else has happened since then, has it?"

She shook her head. "No, nothing."

"But someone might have recognised **you**, Rhys, maybe from the night you were attacked when you followed the group to Holyhead, and made the connection with Hanna," Sergio said.

Rhys looked alarmed as if he'd not realised his actions could have endangered his new family. Several minutes passed, the atmosphere between them tense, the only sound the ticking of the clock on the mantelpiece.

"So, what happens now? What do we do about the trafficking?" asked Rhys finally.

"Well, the Sicilian police have already been investigating this for some time," Sergio replied. "My dad's heavily involved. I know from him that the police are determined to close down the trafficking once and for all, but it's a sensitive operation and they won't make a move until they have all the evidence they need.

With this new proof of the link to other European countries, they may consider they have enough to act on. I'll speak to Dad about it when I get back."

He paused. "The fact that underage girls are involved makes the whole business even more abhorrent. Judges are likely to impose harsh sentences. This story will be as big as that massive EU agricultural fraud, if not bigger."

Hanna frowned. "How long is all that likely to take?"

Sergio shrugged and held up his hands. "If the arrests are confined to Sicily, it could be relatively straightforward as it'll only involve our own police. But if it involves other countries, who knows? It could take even longer. Depends on the level of co-operation we get."

Another silence ensued as they contemplated this. The lull was shattered by Eva bounding in, closely followed by an excited Bryn, barking loudly, both demanding food. The shrill ringtone of Sergio's mobile added to the cacophony, and he disappeared into the garden to answer it. Glad of the distraction, Hanna got up and followed Eva and Bryn into the kitchen.

"What d'you fancy?" she asked the little girl who was rummaging in the cupboard for Bryn's dog chews.

"Cheese on toast, cheese on toast! My favourite! I love cheese on toast!" Eva jumped up and down, almost singing the words, a dog chew in each hand. Bryn snatched them greedily from her grasp.

Hanna smiled and reached for the multigrain loaf in the bread bin. She cut a chunky slice of bread, grated some cheddar cheese on top, and popped it under the grill. Snatches of Sergio's conversation floated in from outside, but it was difficult to hear much with Bryn barking and Eva who'd now launched into her own version of the pop song *Señorita*.

A few minutes later Sergio came rushing in from the garden, his face aglow, almost shaking with excitement.

"Hanna, Sergio, you'll never guess! A real breakthrough! Ceri thinks we've got a witness. Someone who's been a victim of trafficking and is prepared to go on record as a witness, as long as we can protect her. We've really got ourselves a story now!"

CHAPTER TWENTY-FIVE

The following morning Hanna waited until Rhys had gone to work and Sergio had left for the airport before calling Ceri.

"Sorry I've not had chance to speak the last couple of days. It's been pretty hectic here, what with going to Dublin and then Sergio coming over."

"So I saw from your messages. Don't worry, Sergio's been keeping me updated. Sort of. You know how he is. How are things? Did he get away OK?" Ceri sounded a little tense.

"Yes, everything's fine." Hanna glanced at the clock on the mantelpiece. "He should be at the airport by now."

"I heard about Luciano turning up in Wales. That must have been a hell of a shock. Did he try to contact you while he was there?"

A knot formed in the pit of Hanna's stomach at the mention of her husband. "No, Sergio saw him just the once at my old cottage with the girls. He's not been near here as far as I know." The footprint outside the window sprang to mind again.

"He may not even know you're living there. Or he may have moved on, mentally I mean. Getting back at you in some way might not be on his mind."

Hanna gnawed at her lip. "But Eva's still his daughter. You'd think he'd want to see her and not give her up completely, whatever's gone on in the past. I'm worried. I don't want him snatching her back, or for anything else to happen to her. She's already been through enough."

The knot tightened and spasms shot through her stomach. With a groan, she sank into the nearest chair.

"You OK?" asked Ceri, a touch of alarm in her voice.

"Yes, fine." Hanna forced out the words. "Difficult to know what to think without knowing his state of mind."

"Sergio's pretty sure it was only a fleeting visit and that he's gone back to Sicily now," said Ceri, obviously trying to reassure her.

"Let's hope so. He certainly hasn't been seen since, thank God. Anyway, tell me about this witness you've found. Sergio mentioned it but he didn't go into any detail."

"Well, it's not definite yet." Ceri's voice was cautious. "She could always change her mind. Bit of a long story, really. A contact at the refugee centre put me in touch with her. Her name is Zhuri. She's originally from Nigeria and was sold by her parents to traffickers when she was thirteen. Zhuri, along with two friends from the same village, was forced to take an oath in a juju ritual where they all promised to repay the cost of their passage to Europe on fear of death."

"My God, that's terrible..." Hanna remembered Sergio had mentioned juju rituals.

"Unfortunately, it's all too common," Ceri continued. "Anyway, the traffickers forced them to become sex workers: Zhuri here in Palermo, while one friend was sent to France, the other to Germany. Zhuri was picked up by the police a couple of months ago soliciting in one of the city's parks, and is now being looked after and rehabilitated in a specialist refugee centre. She's determined to help other girls in the same position. She's still only fifteen."

"That's some story," said Hanna, almost reeling in disbelief.

"And there's a dozen other girls in the centre with similar tales." Ceri sounded bitter. "And that's only one centre, and the ones who managed to get away. God knows how many girls are caught up in this right across Europe…"

Hanna couldn't imagine. It was unbearable to even think about. "Can Zhuri be a witness, at her age?" she asked.

"Apparently so. It can all be done anonymously to protect her identity, which will be changed anyway. She insists on giving evidence. Her mind's set on helping to bring an end to the whole sordid business. She wants to study and become a lawyer here in Italy."

"She sounds very strong-minded for such a young girl."

"Zhuri's quite a character. Bright and opinionated. She should go far. Let's hope she doesn't change her mind about testifying. She's agreed to give Sergio an interview for the paper, too. It'll be quite a breakthrough, both for the police and for Sergio."

"Yes, it's really good news…"

"Hanna, I'll have to go," Ceri interrupted, "I've got the final fitting for the wedding dress this afternoon and I can't miss it."

"'Course not. Call me in a couple of days, or sooner if there's any news."

"I will, don't worry. You **are** still coming?"

"You know I am."

"I'm counting on it. *Ciao.*"

Hanna sighed. The wedding was only ten days away now. With all her heart, she wanted to be there; the only problem was its location. Even before Luciano's release from prison, she wasn't convinced she wanted to return to Sicily. And now, with Luciano free, she was more nervous than ever. But if he could turn up so close to home, maybe nowhere was safe. Or was it mere coincidence? After all, he'd made no move to get in touch. The thoughts continued to churn around her head, returning to the same point of indecision. Eventually she told herself she was more or less committed to going now. Ceri would be devastated if she backed out at this late stage. Besides which, Rhys had promised to give his sister away.

Next problem, what to wear? She went upstairs and started to rifle through her wardrobe for something suitable. It was unlikely; she'd not had much call for occasion wear over the last two years since settling down in Wales. And she needed something lightweight as it would be hot. Sure enough, the search proved useless. Rhys would need a new outfit too.

Hanna frowned, reluctantly admitting that a weekend shopping trip was called for. Her interest in clothes had waned. These days, clothes shopping was more of a necessity than a pleasure. And with Eva in tow, it would likely become even more of a chore. The youngster would get really bored unless they made it into a fun day. Hanna would have to come up with a plan.

The decision was made. First stop, Conwy. A couple of boutiques there might have something of interest, and there were a few menswear shops for Rhys. Then, if they had no luck there, they'd have to go on to Llandudno where there would be more choice.

The plan was to leave early and get there before the weekend tourists arrived in their hordes, to avoid jostling through the crowded streets of the picturesque little coastal town. Visitors mainly came to see the magnificent thirteenth-century castle but spilled out into the streets afterwards, invading the shops and cafes, making the most of their day out.

When Saturday came, it was a beautiful morning, with clear blue skies and a light breeze, and the promise of warm temperatures later. Much too nice to be shopping, thought Hanna, but it had to be done. Eva's reaction to the suggested shopping trip had been lukewarm, only tempered by the promise of a surprise if she was good. Over breakfast she was still grizzly, although she tucked with gusto into the pancakes Hanna had made as a special treat. Even Rhys seemed unusually subdued; he hated shopping.

"So, what's this surprise?" Eva asked for the umpteenth time, as she spooned a dollop of yoghurt onto another blueberry-loaded pancake. Fruit stains were smeared like warpaint across her face, giving her a slightly scary look.

"If I told you, it wouldn't be a surprise, would it?" In truth, Hanna hadn't yet decided. She had a few ideas in mind, but it depended on how the day panned out. "Eat up, then go and wash your face and get ready. We're leaving in about half an hour or so."

She looked at Rhys for confirmation. He nodded, forced a smile, and rose from the table, mug of coffee in hand. "Just time for a quick shower, then. Great breakfast!" He drained his mug, then kissed the top of her head before disappearing upstairs to the bathroom.

Eva pulled another face when she heard that Bryn was staying behind.

"We can't take him shopping, poppet. He'd only be miserable."

"But so will I, and I've got to go," Eva pointed out.

Hanna smiled. "Yes, but you've got a treat waiting for you afterwards."

The little girl looked at her imploringly.

"And no, I'm not going to tell you what it is."

CHAPTER TWENTY-SIX

By the time they arrived in Conwy, it was starting to get busy with the first early-morning shoppers. They parked with ease below the castle ramparts, a short way from the centre. Eva eyed them up wistfully as she climbed out of the car.

"Are we going to the castle, Mummy? Is that the surprise?" she asked.

"Not today. It'll be too busy. Besides, you went there with school only recently," Hanna replied.

"Yes, but I don't mind going again. It's fun," said Eva, jumping up and down.

"Another time maybe," said Rhys. "Today, we've got other things to do."

Eva looked crestfallen, as if she suspected these would be adult things that would have little appeal to her.

"First, you can help us both choose outfits for Ceri and Sergio's wedding," explained Hanna. "Then you can have your surprise."

Eva pulled a face. "How long is that going to take? And why can't I come to the wedding?"

Hanna stared at her. She had seemed perfectly content to

stay with Nerys when she had spoken to her. "It won't take long. And you'd only be bored at the wedding. All grown-ups and very few children."

The little girl stared back, a sulky expression on her face. "Can we go on the walls first, then?"

Hanna and Rhys exchanged glances.

"Sure, why not?" said Rhys, locking the car. "Just be careful you don't fall."

They headed for the nearest tower and climbed up the stone steps, Eva going up on all fours, to follow the ramparts around the town. Ahead of them stood the magnificent medieval fortress, a dark silhouette looming against an almost perfect blue sky, a monument to Wales' turbulent past.

The castle always reminded Hanna of that first meeting with Rhys after they'd fled Sicily, followed by the drive up to the cottage in the hills in his rickety old Land Rover. There'd been an easy familiarity between them from the start, and an instant attraction that she'd tried hard to ignore. Getting Eva to a place of safety had been uppermost in her mind at the time.

"Come on, you two!" yelled Eva, shaking her from her reverie.

Hanna noticed with alarm that she was some way in front of them now, and was starting to jump down the steep stone steps that descended to the castle car park.

"Hold on there!" said Rhys, quickening his step towards her.

Eva stumbled, and Rhys managed to grab her hand in time before she fell. She giggled as if it was a game and let him help her down the rest of the steps.

Rhys kept hold of her hand as they crossed the junction into Castle Street, leaving Hanna free to browse the shop windows. She automatically headed for her favourite boutique, one where she'd bought a number of items in the past. Expensive, classy, timeless items, all beautifully made, that she wore time and time again. She couldn't remember if they stocked more formal outfits; she'd never had the need for them before.

Leaving Rhys and Eva to pay a visit to the nearby handmade-sweet shop, she pushed open the door of the boutique, activating the bell as she did so. The assistant smiled in greeting, asked if she needed any help, and pointed her towards the back of the shop where the merchandise hung on rails in colour-coded order. Hanna selected five potential outfits and took them over to the fitting room to try on.

By the time she emerged wearing the first outfit, Rhys had returned with Eva, cheeks bulging from their purchases. She tried on each outfit in turn and, with help from her two critics, opted for a sleeveless Masai dress in an abstract flower print in soft shades of coral and caramel, with a matching coral jacket. The style was flattering, long and flowing, cut to accentuate her curves, and comfortable and cool. Perfect for the wedding.

Rhys looked her up and down in admiration. "That outfit," he said, "is simply stunning. You'll have to be careful that you don't overshadow my sister! You could almost wear that to your own wedding..."

A knowing look passed between them. Would that ever happen, Hanna wondered, realising not for the first time that she was still married to Luciano.

"It's lovely, Mummy," echoed Eva. "You look so pretty!"

Hanna smiled, marred by a twinge of regret at having to leave Eva behind while they attended the wedding.

"Thanks, guys! This one's my favourite, too! Never thought I'd find something so easily. Let's hope we're as lucky with a suit for you," she said as she disappeared back into the changing room.

Luck, that day, happened to be on their side. Not the first but the second men's shop they ventured into offered a vast array of suits. Rhys opted for an Italian model in a light grey silk and linen mix. Hanna couldn't remember a time he'd ever looked so handsome. The light grey suit set off his dark Celtic good looks perfectly.

Eva was getting bored now and kept nagging them about her surprise.

"Can we go now, Daddy? Is it time for my surprise?" she asked, pulling at his sleeve as he handed over his credit card at the cash desk.

"Yes, pumpkin, just let me pay first," he said, trying to appease her.

They left the shop with their purchases and wandered down to the waterfront, stopping at a stand to buy ice-creams – mint chocolate chip for Eva and salted caramel for them – before joining a queue of people lining up along the quay. There was no containing Eva now; she'd sussed out that a boat trip was to be her surprise.

"Will we see seals?" she asked, so beside herself with excitement that she almost forgot about her ice-cream which had started to melt and drip down her arm.

"Not today, but there'll be lots of birds and other things to see," said Hanna, wiping the drips away with a tissue.

"Will there be puffins?" the little girl persisted.

"'Fraid not. You can only see puffins in very special places and at certain times of the year," Rhys explained, adding quickly, "but we should see plenty of other interesting birds. You'll have to see how many you recognise."

That seemed to have piqued her interest and she fell silent. The queue was edging forward to board the *Princess Christine*. They found seats in the stern of the boat, the ideal spot for getting the best views. Rhys kept a restraining hand on Eva who, he knew, would otherwise be tempted to run up and down the boat. He shot her a warning glance which she accepted without a word.

Once everyone was on board, the skipper started up the engine and pulled away from the quay, steering the boat into the estuary, making for the open sea. The brisk breeze whipped their hair into their faces, and they were thankful for the fleece blankets provided, wrapping them around their shoulders against the cold.

The commentary pointed out places of interest along the way: the imposing limestone headland of the Great Orme at Llandudno further along the coast, and distant views of Anglesey and Puffin Island in the opposite direction. Eva hung over the side of the boat, more fascinated by the birds than the views: the shrill call of the oystercatchers and the screech of gulls as they whirled overhead, and the cormorants diving into the water in search of fish.

Before long, the boat turned and headed back towards Conwy, passing Deganwy on the opposite bank as it made its way up the estuary. The passengers clicked away, taking photos of the imposing castle as it came into view, the boat passing under the bridge to enter the lower Conwy valley. Here the birdlife changed; Eva pointed excitedly as a heron lifted its massive wings and rose majestically with effortless grace above the riverbank. Mallards and shelducks swam happily in the shallows, and the occasional egret waded through the water. Rhys pointed them all out by name to Eva, who repeated them to herself, trying to remember them.

As they sailed upriver, the foothills and mountains of Snowdonia came into view, the perfect backdrop to the pretty valley. Eva oohed and aahed all the while, pointing at the tallest peak they could see.

"What's that one called?" she asked, looking at Rhys.

"That's Carnedd Llywellyn," he answered, with a knowing twinkle in his eye. "The second highest mountain in Wales after Snowdon. Do you fancy climbing it?"

Eva's eyes widened as she regarded its massive size.

"Don't think so," she said, after some consideration. "I've only got little legs. That's much too high."

Hanna laughed and gave her a hug, which the youngster shrugged off, embarrassed in front of so many people. They were having a great day. It was such a pity they had to leave Eva behind when they travelled to Sicily for the wedding. But it was much too risky to take her with them.

Hanna pushed this thought to the back of her head and focused on enjoying the views on the return trip. It was only as the boat was chugging back into the harbour that she suddenly realised that it might be equally risky to let Eva stay at Nerys', so close to the goings-on at the cottage.

If not more so.

CHAPTER TWENTY-SEVEN

Why hadn't it occurred to her before? What sort of mother was she? Now they knew almost for certain there was a link between the business at the cottage and Sicily, and to Luciano in particular, the situation was totally different.

Despite a pleasant lunch at the Castle Hotel where Eva devoured a 'posh' fish finger butty, the thought continued to plague Hanna for the rest of the afternoon, serving as a dampener to an otherwise enjoyable day.

Several times she caught Rhys watching her, no doubt wondering what was making her so subdued. He said nothing, focusing instead on chattering to Eva and keeping her amused. Hanna tried her best to join in, but her heart wasn't in it. How could they go to Sicily now and leave Eva behind? She would never forgive herself if anything happened to her daughter again. By the time they got home, her head was so awash with anxiety, she felt light-headed. She got out of the car, collected the carrier bags from the boot, and was making her way to the front door when she stumbled and fell. Rhys rushed over to help her up.

"Are you sure you're feeling OK? You've been quiet all afternoon." He glanced back at the car to make sure Eva was out of earshot. "I didn't want to ask before in front of Eva."

"I'm fine," she assured him, dusting herself down, and walking awkwardly down the garden path.

She unlocked the door and Bryn came rushing out to greet them, tail wagging, barking furiously. Eva grabbed his Frisbee from the porch, and they disappeared together round the side of the cottage into the back garden.

"It's just..." She dumped the bags on the floor and flopped onto the sofa.

Rhys waited expectantly for her to finish the sentence.

"I suddenly realised that everything's changed," she explained. "How can we go to Sicily for the wedding and leave Eva behind on her own, with everything that's going on at the cottage? It's unthinkable, especially for her to stay with Nerys. It's much too close. I'm not prepared to jeopardise her safety again. I don't think we should take that risk."

Rhys nodded thoughtfully. "Yes, you're right. It hadn't occurred to me. So, what are you saying, that you don't want to go now? What if she stayed somewhere else, further away?"

Hanna looked at him perplexed. "But where? We've haven't got any family living locally and I wouldn't want to ask Megan's mum. It's too much of a responsibility."

"Before we decide one way or another, let me have a think," said Rhys. "There may be a solution. Let's sleep on it and talk tomorrow. Meanwhile, I'll make supper. Stay where you are, and I'll get you a drink."

Rhys, ever the pragmatist. Hanna summoned a wan smile. "Deal!"

"By the way, did we do anything about getting Ceri and Sergio a wedding present?" Rhys asked.

"You mean, did **I** do anything? Don't you remember me telling you that I talked to Ceri about this? She suggested a painting by some local artist they both like, and that we could all go to his studio when we're over for the wedding so they can choose one."

"Oh, yes. I remember now. That's okay, as long as we're still going..." Before Hanna had chance to reply, Cosmo wandered into the lounge, leapt onto the sofa and curled up in a ball on her lap. Hanna stroked him gently and within minutes, his breathing slowed, and she could hear soft feline snores. He had chosen his adoptive home well. Cosmo's presence had a strange calming influence on her, and she could feel her own eyelids growing heavy.

Rhys insisted on not only making supper – pasta with a tuna sauce, one of Eva's favourites – but also on clearing up afterwards so that Hanna could have an early night. Feeling emotionally drained, she accepted gratefully, although she normally never went to bed much before midnight. But a restful night eluded her, her sleep tormented by images of Eva being abducted again, this time by Luciano's henchmen. Visons of the youngster battered and bruised, hungry, abandoned, or worse...

The dreams were so vivid that she awoke in a panic believing them to be true. Rhys did his utmost to quell her growing hysteria, but it was only when Eva, disturbed by the commotion, popped her head round the bedroom door, that Hanna finally began to calm down and realise the visions were imaginary.

"What's the matter, Mummy? Why are you crying?" asked Eva tentatively.

Hanna beckoned to her daughter, holding her arms out

wide. "Come and give me a hug, sweet pea. It was a bad dream, that's all."

Eva ran over to her. "Oh, you get them, too?"

Hanna hugged her tightly, smoothing her hair and kissing the top of her head. "I didn't know you had bad dreams, poppet?"

"Just sometimes," Eva's voice was faint, almost smothered in her embrace. "About the bad men who took me..."

Hanna released her grip and held the little girl at arms' length, searching her face for more information. But Eva lowered her head and didn't answer.

Rhys placed a hand on Hanna's shoulder. "Best leave it for now," he said gently. "It'll only make the situation worse."

She nodded. "You're probably right. Let's go and get some breakfast."

After breakfast, they all piled into the pick-up, Bryn included, and headed for the little village of Abergwyngregyn. It was Rhys' turn to lead the Sunday walk, part of the Snowdonia wardens' summer programme. Today's walk would follow the pretty steep-sided valley up to the spectacular Aber Falls, a popular spot for visitors and locals alike. The subject of the wedding had been dropped for the time being, although it preyed on Hanna's mind. She tried to shake it off and focus on the day ahead.

"Are we going on Daddy's walk with all the tourists?" asked Eva.

Hanna turned around to find Eva wriggling in the back seat and Bryn straining on his harness to reach the open window. "No, sweetheart, we're going to go off on our own to see if we can find any mountain ponies. Then we'll go up to the waterfall and meet up afterwards for a picnic. Is that okay?"

"Awesome!" Eva grinned and clapped her hands together excitedly.

"But there's no guarantee the ponies will be there. They roam wild, so they come and go as they please. We'll be lucky to see them," Hanna continued, trying not to build the little girl's hopes up too much.

"But we saw them last time, I remember!" said Eva.

"Apparently, there've been sightings in the last few days so there's a good chance they'll be there," added Rhys.

Eva's face lit up. "Ooh, I hope so."

"Aber Falls might not be as impressive as the last time we were up here," he continued. "It was winter, remember, and we'd had lots of rain. This summer has been so dry so there won't be as much water coming down from the mountains."

"It's a lovely day and such a pretty spot. I'm sure we'll enjoy it, whatever," said Hanna, trying to keep the tone positive.

Before long, they pulled up in the small car park by the river and crossed the bridge towards the small information centre that was to be the start of the organised walk. Bryn ran to and fro, tail wagging frantically, delighting in so many new smells and doggy friends. As Hanna had suspected, Eva was constantly distracted by the wildflowers and birds, hanging back to indulge her curiosity.

"What are those big black birds with the red beaks and legs?" shouted Eva, pointing at a pair swooping and whirling above their heads.

"Those are choughs," said Rhys. "You see them quite a lot in Wales."

"Come on, Eva, get a move on. We don't want to make Daddy late," said Hanna.

"OK, I'm coming," said Eva, reluctantly tearing herself away from watching the two birds' aerobatic antics.

By the time they reached the information centre, a group of

a dozen or so people were already waiting, wearing walking boots, and kitted out with rucksacks and walking poles, chatting animatedly among themselves. As they approached, snippets of conversation drifted over. One voice stood out, the words melodic, uttered in a foreign but familiar tone. The speaker turned round, and a cold shiver coursed through Hanna's body.

It was the driver of the white transit van.

CHAPTER TWENTY-EIGHT

Rhys was about to greet the small group of people assembled for the walk when Hanna grabbed his arm.

"D'you see who's here?" she almost hissed in his ear.

An anxious look flitted across Rhys' face. "No, who d'you mean?"

"Over there, the guy with the loud voice. It's Ottavio's father, the guy you recognised, the van driver from the cottage. Remember? He was in Holyhead the night you were attacked. He might even be the one behind the attack. Any chance he'll recognise you?"

Rhys frowned. "Christ, let's hope not, or we could really be in trouble. But it was pretty dark that night, so the chances are slim. Anyway, I don't think he was my attacker."

Hanna glared at him. "How can you be sure he wasn't?

Rhys shrugged. "I can't, *cariad*, and I was pretty wound-up at the time. But we have to get on with our lives. We can't be looking over our shoulders the whole time. I have to lead this walk, whatever else."

Hanna was dumbfounded. "You've certainly changed your tune."

He made to pull away, but she still had a tight grip on his arm. "By the way, have you been checking the surveillance camera? Has Luciano showed up again?"

"**Now** you ask me." Rhys sighed. "Yes, and no. No sign of him. Now can I go?"

Hanna reluctantly relinquished her grip.

"Look, I've got to get this thing started. Try and enjoy your walk and I'll see you later." He kissed her lightly on the cheek. "And don't worry. Even if he does recognise me, he won't be able to do much about it in front of a group of people. I'll be fine."

With that, he stepped towards the people waiting for the walk to begin. Hanna grabbed Eva's hand and quickly steered her away as Rhys began to introduce himself and explain the walk itinerary.

She wondered if she'd overreacted. It was bad enough worrying about Luciano from afar, but this latest development was, quite literally, too close to home. Despite the warm sunshine, she felt as if a dark cloud hung permanently over her, whatever she did, wherever she went.

Would she ever be free?

Outside the information centre, Eva tugged Hanna's arm, eager to get going. Bryn stayed behind with Rhys. The dog was in his element, wagging his tail and lapping up attention from the walkers.

Hanna forced a smile as Eva broke free and scampered up the path that led towards the waterfall. "D'you know where you're going?" she shouted after her.

"There's only the one path," said the little girl logically, before running off again.

"Well, be careful, then. Mind you don't fall."

Hanna quickened her pace to keep up. The path undulated gently up through the steep-sided valley, with a fine view of the Carneddau mountains ahead. She made an effort to push her concerns aside and, despite herself, started to relax and enjoy the walk.

She remembered the first time Rhys had brought them here, not long after she and Eva had arrived from Sicily, and how much they'd enjoyed it then. It was a while since they'd visited, although it remained one of their favourite places. Not just for them: it was popular with both locals and tourists and could get quite crowded in the summer, especially at weekends. But today few people were about as it was still early in the day; only the odd hiker and dog-walker.

The sun was warm on her face and a gentle breeze ruffled her hair. Eva was some way ahead but still in view. Suddenly the little girl stopped and cried out excitedly, her words indistinct, caught in the air. Hanna followed her pointing hand and saw a small group of stocky ponies grazing nonchalantly nearby.

She hurried to catch her daughter up and whispered in her ear, "Remember they're wild, Eva, so don't approach them or do anything to spook them."

Eva's eyes filled with disappointment; she was dying to stroke them, Hanna could tell. They sat down on the remains of a low stone wall to watch them for a few minutes, the ponies oblivious to their presence. Gradually the ponies moved further away until one, a handsome chestnut mare, broke into a canter and headed for the hills, closely followed by the others. Hanna captured it on her phone to share with Rhys later. Sightings of the ponies were still rare, and these would be long gone by the time Rhys and his group passed through.

They continued on, their walk punctuated by numerous

stops and endless questions, not all of which Hanna was able to answer.

"You'll have to save the rest of your questions for Daddy. He's the expert, not me," said Hanna eventually, tired of fending off the constant volley of queries.

"It'll be too late by then. I'll have forgotten them all," grumbled Eva.

"Come on, grumpy-head! We're nearly at the waterfall now. If you listen carefully, you can hear it from here."

Eva tilted her head and listened. "Ooh, yes! It's a bit like those shells on the beach that let you hear the sea."

"Come on, race you up the hill!" said Hanna, trying to distract her from asking anything else.

Eva grinned and spurted ahead, eager as always to win. Hanna let her and reached the top of the incline panting. The waterfall was in full view now, impressive as ever, the water creating its own spray as it plunged more than 100 feet over a rocky escarpment. As they got nearer, Eva ran through the spray, whooping loudly, her arms wide apart as if determined to soak up every last drop. Hanna grinned. It was a warm day and she'd soon dry off.

"Can I go for a paddle?" Eva pleaded, moving closer to the pool at the bottom of the fall.

"No!" said Hanna sharply, wondering why water held such a fascination for youngsters. "Sorry, sweetheart, it's too deep there for paddling. We don't want any accidents, do we? Maybe you can have a paddle in the river later."

The little girl accepted this without question, but pulled a face when Hanna grabbed her hand.

"I'm not a baby, you know," she said indignantly.

"I don't want you slipping, that's all," Hanna reasoned.

Together, they gazed up in awe at the spectacular waterfall, almost hypnotised by its rhythmic torrent, their faces sprinkled with spray.

"Awesome!" declared Eva, after a minute or two. Her word of the moment.

"Let's go before we get totally drenched!" said Hanna, pulling the reluctant little girl back to the path. "Then we can have our picnic with Daddy and Bryn."

That did the trick. Eva quickened her pace, running ahead again as they started out on the return leg of the walk. Choughs squawked in the surrounding cliffs as the sun intensified. More people were about now, walking their dogs and enjoying the fine weather. Suddenly, the little girl stopped and pointed to a wildflower meadow some way from the path.

"Mummy, look at those lovely flowers! Can we go over and see them?"

Hanna hesitated and looked at her watch.

"Pleee...se?"

"C'mon then, but we can't be too long," Hanna answered.

She followed Eva, clambering over boulders to get there, almost regretting her decision. By the time they reached the meadow, they were both breathless, but the effort was worth it. Close-up, the flowers were even more stunning: bright blue cornflowers, scarlet and tangerine poppies, pink and white foxgloves, and white ox-eye daisies, all dancing in the sunlight.

"Can we pick some to take home?" Eva pleaded.

Hanna shook her head. "You know you shouldn't pick wildflowers, Eva. They're much prettier left where they are so other people can enjoy them, too."

Eva's face fell. Hanna rummaged in her small rucksack and brought out a packet of Haribo Starmix. The little girl's face lit up. They sat on a low stone wall and munched their way through a handful of the gummy sweets, Eva picking out all the fried eggs, her favourite.

Hanna suddenly remembered the time. "C'mon, we need to meet up with Daddy. Don't have any more sweets, otherwise you won't have any room for lunch."

"OK, OK," grumbled Eva as she jumped off the wall.

Hand in hand, they meandered back to the information centre. As they approached, Hanna kept an eye out for the group to see if there was any sign of Ottavio's father. But the group had already dispersed, and Rhys was sitting outside, talking to another warden. He smiled and waved when he spotted them, got up and left his colleague, Bryn bounding around his feet.

"So, how was the walk?" asked Hanna. "Any trouble? Any sign he recognised you?"

"No, nothing at all," said Rhys, shaking his head. "Great group, lots of questions. Ottavio's a cute little boy and his father behaved like everyone else, no different. There was a woman with them too. His partner, I presume. I caught the odd word of Italian."

Hanna felt a momentary wave of relief. At least, Ottavio's father hadn't recognised Rhys from the other night. Or had he, but it just wasn't the time or the place to follow it up?

Her chain of thought was broken by Rhys' cheery call: "C'mon, gang, let's go down to the river and have lunch. I'm famished!"

Eva shrieked in approval.

But for Hanna, the gnawing anxiety about whether she should leave Eva in the midst of all this had returned.

CHAPTER TWENTY-NINE

The rest of the afternoon passed pleasantly enough. The walk had sharpened their appetites, and they devoured the picnic lunch that Hanna had crammed into Rhys' rucksack.

"You know we could have left all this in the car if we'd thought," said Hanna, as she gathered up the empty containers. "It would have saved you carrying it up to the falls and back."

"But then I'd only have had to trek back to the car to pick it up," said Rhys. "This way, we've been able to have lunch sooner and I got to avoid the extra exercise!"

Hanna grinned as she poured the last of the homemade lemonade out of the flask and handed him a cup. She glanced over at Eva who was paddling in the river, shrieking with delight as she splashed an excited and barking Bryn with water. By now, a few other groups had gathered further along the riverbank, making the most of the fine weather.

She continued to watch their antics, deep in thought. What was it to be: Eva's safety or her best friend's wedding? There was really no contest, she decided. It had to be Eva. Ceri would understand and forgive her absence in the circumstances. She felt Rhys' gaze on her.

"Penny for them?" he asked.

"I don't think we can go to the wedding and leave Eva with Nerys," she said slowly, as if to convince herself. "I'd never forgive myself if we went and something happened to her. The other option would be for you to go on your own. Then at least you wouldn't miss your sister's wedding."

Rhys nodded thoughtfully. "I suppose so. You wouldn't be able to relax and enjoy the festivities if you were worrying about Eva the whole time."

"So, what do you think you'll do?" Hanna asked.

"Not sure. I don't want to go without you, but equally I don't want to let Ceri down. We've always been so close, even if we live in separate countries now. And she's counting on me to give her away."

A few minutes silence ensued until Eva decided she'd had enough of the river and dragged herself away. For someone who'd only been playing in the shallows, she was pretty wet, her rolled-up trousers soaked to well above the knees. Bryn emerged from the water dripping and looking bedraggled, waiting until they were all reunited before shaking himself briskly, showering drops of water in all directions.

"Thanks, Bryn, I really needed that!" Rhys said with a grin.

Hanna grabbed Eva and rubbed her damp legs down with a microfibre towel, then tossed it to Rhys.

"Did you bring Bryn's Frisbee?" she asked.

Rhys rummaged in the rucksack and pulled it out. "Yep, here it is! Who's up for a game, then?"

"Me! Me!" said Eva, jumping up and down, alongside a delighted Bryn, ready for yet another game.

"C'mon, Hanna! You, too!" Rhys pulled Hanna to her feet, leaving her no choice in the matter.

Hanna continued to mull over her dilemma in the car on the way home. She felt that she was the one who had to make the final decision whether to go to the wedding. Only she had lived through the ordeal of Eva being kidnapped, only she knew what Luciano was capable of. Rhys had only been a casual friend at the time, someone who was helping out his sister's best friend.

She'd have to call Ceri the following day and let her know what she'd decided. Her last chance to cancel, with the wedding being less than a week away now. As she weighed up the pros and cons, she began to think more and more that it would be too risky to leave Eva behind.

Her thoughts persisted as she mechanically peeled potatoes and carrots for dinner. By the time she took the shepherd's pie out of the oven, her mind was made up: she would stay in Wales with Eva and Rhys could go to Sicily on his own. She'd tell him after dinner, once Eva had gone to bed.

But it was Rhys who brought the subject up later that evening as they sat next to each other on the sofa. "So, have you thought any more about Eva and what we should do?" he asked softly.

"I've thought of nothing else, especially with Ottavio's father turning up like that today," she replied with a frown.

"And have you reached any conclusion?"

She sighed. "It's just so difficult. I don't want to let Ceri down – I wouldn't miss her wedding for the world – but I can't risk anything else happening to Eva."

Rhys shook his head. "It's a hell of a quandary, I admit. I wish I could come up with a better solution. I suppose there's always the option you suggested – I go on my own and you stay here with her."

"Yes, I've given that some more thought. But unless all this local business gets sorted out sometime soon, we could be in a vulnerable position if we stay here."

Rhys looked shamefaced. "I wouldn't want that. I'm only trying to help, not make things worse."

"Yes, I know," said Hanna, with another sigh. "There's no easy solution."

"Have you heard how Sergio's getting on with the investigation?" Rhys asked.

As if on cue, Hanna's mobile rang. She fished it out of her handbag and glanced at the screen. "This is Ceri now. She may have some news."

Rhys watched as she listened intently for several minutes without interrupting.

"Christ, I can't believe it," she blurted out finally. "You don't think it could be a trick of some sort, do you?"

"Why would it be?" Ceri's voice was so clear, it was if she was in the room in person. "Luciano can't have had any inkling that his phone was being tapped, and he was speaking to his father, not just any old acquaintance. I think we can take it as being genuine."

Hanna exhaled slowly, gripping the arm of the sofa as she did so. "If this is true, it changes everything. It means we've got our lives back and we're safe, no longer having to look over our shoulder. But what about the girls in the cottage? How's Sergio getting on with the story? That's still something we could be implicated in..."

"But Luciano's made no attempt to contact you, has he? He probably doesn't know you're there, and even if he does, it seems he's not bothered, given what he's told his father." Ceri seemed animated, clearly enjoying being the harbinger of good news.

"No, that's true but—"

"But nothing, Hanna! And, according to Sergio, the police should be in a position to round up the traffickers within a few weeks, so that'll be the end of that."

"After the wedding, then?" asked Hanna gingerly, trying to weigh up the situation.

"Probably, but does it really matter now? You and Eva are off the hook, as far as Luciano is concerned. You're safe, Hanna, free to get on with your life."

Hanna gulped, her throat dry, as she tried to take all this in. She desperately wanted to believe it but didn't know if she dared. She glanced at Rhys, who was looking at her quizzically.

"So, no excuses now for not coming to the wedding!" Ceri's voice tinkled like sharp notes being played on a piano. "We'll be expecting you both!"

"No, I guess not," said Hanna. Circumstances had made the decision for her.

"So, what was that all about?" asked Rhys, when Hanna came off the phone.

"The police managed to put a tap on Luciano's home phone line as part of their ongoing investigation. Yesterday he was talking to his father, who asked about the situation with me and Eva. Apparently, he was very dismissive and said that part of his life was over, as if it had never happened as far as he was concerned. He has no intention of trying to get custody of Eva, by fair means or foul. Vincenzo felt it was such a key revelation that I should be told immediately to put my mind at rest, especially with the wedding coming up. It's against police protocol, but it's family, or as good as..."

Rhys' brow furrowed. "You think it's genuine?"

"Well, the police and Sergio and Ceri seem to think so. And, apparently, Luciano's been seen out and about on several occasions with one of his old flames. Someone I've met, actually – she owns a shop in Palermo selling local artwork and handicrafts. Very glamorous, not like me." Hanna laughed briefly, but it sounded hollow, even to her.

A worried look flitted across Rhys' face. "You don't regret... you know...getting together with me, do you?"

"Of course, I don't! Don't even think that. I'm happier now than I ever was in the past, and Eva adores you!" Hanna leaned across and snuggled up to him. "You're happy, too, aren't you?"

"'Course, I am. Can't you tell?" He kissed the top of her head and held her in a tight embrace.

Bryn stirred from the rug and sneaked up onto the sofa, settling down next to them, determined not to be left out. Hanna and Rhys laughed at his antics, and any slight tension between them completely disappeared. He tilted her face towards him, kissing her gently at first, then more urgently until he pulled her up from the sofa and steered her upstairs towards the bedroom.

CHAPTER THIRTY

The following morning, Hanna felt almost euphoric, relieved that the decision had been taken out of her hands and she didn't have to disappoint Ceri after all. The good news about Luciano couldn't have come at a more opportune time.

She got up early and had a coffee with Rhys before he left for work, filled with renewed energy that she put partly down to the news and partly to their frenetic lovemaking the night before. She hummed softly to herself as she prepared breakfast. By the time it was ready, there was still no sign of Eva. Strange, as she was usually up and raring to go in the morning.

Hanna popped her head round the little girl's bedroom door. The bed was empty, the covers thrown back as if in haste, but no Eva. She called her daughter's name loudly several times. No response. No sign of her in the bathroom or the lounge. Hanna's stomach knotted in fear. Where the hell was she?

A vague recollection of the kitchen door being slightly ajar made her dash outside into the garden. There, from behind the hedge that ran the full length of the garden came a reedy sing-song voice. Peeping around the hedge, she saw Eva, still in her pyjamas, busy watering her pansies and evidently giving them a good talking-to.

Hanna relaxed and smiled. But she remembered her initial reaction. How long would it take to convince her that Luciano was no longer a threat, and her anxieties disappeared once and for all?

The next few days were a flurry of activity. It was almost as if they were preparing for some expedition into the unknown, rather than a long weekend in Sicily for a friend's wedding. Hanna had briefly considered taking Eva with them, but decided against it. She realised with alarm that the last time she'd been apart from Eva for so long was during the kidnapping. A disturbing thought. She threw herself into making sure that this time, her daughter would have a pleasant experience, calling Nerys to finalise arrangements, talking at length and giving her detailed instructions.

"Hanna, for God's sake, I have looked after children before," said Nerys, clearly exasperated. "Matt and Olivia, my nephew and niece, were up here from London for a few days last week. They were a real handful. I'm sure we'll be able to cope okay with Eva."

"Sorry if I'm being over-protective," said Hanna. "It's just that—"

"I know. The circumstances. I understand."

"I'll send over a list of emergency contacts – doctor, vet etc. You **will** call me if there are any problems, won't you, however small?"

"Stop worrying, Hanna! We'll be fine," said Nerys. "You're only going for a couple of days and I won't let her out of my sight. There's plenty here to keep her occupied, what with looking after the animals, and helping in the pottery. She can spend some time painting with Lars and doing some baking with me. The time will fly by! Go and enjoy yourselves and have fun!"

"OK, OK. I wanted to make sure that both of you have got all you need. I've not left her overnight since—"

"I know, I know," replied Nerys quickly. "Lars and I are looking forward to having her here. She's such a lovely little girl, always so lively and inquisitive!"

"She's that, alright," said Hanna. "Just hope she's not too boisterous."

"No such thing! We'll have fun, you'll see."

"Fine. We'll bring her up early Thursday afternoon, then, if that's okay?"

"We'll be ready. I'm planning on making chocolate brownies that day so Eva can help me with those."

"Good luck with that!" said Hanna with a smile, picturing the mess Eva would make, her mouth caked with uncooked mixture as she sampled it before baking.

As she rang off, Eva tottered precariously into the bedroom in an old pair of Hanna's high heels, grinning.

Hanna frowned. "Where did you find those? I've not seen them for ages."

"They were at the back of my toy cupboard," said Eva.

"Aren't you supposed to be getting your things together to go to Auntie Nerys'?" Hanna asked, wondering how the shoes had ended up there.

"I was. That's how I found them. Everything I want to take is on the bed. Come and see." Eva pulled Hanna towards the door.

"You'd better take those off first," said Hanna, pointing to the shoes. "Otherwise, you'll fall and hurt yourself."

"OK, OK," said Eva, reluctantly kicking them off, leaving them in the middle of the floor.

Hanna sighed and picked them up. Not much call for high heels in Wales. She ran her fingers over the soft leather. Beautiful. She remembered buying them one spring during a trip to Rome with Luciano, in a shop on Via Cola di Rienzo. She pushed the thought from her mind, stuffed the shoes into a carrier bag and pushed it to the back of her wardrobe.

She followed Eva to find her bedroom in chaos. The bed was covered in clothes and toys, with Cosmo curled up asleep in the middle of it all. Bryn stood at the foot of the bed, wagging his tail furiously. Nerys had offered to look after him too, as well as Cosmo. Two more animals wouldn't make much difference to her growing menagerie, she'd said.

"You won't need all this stuff," said Hanna. "It's only for a few days. Let's sort out the most important things and you can put the rest away."

Eva clambered onto the bed, her face set in a scowl. She sat cross-legged next to Cosmo, picked up her empty alpaca rucksack and waved it in the air. "This is for the important stuff," she declared.

"Which is...?" Hanna asked.

Her daughter grabbed her battered old teddy, Orsina, that had been her favourite toy for years, and put her in the bag. The bear was now missing an ear and a bit grubby, but Eva insisted on sleeping next to her every night. Hanna could see that clothes were going to be secondary in Eva's eyes.

"Let's pack your clothes first, then we'll see how much space is left. I don't think you'll need too many toys. There'll be so much to do at Auntie Nerys', looking after the animals, making pots and painting."

Eva's face brightened. She'd developed a keen interest in painting at school during the last term, although at the moment all she seemed to draw was birds. Maybe Lars could help widen her repertoire during her stay.

Together they picked a selection of clothes suitable for the capricious Welsh climate, squeezing some into the rucksack and the rest into a small holdall. Eva added a few toys, including her paints and a couple of brushes.

"Ready!!" she announced finally, laying the stuffed rucksack on the bed. Cosmo opened his eyes, slowly got up and stretched, before curling up once more, this time on top of the bag.

One down, Hanna thought. All that remained now was sorting out the animals and her own things. Her phone rang and she raced over to her bedside table to retrieve it.

"You sound out of breath!" It was Ceri.

"Out of condition!" panted Hanna in reply. "Not enough walks in the hills with the family!"

Ceri laughed, a light tinkling, happy sound.

"How's everything going? Excited? Nervous?" Hanna asked.

"All the arrangements have been checked and double-checked a thousand times. We can't do anymore. And, yes, I'm feeling a bit jittery, but that's only to be expected, isn't it? It's a life-changing step to make, after all. Weren't you nervous?"

"Absolutely. But I had my prospective mother-in-law taking care of the preparations. She fussed over me like a mother hen 'cos I was pregnant, remember?"

"Well at least I don't have that to worry about," said Ceri. "I'm so pleased that you're both coming. It'll really make my day!"

Hanna felt a warm glow inside. "You know I wouldn't have missed it, unless there was good reason."

"I know," said Ceri, "Anyway, how's the business at the cottage going?"

"Same as before. No new girls or other visitors. How's the police investigation going?"

"According to Vincenzo, they're nearly ready to make the

arrests. This time they've got enough evidence on the ringleaders, thanks in large part to Sergio. He's mega-excited about getting the story published as an exclusive. Reckons it will be the scoop of his career!"

"And what about Luciano and the rest of his family? Are they likely to be arrested again?"

"Looks like it. But proving they're major players in the network will be the problem. But from what Vincenzo has said, the police have more than enough this time to round up all the main culprits."

"Let's hope this time they manage to put a stop to the whole sordid business," said Hanna. "By the way, has anything else come up about me on the wiretap?"

"No, nothing. You're not still worried about coming back here, are you?"

"After everything that's happened, I'm bound to be a bit. Even if Luciano is true to his word and won't be coming after me."

"Don't forget the undercover officers will still be at the wedding. Vincenzo is keeping them in place just as a precaution."

"That's something, I guess," said Hanna, still slightly worried whether she was doing the right thing.

"I can't wait to see you both! It'll almost be like old times..."

CHAPTER THIRTY-ONE

Hanna gazed out of the window, deep in thought. Cruising at this height above the clouds, there was little to see. Outside, all was serene, the sky the palest of blue. Inside, Hanna felt anything but serene. Her stomach was churning despite the smoothness of the flight, a swell of mixed emotions washing over her.

Understandable, she thought. After all, she was returning to Sicily for the first time since the kidnapping two years ago. She felt light-headed, almost nauseous, and took a gulp of tonic water from the glass on the fold-down tray in front of her.

"Are you okay?" asked Rhys, taking her hand in his and giving it a squeeze. "You've gone really pale."

"I'm feeling a bit queasy, that's all," Hanna replied. "Nothing to do with the flight. It's just..." She paused, finding it difficult to put her thoughts into words. "You know. Confused. Thrilled about the wedding, but trepidation at going back. Not knowing for sure if it's really safe or not."

"Well, it's only for a few days, then we'll be back home." Rhys patted her hand as if to reassure her. "And there'll be security at the wedding, so everything should go smoothly."

"I hope so," said Hanna, not wanting to explain her feelings any further.

It had been traumatic enough leaving Eva behind with Nerys and Lars. Traumatic for her, not for Eva who seemed to be taking it all in her stride, treating it like a great adventure. She reclined her seat and settled back. Closing her eyes, she dozed off almost immediately, only opening them again when the plane started its descent towards Palermo's Falcone Borsellino Airport. Her head felt muzzy, and it took her a minute or two to realise where she was.

"Welcome back to the land of the living!" said Rhys, smiling at her.

She forced a weak smile in response. "Sorry, I've not been much company, have I?"

"As long as you're okay for the wedding tomorrow, that's all that matters."

Hanna nodded and fastened her seatbelt. "At least we haven't got far to go when we arrive. We were lucky to get a flight to Palermo. Saves us the trek from Catania."

"Don't most flights from the UK go to Palermo?" asked Rhys, with a puzzled face.

"Charter flights usually go to Catania. It's nearer the popular beach resorts on the east coast. There are fewer flights into Palermo, and it tends to be a more expensive option," Hanna explained.

"D'you know I've only ever been to Sicily once? That was years ago, when Ceri was still a tour guide. I came over at the end of the season and stayed for a week. It's a wonder our paths didn't cross then."

Hanna frowned. "I vaguely remember Ceri saying something about you coming to visit. Can't remember where I was at the time, or even what year it was..."

"Me neither," said Rhys, laughing. "But I can recall being

smitten by the beauty and colour of the place – the contrast between the coast and countryside, the hills and mountains, the history and architecture. Not forgetting the wonderful food!"

"I guess Sicily worked its magic on all three of us. I still have happy memories, of the days before I found out I was living a lie," said Hanna sadly. "I only hope Ceri has more luck."

"Sergio seems like a pretty sound sort of guy. He and Ceri make a good couple."

That's what people said about me and Luciano, thought Hanna. *And look how that turned out.* She smiled and nodded, saying nothing. The cabin filled with increased engine noise, making further conversation difficult.

Once the plane emerged from the clouds, the sea and the silhouette of the mountains gradually came into view, followed by the distant sprawl of the island's capital city nestled between the two. A lump rose in Hanna's throat. She swallowed hard and took a few deep breaths. She had to get a grip of her emotions, otherwise she wouldn't make it through the weekend. The plane jolted as it hit the runway and taxied to a halt.

Their seats being near the front of the plane meant they were among the first passengers to leave. The searing heat hit them as soon as they stepped outside. The digital display outside the airport building indicated 32 degrees Celsius, but it felt hotter, almost stifling, despite the lightest of breezes. Like stepping into a sauna. Hanna held up a hand to shield her eyes from the blinding sun and took in gulps of humid air as she descended the aircraft steps.

Within minutes, they were back in the shade within the confines of the air-conditioned airport building. Hanna shivered violently at the sudden extreme change of temperature. Rhys was saying something, but his words were drowned out by an announcement over the loudspeaker system.

They followed the signs towards Passport Control. Hanna

rummaged in her handbag for their documents. With few people in front of them, they passed through quickly and moved on to the baggage retrieval area. Rhys would have been quite content to cram his wedding suit into a carry-on bag, but Hanna was adamant about taking a suitcase. No way was she wearing a crumpled outfit to her best friend's wedding.

Ceri and Sergio would be in the Arrivals hall waiting for them. Ceri had insisted on picking them up despite Hanna's protestations. Hanna sent her a quick text to let her know they'd landed. The bags could take a while to come through. She glimpsed the baggage handlers through the window, conversing loudly with a lot of arm-waving, processing the cases with customary lethargy.

"Won't be long now!" said Rhys, with his usual optimism.

"You reckon?" said Hanna, feeling less confident. She yawned. It had been a fraught couple of days, preparing both themselves and Eva for the break. And it had been a long day; up early for the drive to Manchester airport, then the wait there, followed by the three-hour flight.

Another twenty minutes passed until they spotted their case and dragged it off the carousel. As soon as they passed into the Arrivals hall, a whoop of joy arose from the waiting crowd and Ceri ran towards them, her arms waving wildly, followed by a smiling Sergio.

The two young women fell into each other's arms and hugged for what seemed like ages. Anyone watching would have taken them for long-lost friends. In fact, it was only a few months since they'd seen each other last, when Ceri had come over to Wales for a week at Easter.

Hanna felt so close to Ceri; she wished they could live nearer to each other. But in a way it didn't matter. It was one of those friendships that you could quickly pick up where you'd left off, regardless of the time spent apart.

"I'm so pleased you're here!" said Ceri, slightly breathless, the delight evident in her voice. "The wedding wouldn't have been the same without you!"

"Just hope we're doing the right thing..." replied Hanna tentatively.

"Of course you are! Everything will be fine, you'll see!"

"C'mon on, guys, let's get out of here!" said Sergio, shouting to make himself heard above the noise of the crowd.

As they followed in his wake, Hanna felt as though they were being watched. She glanced around, but it was difficult to pinpoint the source with so many people around. Probably nothing, merely her imagination again, she thought, as she hurried to catch up with the others.

CHAPTER THIRTY-TWO

Sergio led the way through the throng of people in Arrivals and steered them towards the exit. As soon as they stepped outside the building, they were confronted once again by the searing heat. Hanna could feel beads of sweat forming on her forehead and wiped them away with the back of her hand.

"Wait here while I go and collect the car. Won't be long," said Sergio, as he turned away and quickly disappeared from view.

Hanna still felt uneasy, as if they were the focus of someone's attention. Although they were fewer people out here, she still couldn't identify the culprit. None of the others seemed to have noticed anything amiss. She chose to keep quiet. They'd soon be well away from the airport and any prying eyes.

Rhys looked uncomfortable, his face flushed and clammy. "Is it me or is it really humid?" He shouted to be heard among all the comings and goings.

Ceri laughed sympathetically. "Welcome to Sicily in August, bro! Not like Wales, eh? Don't worry, you'll soon get used to it."

Hanna opened her mouth to speak but the noise level

around them drowned out her words. She grinned and mouthed that they'd talk later and got a thumbs-up from Ceri. The atmosphere felt so alien after the tranquillity of Wales.

Ceri looked so radiant and relaxed, her deep tan evident in a pair of skimpy shorts and a low-cut T-shirt. Hanna could feel her clothes sticking to her. But it wasn't long before Sergio pulled up and they all piled into the car, grateful for its cool interior. Hanna climbed in the back alongside Ceri, leaving Rhys to sit in the passenger seat next to Sergio.

Sergio threaded his way through the heavy traffic towards the *autostrada* for Palermo. The airport, Hanna remembered, lay about 20 kilometres north-west of the city. Gradually she began to feel better in the air-conditioned confines of the car. She sat back and started to relax, listening to Ceri's excited chatter about the wedding. *She seems so happy*, thought Hanna, watching her closest friend talk animatedly, waving her arms in the air to emphasise certain points. She felt a twinge of excitement herself, forgetting for a moment her anxiety about the whole trip.

Glimpses of the wide bay of Castellammare flashed by as Sergio drove with his customary confidence and no lack of speed. Every so often, he'd interrupt Ceri's constant flow with a brief comment, but otherwise he seemed content to let her do all the talking.

"See how I can't get a word in edgeways!" he grumbled good-naturedly. "God knows what it'll be like when we're married!"

Ceri stretched across the gap between the seats and gave him a playful dig in the ribs. "You've usually got plenty to say for yourself, so don't complain!"

Changing the subject, she carried on: "We're going to drop you off at the hotel and let you get settled in. We've got a couple of last-minute things to sort out before tomorrow. But we'll be back for dinner tonight. The table's booked for eight o'clock; hope that's okay?"

Rhys nodded. "That's fine with us."

"Good," Ceri continued. "The hotel is really something. It's a bit off the beaten track but it's truly amazing. I'm sure you'll love it as much as we do. We were lucky to get the booking for the wedding reception, given its reputation."

"And that was only because I managed to pull a few strings, remember, *cara*?" said Sergio.

"Oh, yes, I'd forgotten that," said Ceri, offering no further explanation.

Rhys and Sergio struck up a conversation between themselves, their voices so muted that their words were impossible to make out in the back seat.

Ceri turned to Hanna. "So, how's that little rascal daughter of yours?"

"Fine. She's really settled down in Wales," Hanna replied. "She loves the countryside, the beaches, and all the wildlife. She's getting on well at school and has made a couple of good friends. And she adores Rhys – calls him Daddy now. She's stopped asking about Luciano, thank God."

Ceri raised an eyebrow. "It'll be you next, then!"

Hanna frowned. "Maybe, who knows? But I'd have to get divorced first." And that would mean inevitable contact with Luciano again. A dispiriting thought.

Hanna had told Ceri about Rhys wanting a child of their own. But neither of them brought the subject up now. Instead, Hanna said, "So what did you decide to do about the honeymoon?"

Ceri shrugged. "We can't begin to think about going away at the moment with the police investigation going on. Soon as it comes to a head and the arrests are made, Sergio will have to go to press with the story. There'll be time enough afterwards..."

Before reaching the city, Sergio turned off the *autostrada* and headed inland on a winding road.

"So, this hotel, where is it exactly?" asked Hanna.

Ceri frowned. "I sent you all the details. Didn't you look at them?"

Hanna shrugged apologetically. "I did, but with everything going on..." Truth was that she'd given them no more than a cursory glance, convinced that they'd never get to make the trip there.

"It's a boutique hotel some way outside Palermo, in the middle of nowhere, a *contrada* all of its own, miles from the nearest village. Sooo beautiful and peaceful," Ceri replied.

"Bet it won't be so peaceful during the wedding reception," said Rhys with a wry smile.

"Hopefully not!" said Sergio. "We've taken the place over so we can make all the noise we want without disturbing other guests."

Hanna could feel her old anxieties nudging their way back into her consciousness. "How many guests did you say are coming?"

"There'll be thirty to forty guests at the ceremony itself in Sergio's childhood village church. Just close friends and family. Then we'll come out here for the wedding breakfast. More people will join us for the evening do."

"Is Mum going to be able to make it after all?" Rhys butted in, turning round to face the two girls.

Marilyn, Ceri's and Rhys' mother, lived in Melbourne, Australia. She'd walked out of the family home when they were little, leaving their father to bring them up single-handed. He had died of a massive heart attack a few weeks before his sixtieth birthday. The relationship between Marilyn and her children remained strained, and any contact was sporadic. A few days ago, they heard that she'd broken her ankle, having fallen awkwardly playing tennis.

Ceri pulled a face. "She reckons she needs urgent surgery, so she won't be here. Or, at least, that's the tale. If it's true…"

"Shame, but she was never much into families, was she? Certainly not ours, anyway," commented Rhys, with a touch of bitterness. "She couldn't even be bothered to turn up for Dad's funeral."

"No surprise and no great loss. A pity Dad couldn't be here, though."

Tears welled in Ceri's eyes. Hanna gave her a hug and said, trying to lighten the mood: "Never mind, you've got us instead. What more could anyone wish for?"

A faint smile flickered across Ceri's face. "It means so much, you know, the two of you being here."

"Getting married is a big deal. One of those life-changing events that you'll remember for years to come," said Hanna, remembering how excited she'd been to marry Luciano.

A glance from Rhys cut her short. She realised the insensitivity of her words. Was their long weekend going to be marred by old memories and difficult decisions about her own life? Whether to have a child with Rhys, and what to do about getting a divorce? She'd have to face them sooner or later, but this weekend was about Ceri and Sergio. Not her and Rhys.

Or Luciano.

CHAPTER THIRTY-THREE

The dusty single-track road continued to wind through a landscape of rolling hills that stretched for miles with little sign of human habitation. Golden fields of wheat danced in an almost indiscernible breeze below the unforgiving afternoon sun, set high in the perfect azure sky.

Hanna was getting restless. The drive to the hotel seemed to be taking forever. Feeling hot and clammy despite the Fiat's fierce air-con, she longed to peel off the clothes glued to her body and dive under a cool shower. More than anything else, she was dying for a long, cold drink.

"Not much further now!" Ceri announced cheerfully, as if sensing her discomfort.

Hanna's couldn't respond, her mouth was so dry. Instead, she managed a feeble smile. They drove on for a few more kilometres, admiring the beauty of the countryside in silence. As they came over a hill, a large stone farmstead appeared ahead as if by magic, set back from the road.

"Look, there it is now!" said Ceri, pointing excitedly at the cluster of buildings. "Masseria Cianduca! That's the place! Isn't it in an amazing location?"

"Well, it's certainly isolated, I'll give you that," said Rhys.

Ceri punched his shoulder playfully. "Not half as isolated as parts of Snowdonia. You should feel at home!"

"If it wasn't for this baking heat," said Rhys, wiping his brow with the back of his hand. "I'm gagging for a cold beer."

Sergio smiled ruefully. "Aren't we all, *amico*? Our August temperatures can be quite trying if you're not used to them."

"You can say that again," Rhys growled, wriggling uncomfortably in the passenger seat. "Maybe you should have chosen a cooler month to get hitched."

"Don't be such a grump!" said Hanna, secretly thinking that he had a point.

"This place dates back to the eighteenth century. The same family have farmed here for generations. Nowadays, they still grow a lot of their own produce for the restaurant – vegetables, fruit, olive oil, and so on," said Ceri, sounding like her former tour guide self.

"How on earth did you manage to find a place out here?" asked Hanna.

Ceri tapped her nose. "I have my ways."

Minutes later, they drew up outside the farmstead, a set of impressive stone buildings laid out in a massive square as if protecting its inhabitants against marauders. Sergio drove inside around a gurgling stone fountain, pulling up alongside a handful of top-of-the-range cars and 4x4s.

"As you can see, we fit perfectly with their usual clientele!" joked Sergio as they untangled their limbs and emerged stiffly from the interior of the little car.

"I keep telling you that we need something bigger," said Ceri with a smile. "Fiats are OK when you're young, but in your thirties, you need something slightly more impressive, not to mention comfortable."

"Well, we'll see once this story gets published," Sergio said, locking the car. He strode in front, leading the way up a set of fan-shaped stone steps towards an entrance flanked by exotic-looking spiny aloe shrubs, full of red-orange blossoms on tall stems.

Hanna breathed a sigh of relief as she stepped into the cool reception area. They were greeted by two young women dressed in dark jackets and crisp white blouses. Their luggage and passports were whisked away and one of the receptionists checked them in, while the other showed them to a seating area and brought a tray laden with glasses of *latte di mandorla*, almond milk, a speciality of the island, served with chunks of ice. Tempting though it was to down it in one go, the iciness set Hanna's teeth on edge, making her drink it more slowly. Not so for Rhys, who polished it off with one gulp.

"That," he said, licking his lips with a smile of satisfaction, "was wonderful. Whatever it was..."

As Ceri started to explain, the receptionist emerged from behind the desk to escort them to the room. Hanna and Rhys got up to follow her.

"We'll leave you to get settled in," said Ceri. "There's a great pool if you fancy a swim, and fabulous gardens. Dinner's at eight, don't forget!"

"As if!" said Rhys, grabbing her arm and kissing her on the cheek.

"Are you sure there's nothing we can do to help?" Hanna asked.

"Absolutely not. You're here to relax and enjoy yourselves, starting now!" said Ceri, with mock sternness as she hugged Hanna.

"OK, OK, we're only too happy to do as we're told!" said Hanna, following Rhys and the receptionist into the dark interior of the hotel, glad of the chance to relax a little before the real celebrations began.

Hanna finished off with a spritz of her favourite perfume, a light blend of bergamot and mandarin. She gazed at herself critically in the bathroom mirror. Rhys appeared behind her, towelling his still damp hair.

"Wow! You look stunning! Anyone'd think that it's you getting married tomorrow!" he said admiringly, gently kissing the back of her neck. Hanna's whole body trembled in response.

"Thanks! You don't look so bad yourself!" she said, thinking how handsome he looked, relaxed and tanned, dressed in a pale lemon shirt and navy chinos.

Rhys reached for the hairdryer hanging on the wall next to the mirror, switched it on and ran the airflow quickly through his dark curls. For a moment or two, Hanna thought he bore more than a passing resemblance to Luciano, before she dismissed the thought out of hand. Returning to the bedroom, she put on a pair of coral sandals and the silver bracelet with the sea urchin charm that Ceri had given her as a present.

"Well, I'm ready. C'mon, we don't want to be late," she called, reaching for the gold gift bag lying on the bed.

"Tell me about it," said Rhys, emerging from the bathroom, his hair nearly dry. "My stomach's been growling for the last hour."

He smiled and reached for her hand as they left the room and threaded their way through the lush gardens full of palms and prickly pears towards the main building. Climbing a flight of stone steps, they found Ceri and Sergio already seated at a table in the rooftop terrace restaurant, their heads bent close together in the candlelight, almost in an embrace, laughing softly. Hanna felt her emotions stir just looking at them.

"How happy they look together," she murmured. "It seems almost a shame to invade their privacy."

Before Rhys had time to answer, a fierce growl emanated from his stomach, ruining the magic of the moment.

"That says it all," he said, laughing as Hanna gave him a playful punch. "C'mon, let's go and eat. The food had better be good 'cos I'm famished!"

A young waiter, dressed in crisp white shirt and tight-fitting black trousers that showed off his muscled physique, greeted them and showed them to the table. Ceri and Sergio sprang apart as if they'd been doing something illicit.

"Not interrupting anything, are we?" said Rhys, with a grin.

"No, of course not, cheeky!" replied Ceri, as the newcomers took their seats. "How was your afternoon?"

"Exhausting!" said Hanna. "A stroll around the grounds, a swim in that amazing pool, and a snooze in a hammock under the umbrella pines. What a place! So peaceful, and the views are spectacular."

"And your room?" Ceri asked.

"Simply perfect. French windows that open onto the garden, with fabulous views of the surrounding countryside. Great air-con, designer toiletries, beautiful décor," Hanna replied.

"You've forgotten to mention the wonderful little coffee machine and the mini-bar," Rhys added.

"How could I possibly forget?" Hanna smiled and sat back, taking in their surroundings. A slight warm breeze carried wafts of lavender and citrus across the terrace. The sun was disappearing in an orangey-pink haze, and the only noise was the chirping of crickets and the low murmur of conversation from the handful of other diners.

"Before I forget," said Hanna, handing Ceri the gold gift bag. "A little something from Wales."

Ceri's eyes lit up. "You shouldn't have," she said, diving into the bag. "Ooh, a bottle of rhubarb and ginger gin! We'll enjoy this, won't we?" Sergio smiled and nodded. Ceri rose from her chair and hugged Hanna and Rhys in turn. "Thank you both so much."

She had just sat down again when the waiter approached, bearing menus. *"Gradite un aperitivo, signori?"*

Hanna needed no prompting. *"Un Aperol per me."* The others nodded in agreement and the waiter disappeared to fulfil their order.

"So, guys, what do you recommend?" asked Rhys, scrutinising the menu, trying to use his scant knowledge of the language to decipher the words.

"Maybe we'll leave the choice up to you," Ceri teased. "God knows what we'd end up with!"

Rhys adopted a mock hurt expression. "For once, dear sister, I will bow to your superior knowledge. Hanna, does anything take your fancy?

"I wouldn't know where to begin. Every dish sounds delicious."

The waiter returned and placed their drinks, together with a small plate of appetisers, on the table with a flourish, promising to return promptly to take their food order.

Rhys took a sip of his drink. "How about the groom-to-be? Any last wishes as a single man?"

Sergio smiled and continued to study the menu. After a few minutes, he said thoughtfully: "I reckon I've got a fair idea of everyone's likes and dislikes. Shall I order for us, so each course is a surprise? Or is that too risky?"

A murmur of consent around the table. Sergio turned to call the waiter.

Hanna suddenly felt her spine tingle. She turned around to see three smartly-dressed middle-aged men sitting on the other side of the terrace, observing their table with great interest. They looked away quickly as she met their gaze.

CHAPTER THIRTY-FOUR

"Do either of you know those men at the table behind me?" Hanna tried to make the question sound casual but even she could hear the note of alarm in her voice.

Sergio and Ceri both glanced across the terrace.

"No, I don't think so," said Sergio slowly. "Why do you ask?"

"It's just that... they seemed to be staring at us before," Hanna replied, stopping herself from turning round.

"Really? Well, they're deep in conversation and not paying us any attention now," said Ceri. "Probably eyeing us up. You know how Sicilian men can be. Not always subtle."

"Hope you're not including me," said Sergio with mock offence. "I don't think I've ever ogled a woman in my life."

"You must be the exception then, *amore*," said Ceri with a smile, squeezing his hand. "But Italians do love to people-watch. Must be their innate curiosity."

"You're probably right," said Hanna, though she was far from convinced. The steely glint in the men's eyes had conveyed anything but a passing interest in the opposite sex. A familiar sense of foreboding washed through her. Was she reading too much into what could be an innocuous situation? An overreaction on her part?

Sitting with her back to the men's table, there was little she could do to monitor the situation. Sergio and Ceri didn't seem unduly concerned. She decided to let the matter drop.

The waiter returned with an ice bucket containing a bottle of chilled Grillo, which he uncorked and poured a little for Sergio to approve, before filling their glasses and disappearing again.

"Well, I would like to propose a toast to the happy couple," said Rhys, raising his glass. "To Ceri and Sergio, may you have a long and happy life together."

"Hear, hear! *Auguri!* All the best for the future!" echoed Hanna. They all chinked glasses, teary-eyed, overcome with the emotion of the moment.

Ceri looked radiant, a beaming smile on her face as she looked adoringly at Sergio, who reciprocated in kind. Hanna and Rhys exchanged appreciative glances. *La vita è bella,* thought Hanna happily. Life is good.

The waiter wasted no time in bringing their starter, *arancini di riso*, rice balls served with a delicate red mullet and wild fennel sauce. They smiled at each other in anticipation, before devouring the delicious food.

Halfway through their main course – succulent local Nebrodi pork cutlets in a tomato and fresh herb sauce – Hanna began to feel uncomfortable again, as if eyes were boring into her back. But without turning around, she couldn't verify this. No one else on the table seemed to have noticed anything. She took a gulp of wine, relishing the warm glow as the alcohol began to take effect.

"So, what's happening with the police investigation?" Rhys

asked, changing the subject from endless chatter about the wedding arrangements.

Sergio wiped his mouth with his linen napkin. "Still a few loose ends to tie up," he replied in a low voice. "Once the police are satisfied that they have everything they need, they'll be able to co-ordinate with the police forces abroad to make sure they get everyone involved. If all goes well, the swoop is likely to be the week after next."

"Swoop?" asked Hanna, frowning.

"A dawn raid on a massive scale. I don't have all the details yet. Can't wait to run the story." He sounded excited, his voice rising in pitch as he talked.

"Does that mean they'll get the people in North Wales, too?" Rhys looked concerned.

"As far as I know, yes. At least, that's the plan. Dad said the Welsh police have been very co-operative. They're keeping the gang under close surveillance."

"And Luciano?" asked Hanna.

Sergio shrugged. "He, and the rest of the family, are the main players in all of this. Top of the arrest list. This time, he'll go down for a long stretch, and no early release."

A wave of relief flooded through Hanna. Finally, it looked as if Luciano would get what he deserved, and his heinous sex-trafficking network be smashed for good.

"At last, thank God," she murmured, glad it would all soon be over.

"You don't anticipate any – you know – problems?" asked Rhys.

"What do you mean, problems?" asked Ceri, looking anxious.

"Well, you know, obstacles – anything that could stop the arrests going ahead?" Rhys looked slightly uncomfortable for having brought the subject up.

"According to my dad, the police are confident that they've nailed it," said Sergio, scooping a forkful of food into his mouth.

A few moments of silence ensued as they resumed eating.

"Well, that was delish!" Rhys declared, polishing off the last mouthful and laying his fork to rest on the empty plate. "Your Nebrodi pork is a worthy match for our Welsh lamb and black beef."

"Glad you approve!" said Ceri with a touch of sarcasm. "Maybe you'll come and visit us more often now, if only for the food!"

"Absolutely!" Rhys said, patting his stomach happily. "What's for dessert?"

The waiter appeared and whisked away their empty plates, returning promptly with terracotta dishes bearing their dessert.

Rhys regarded his with a puzzled look. "And dessert is...?"

"Taste it first and see!" said Hanna.

He dug his spoon into the little mound set before him and brought it to his mouth.

"Mmm!! That, whatever it is, is a little piece of heaven!" he declared, rolling his eyes upwards in mock ecstasy. "I still don't know what it is, though."

Ceri laughed and explained. "It's an almond *semifreddo*, a kind of semi-frozen ice-cream cake. It's a house speciality. I had it the first time I came here, and it was so good that I ended up taking one home, all packed up in a freezer bag."

Hanna tasted hers. Nibbed almonds ran through the creamy concoction which, although rich, retained a slight bitterness. "Fabulous," she agreed. "I can see why you like it so much."

The *semifreddo* quickly vanished before it even had a chance to melt.

Sergio rose from the table, excusing himself as he made for the toilet, promising to order coffee and *digestivi* on the way back. No sooner had he disappeared from view than Hanna heard raised voices and chairs being moved on the far side of the terrace as the three men got up to leave, passing their table without a second glance. *Maybe I was mistaken about them,* thought Hanna, as she watched them pay the bill and leave, smiling and bidding goodnight to the restaurant staff.

But when Sergio returned a few minutes later, he collapsed onto his chair, visibly shaken, his face ashen.

"Oh my God, what's happened?" asked Ceri.

He gasped, "Those three men... They followed me into the toilet."

"Did they hurt you?" Ceri looked him up and down for any signs of injury.

Sergio shook his head. "No, no, they didn't touch me. Just pointed a gun to my head and threatened me. Told me to halt the police investigation, or else. And, under no circumstances, to run a story in *La Gazzetta*."

"Christ, what did you say?" asked Hanna.

"I told them the police investigation wasn't my call. And as for the story, I told them no chance and to fuck right off," Sergio replied, with more than a hint of triumph in his voice.

CHAPTER THIRTY-FIVE

The three of them looked at each other, aghast.

"You did WHAT? Sergio, you're such an idiot," growled Ceri, tears in her eyes. "You're lucky to have got out of there in one piece. Do you want to get yourself killed?"

"But that's exactly the point," said Sergio, gradually becoming more composed. "These people have always used bully-boy tactics to get what they want, and in the past people have been too scared to take a stand against them. It's time that changed. We have to destroy their toxic influence once and for all."

"But at what cost?" said Hanna, quietly. "God knows what the consequences might be. Look what happened to Eva and me."

"Do you really think it's wise to go ahead in the circumstances?" asked Rhys. "You could be putting the two of you in danger, as well as your dad."

Sergio made a dismissive gesture with his hand. "It's the only way. Once the whole sorry affair is out in the open, they won't dare retaliate."

Hanna begged to differ, but said nothing; she could remember numerous cases where acts of retribution had been swift and deadly. Was Sergio intent on wiping out the trafficking, or was he simply trying to make a name for himself? Either way, he was playing a dangerous game.

In sombre mood and deep in thought, they drank their coffees and downed the *amari*. The alcohol soothed their nerves, and talk turned to the following day. The candle on the table flickered in the breeze as they got up to leave. Myriad stars twinkled in the inky sky, mesmerising Hanna who couldn't ever remember seeing so many. No lights shone across the countryside, a reminder of the *masseria*'s isolated position. Hanna felt a shudder of apprehension.

Despite the grim end to the evening, Hanna quickly fell into a deep sleep. She awoke shortly after eight-fifteen to an empty bed. Her initial reaction was a twinge of alarm as memories of the previous evening's threat came flooding back.

Warm, slightly-perfumed air wafted through the open French windows. There was no sign of Rhys. He'd left his mobile and wallet on the bedside table, so he couldn't be far away, could he? Trying not to consider the worst, she threw back the covers and ran down the stairs of the split-level room, calling his name. No response, but no sign of any disturbance.

Outside, the little mosaic table on the patio was laid ready for breakfast. Hanna scanned the gardens for any sign of life, shielding her eyes from the bright morning sun. All was peaceful, the only sounds a soft breeze rustling through the umbrella pines and the birds chirping merrily. Her heart was beating wildly now, convinced that something was wrong. Suddenly she heard a shout and turned to see a dripping wet

Rhys, dressed in a pair of swim shorts, scamper across the lawn towards her.

What the hell...

"I thought something had happened to you," said Hanna, angry but relieved to see him.

"Sorry, I didn't mean to give you a fright," he said, holding up his hands in a gesture of surrender while trying to regain his breath. "Just thought I'd go for a quick dip in the pool before you woke up. Didn't want to disturb you, you looked so peaceful." He slipped a wet arm around her waist and laughed when she shrieked, trying to shrug it off.

"Get away with you, you're soaking! Go and dry off!" she cried, struggling to escape his grip. He laughed again, stole a quick kiss, and ran off to get a towel. "And don't do anything like that again. I was really worried," she called after him. He raised an arm to acknowledge that she had a point.

Returning to the table, she sank onto a chair and fished her mobile out of her pyjama pocket. It was still a bit early to call Nerys with the hour's time difference. She'd called briefly the day before, but she wanted to hear her daughter's voice again and make sure she was okay. No matter, she'd call later.

Rhys appeared minutes later, somewhat drier, still in his shorts, a towel slung across his shoulders. "I've asked them to bring breakfast over now. Hope that's okay?" He still looked sheepish.

"'Course it is. We've got loads of time for a leisurely breakfast, then the rest of the morning to get ready before the car picks us up," said Hanna.

She settled back in the chair, enjoying the warmth of the sun on her face, and began to relax, her usual composure gradually returning. All around, the garden was a blaze of colour: swathes of deep pink and purple bougainvillea, yellow and orange hibiscus, and a showy scarlet flower that Hanna recognised but didn't know the name of. All offset by an impossibly green lawn which must have been a nightmare to maintain in the hot summer sun. Coming back to Sicily seemed to have heightened her senses and emotions somehow, leaving her feeling a little off-balance.

The arrival of the waitress a few minutes later shook her from her reverie. Breakfast turned out to be a veritable feast. Not just the usual pastries and coffee, but an assortment of local cold cuts and cheeses, a courgette *frittata*, sweet cherry tomatoes and olives, a medley of citrus fruits and watermelon, fresh bread, and a selection of jams. According to the young waitress, the pastries – croissants filled with a vanilla, hazelnut, or pistachio *crema* – were made fresh on the premises each morning.

Rhys eyed up the food with glee. "Can't wait to get stuck in! My early morning swim must have given me an appetite!"

Although Hanna didn't have the same excuse, she had to admit the spread looked tempting. Rhys passed her a plate and began to load his with a generous selection of food.

"What time will the wedding breakfast be?" he asked between mouthfuls.

"Probably not until about mid-afternoon," Hanna replied, adding with a note of sarcasm, "D'you think you'll last out till then?"

"You know that appetite I mentioned?" he said, with a twinkle in his eye as he continued to attack the food with enthusiasm.

"You can think again!" said Hanna, laughing as she realised what he was referring to.

They continued to demolish the food until there was little left.

"That was such a fantastic breakfast," said Hanna. "I can

hardly move, I'm so stuffed. I'm just going to make a quick call to Eva and Nerys to make sure everything's okay, then I'm off to have a shower."

Rhys' face fell with disappointment, and she could feel his eyes watching her as she disappeared into the room.

CHAPTER THIRTY-SIX

As they waited for the car in the hotel's cool reception area, Hanna caught sight of their reflection in the enormous gilt-framed mirror hanging on one of the stone walls. Decked out in their wedding outfits, their arms interlinked, any onlooker could be mistaken for thinking that they were the couple about to be married. Except for the coral and caramel tones of her dress, rather than the traditional white. *What would it be like to marry Rhys,* Hanna wondered? Not that he had asked her, but then, she was still married to Luciano. But he was keen for them to have a baby together. No time to think about that now. This was Ceri and Sergio's day. Everything else would have to wait.

A screech of brakes outside indicated their transport had arrived. Rhys pulled Hanna closer and kissed her tenderly on the lips.

"I wish it was us getting married," he whispered as they pulled apart.

Flummoxed and at a loss what to say, Hanna merely smiled and squeezed his hand in what she hoped was a positive gesture. Still entwined, the two of them made their way to the little sporty convertible that was waiting outside. The driver, a handsome, immaculately-dressed, middle-aged man with greying hair, leapt out, his hand outstretched.

He introduced himself in Italian as Ignazio Spadoni, a journalist colleague of Sergio's. It was, he explained, only a short drive, some eight to ten kilometres, to the little village church of Brocco where the wedding ceremony was to take place.

But to Hanna the drive seemed much longer, the car kicking up dust in its wake as Ignazio sped along the country lanes. Sicilian kilometres must be a bit like Welsh miles, she thought with a wry smile. For once, Hanna was grateful for the lack of breeze; her carefully-curled hair would stay in place.

Finally the village came into view: a collection of old stone buildings perched higgledy-piggledy on the top of a hill. By the time they pulled up in the *piazza* outside the little seventeenth-century church, her head was muzzy from the heat and the winding roads. Ignazio delved into the glove compartment and passed her a small bottle of water with a knowing wink. She took it gratefully and took a large gulp before consigning the rest to her handbag.

They left the car and entered the flower-adorned church. It was still early, and only the main party had arrived. Sergio, dressed in a smart midnight blue suit offset by a lemon and white buttonhole, stood near the altar looking nervous and talking in a low voice to the best man. Hanna remembered Ceri telling her that he was one of Sergio's childhood friends. Sergio's father, Vincenzo, was sitting in a nearby pew, next to a frail-looking grey-haired woman in a wheelchair who Hanna presumed must be his wife. Vincenzo beckoned them over and introduced them to Marta.

"Is Rhys okay with the arrangements?" whispered Vincenzo in Italian to Hanna. "He knows what he has to do?"

"*Certo*," Hanna assured him with a smile. "He's rehearsed it over and over again. He'll be fine."

She glanced at Rhys, who was now looking almost as anxious as Sergio. His face was flushed, and a few beads of sweat had appeared on his forehead.

"Are you OK?" she asked.

He gulped and wiped his forehead with the back of his hand.

"Just don't want to mess up Sis's big day. I better go and wait outside for her. See you later."

He pecked her on the cheek, then retreated down the aisle towards the front door and disappeared outside.

Hanna felt for him; it wasn't every day that you gave your sister away. With their mother injured, there was no-one else to do it. Not that Ceri was close to her anyway, not after the way she'd walked out on them when they were little. It was typical of her to leave them in the lurch again.

The organist started to play, and the church filled with the strains of rousing music. The priest shuffled into place in front of the altar. Ceri and Sergio had insisted on a low-key affair, no bridesmaids, and only thirty or so guests at the church, with others coming to the reception later that evening. More guests began to arrive and fill up the remaining pews, chattering excitedly among themselves. Eager anticipation hung in the air.

Hanna turned her head and noted that the little church was now almost packed to capacity. Three men sitting towards the back caught her eye. Although suitably dressed, they seemed oddly out of place. Could they be the same men responsible for the threat at the hotel, she wondered with a shudder? But on closer scrutiny she realised they were different: younger, remaining curiously aloof and distant from what was going on around them. Maybe they were the undercover police that Vincenzo had promised.

She was on the verge of asking him who they were when the organist launched into a rendition of Debussy's *Clair de Lune,* signalling the bride's arrival. Minutes later, Ceri made her entrance, walking slowly down the aisle on Rhys' arm, clutching an elaborate bouquet of lemon and white flowers, matching Sergio's buttonhole. She looked relaxed and radiant, smiling at the guests on both sides as she went.

The white wedding dress fitted her petite frame perfectly: a sleeveless lace bodice, cut wide across the shoulders with a deep V-shape neckline that revealed her dark tan, ending in a satin bow above a tight-fitting waist. From there, the material fell in soft layers to the ankle. A simple net veil, adorned with clusters of matching lace, revealed her blonde-streaked hair that had been coaxed into an elegant chignon for the occasion and woven with wildflowers. Her only jewellery was a pair of large pearl teardrop earrings. She was dazzling, glowing with happiness. Hanna reached into her handbag for a pack of tissues as she felt the first tears begin to trickle down her cheeks.

The service passed in a blur, although Hanna remembered the priest's voice droning on for what seemed like forever. At last, she heard the words *"Vi dichiaro marito e moglie"* as he pronounced the couple man and wife. Their first marital kiss sent her into another flurry of tears. As the organist struck up the Wedding March, and Ceri and Sergio began to make their way back down the aisle past the guests, Rhys reappeared at her side, looking much more at ease now.

Hanna dabbed at her face with a paper hankie, hoping her waterproof mascara would live up to its claims and she wouldn't end up with panda eyes. Rhys took the hankie from her and finished off the job. Bending his head close to hers, he brushed his lips against her ear and whispered, "Us next!" More tears threatened and Hanna bit the inside of her cheek as she struggled to regain control of her emotions. Rhys hugged her tightly against his chest.

The music blotted out any further attempts at conversation, and they fell into step behind Vincenzo as he slowly pushed Marta in the wheelchair towards the exit. There was no sign of the three men who'd been at the back of the church earlier.

The guests drifted out into the bright sunshine, their loud chatter drowning out the faint strains of music coming from within the church. Some jostling followed as the photographer identified the key players and elbowed them into position, shouting encouragement to relax and smile as he expertly captured various poses. Then it was over, and the guests gathered round the happy couple, showering them with handfuls of rice and paper confetti.

Ceri and Sergio squealed with delight as they fought their way down the path towards the waiting vintage car. Before she stepped inside, Ceri turned and threw her bouquet into the crowd. Hanna saw the flowers hurtling towards her and just managed to catch them before they hit the ground.

Rhys winked. "See? I told you it'd be us next."

CHAPTER THIRTY-SEVEN

A fleet of minibuses waited in the piazza outside the church to whisk the guests off to the wedding reception at the *masseria*. Ignazio introduced his partner, Elena, who he'd met up with at the church after collecting Hanna and Rhys from their hotel. The Sicilian couple insisted on running them back. It would have been rude to refuse, but there was barely enough room in the back seat for two adults, especially someone of Rhys' height. Somehow, they managed to squeeze in, although Hanna could tell from his face that Rhys was uncomfortable.

Nevertheless he bravely tried to practise his few phrases of Italian on their new friends, but quickly gave up when he discovered that they both spoke passable, if heavily accented, English. Elena explained that she was a nurse at a Palermo hospital and had been lucky to get time off for the wedding.

Chatting away, the return journey flew by and they were soon back at the *masseria*, where they were greeted with flutes of vintage Prosecco and escorted to a terrace with breathtaking views over the surrounding countryside. Spectacular arrangements of white flowers graced the long table laid out ready for the wedding breakfast, and tiny fairy lights festooned the nearby trees.

"Wow, this is so..." Hanna struggled to find the right word, as she surveyed the scene.

"Magical?" Rhys suggested, slipping an arm around her waist.

"Yes, that's it. Spot on," replied Hanna, a little breathlessly. "So much for a low-key affair!"

Rhys shot her a meaningful look. He didn't have to say anything; she knew that he was thinking about their future as a couple and whether they would ever get married.

As the minibuses arrived and more people started to flood onto the terrace, collecting in small groups, sipping Prosecco and chatting animatedly, the air filled with tinkling laughter. Rhys' eyes lit up at the sight of waiters starting to circulate with trays of delicious-looking canapés.

"Thank God for that!" he said with a grin. "My stomach was beginning to think I'd never eat again!"

Hanna laughed; she felt much the same way. "Well, it has been a long time since breakfast. Be warned, the main meal may still be some way off yet..."

Rhys needed no further prompting; he secured two miniature dishes from a passing waiter, passed one to Hanna and proceeded to load his up.

"I don't know what half of this stuff is, but it all looks luscious," said Rhys, taking a bite from the top item on his dish.

The canapés could almost have been a feast in themselves, such was the choice and the quantity: tiny skewers of seafood, mini *arancini* (risotto balls), *panelle* (chickpea fritters), crostini topped with various chargrilled vegetables, smoked swordfish and eel, and cured meats.

"By the way, you don't have to taste every single item," Hanna added, with a grin. "You need to save some space for later, although the main meal is likely to be spread out over several hours. And don't forget," nodding at his glass, "that you've still got to deliver your speech."

"Thanks. I'll try and remember to pace myself, then," Rhys replied between mouthfuls, looking as though that was the last thing on his mind.

Hanna was proved right: the wedding breakfast went on for ages. Course after course of sumptuous food, washed down by copious amounts of wine, prompting flashbacks of Hanna's own nuptials. A time that was meant to be one of the happiest days of her life. And it had been. Then. Before she found out the shocking truth about Luciano, a whole other life that he'd managed to keep secret from her until years later. She tried to brush the thoughts aside, but the nagging question about her marital status continued to plague her. She'd have to find a solution, but today was not the day.

Everyone was in high spirits, and Hanna and Rhys chatted to the other guests, the conversation emerging in a curious blend of local dialect, Italian and English. Rhys' inhibitions at testing his newly acquired linguistic skills paled the more wine he drank.

Between courses, people left the table for a break (cigarette or comfort) or simply to talk to other guests sitting further away. The handful of children present, all impeccably dressed like child models in a magazine, used the breaks to let off steam and run around noisily before they were admonished by their parents and summoned back to the table.

By the time they'd finished eating the light was starting to fade, and the fairy lights twinkling in the dusk were making the terrace look even more magical than before. Vincenzo stood up and tinged his glass several times to ask for silence, but the sound got lost in the noisy crowd and he had to resort to bellowing across the terrace, *"Signori, vi prego, silenzio!"* several times until the assembled guests reluctantly fell silent.

He launched into a short speech, relating how he and Marta never reckoned they would see the day when their son got married, so intent was he on his career.

"What's he saying?" Rhys whispered in Hanna's ear.

"The usual wedding stuff," Hanna replied. "I'll translate for you as we go along."

Vincenzo continued his speech: how they'd hoped Sergio would follow him into the police force. There was no mention of Sergio's strained relationship with his brother, Pino, the black sheep of the family. Pino had been involved in the rival clan responsible for Eva's kidnapping and had ended up dead in a shoot-out with Luciano and his associates.

Hanna shuddered at the sudden memory, and shivered despite the heat. It was as if someone was running an icy finger down her back. Would the spectre of Luciano never disappear, even on such a happy occasion that had nothing to do with him?

Vincenzo finished with a couple of jokes in dialect that she could barely understand, before handing over to his son. Sergio stood up, looking flushed and a little nervous. He kept his speech short – how lucky he was to have met Ceri, and how he was looking forward to their future together. Ceri also said a few words, echoing similar sentiments, adding in English how much she owed to her big brother. As they spoke, the newly-weds kept looking into each other's eyes, clearly besotted. Hanna felt her eyes prick with tears again.

They fell silent and Hanna nudged Rhys, who seemed to be miles away. Nodding, he shuffled to his feet, clutching his notes in one hand. He began by apologising in faltering Italian for his poor grasp of the language, before switching back to English, aware that several of the guests had some knowledge of that language. He kept the rest simple – how happy he was that his sister had found a soulmate in Sergio and how much she loved life in Sicily – in the hope that some of his words would be understood. He sat down to rapturous applause. Whether the guests had understood, or were merely being polite and appreciative of his efforts to speak to them in their own language, was uncertain.

"That went down really well!" said Hanna, squeezing his hand. "You can relax now."

With a sigh of relief, Rhys reached for his glass of wine and took a large gulp. "Thank God. I hate this kind of thing, especially when you've got to speak in an alien language."

Hanna laughed. "You make it sound as if we're in outer space, rather than a European country."

"It feels a bit like that to me," said Rhys, with a grin.

Vincenzo stood up again and called everyone to order. "And now," he announced in a booming voice, raising his glass of Prosecco. "I invite you all to join in a toast to the happy couple."

A loud shuffling as everyone rose to their feet and raised their glasses.

"*A Ceri e Sergio, evviva gli sposi!*" he proclaimed.

"*Evviva gli sposi!* – Long live the newly-weds," echoed the guests.

"And now, to the cake!"

Responding to his cue, Ceri and Sergio moved across to a separate table, where a magnificent multi-layered cake embellished with a colourful cascade of intricate iced flowers awaited their attention. Together they gripped the knife and cut into the bottom layer, to more tumultuous applause from the assembled guests.

As the waiters began to distribute portions of the cake, Vincenzo announced that the dancing would begin shortly on the lower terrace. Ceri and Sergio mingled with the guests, accepting their exuberant embraces and endless good wishes for the future.

Gradually everyone began to drift down the stone steps towards the lower terrace and the sound of music playing. Hanna and Rhys linked arms as they followed. It was dark now, the fairy-lights glinting in the trees, the air still heavy and claustrophobically warm. Endless stars sparkled in the sky and crickets chirped loudly.

She felt strangely euphoric and full of optimism for the future. Life had finally settled down. They all had the rest of their lives to look forward to. More tears threatened to flow. What was happening to her? She was turning into a romantic old fool. Or too much Prosecco, maybe? Oh well, she was allowed – it was a special day after all. She could be forgiven for being lost in the moment.

At that moment, Ceri and Sergio came over, all beaming smiles, radiating happiness, arms around each other.

"What a fantastic day it's been," said Ceri, breathlessly breaking free from Sergio to throw her arms first around Hanna, then Rhys. "Thank you both so, so much for coming. It wouldn't have been the same without you."

"We've enjoyed every minute," said Hanna. "It's wonderful to see you both so happy."

"It's wonderful to feel so happy," said Sergio. "Almost like a dream. Never thought it would happen to me."

Ceri laughed. "You're getting sentimental in your old age, *amore!* Next thing, you'll be talking about starting a family."

"Funny you should say that..." Sergio began, with a wistful look in his eyes, only to be interrupted by a shout from his father, beckoning them over. "Oh, oh. Must be time for our first dance. Ready?" he asked Ceri.

Ceri tucked a stray strand of hair behind her ear and nodded. "See you both later. Hope you'll join in the dancing."

Rhys pulled a face. "Not my thing. But for you, Sis, I'll make an effort."

Ceri smiled and kissed him quickly on the cheek before Sergio pulled her towards the space cleared by the guests in the middle of the terrace. The opening bars of their chosen song, the romantic *It's You* by Ali Gatie, sounded through the speakers. Sergio took Ceri in his arms and they started to dance slowly, lost in the moment and in each other.

Watching them, Hanna felt so happy that the tears began to flow freely down her cheeks. Rhys wrapped his arms tightly around her. Hanna thought she glimpsed a tear in his eyes too. Together they swayed in time to the music, closing their eyes, entranced.

Then, a fleeting glare of headlights. A screech of brakes. Cracks of gunfire. Screams. And Ceri slumped in Sergio's arms, a crimson stain spreading across the back of her white wedding dress.

CHAPTER THIRTY-EIGHT

Sergio collapsed to his knees, cradling Ceri's inert body in his arms, his face a picture of horror and despair. She lay still, her eyes closed, her face contorted in agony. No visible sign of life. A single low, guttural growl emanated from his throat.

Hanna tried to move, but her body refused to obey her brain's instruction. Her blood felt like ice, and her head and heart pounded in unison.

None of the guests moved, looking on in shock and abject dismay, incredulous, as if staring at a still from a film.

An eerie silence descended, broken only by the roar of a high-powered 4x4 accelerating away at high speed. Racing across the lower terrace, guns raised, the three men Hanna had noticed in the church launched themselves into an unmarked car and set off in hot pursuit.

Rhys and Vincenzo were the first to react, running over to the newly-weds. Rhys gently prised Ceri away from Sergio's grip to check for a pulse.

"She's still breathing," he murmured, then yelled at Vincenzo. "Call an ambulance!"

Vincenzo stared at him with uncomprehending eyes.

"NOW!" Rhys roared, shocking the other man into action. Vincenzo fumbled in his pocket, drew out his mobile and began dialling slowly with trembling fingers.

Rhys snatched it off him. "What's the emergency number?" he asked.

"118," Vincenzo replied.

Rhys punched in the numbers, flinched at the response, and handed the phone back to Vincenzo. Rapid words at breakneck speed punctured the silence as the older man explained to the operator what had happened.

Hanna forced her reluctant limbs into action and dashed over to where Ceri lay. She knelt down, noting her friend's ashen face, lips pale and unmoving, eyes glued shut. A slight chest movement was the only indication she was still breathing. Hanna felt her pulse; it was faint, erratic. She gulped, a huge lump in her throat, fearing that she was about to lose her best friend.

"Oh my God, we've got to stop the bleeding," said Rhys, the panic rising in his voice.

Then a familiar voice rose from the crowd. "Let me through! I'm a nurse!" Elena barked at the staff to bring some towels. "Help me move her onto her front. Gently now!"

Hanna nodded, unable to speak. She and Rhys did as Elena asked. Sergio watched, distraught, his head in his hands, as Elena gently examined the wound which was still bleeding profusely.

"Where are those damn towels?" she yelled.

Two of the waiting staff rushed in with a fresh batch of towels. Elena grabbed one and pressed it to the injury. She held it in place for several minutes, applying pressure directly to the wound. The towel quickly deepened in colour as it absorbed the blood flow. Adding another towel on top of the first, she said brusquely, "Hanna, talk to her, reassure her everything's going to be okay. Rhys, get a coat or blanket to put over her. We need to keep her warm until the paramedics arrive."

Rhys nodded and rushed off, while Hanna held Ceri's hand and whispered softly in her ear, trying to keep her voice steady. "You're going to be just fine, Ceri. Nothing to worry about. The ambulance is on its way. Won't be long now. Hang on in there."

Sergio held Ceri's other hand, tears flooding silently down his face. He looked helpless, a broken man.

"Is she on any medication, Sergio? Any drug allergies?" Elena asked, never taking her eyes off the task in hand.

He shook his head and mumbled, "No, nothing. No medication, no drug allergies."

Rhys sprinted back, carrying several blankets which he laid on the stone floor by Ceri's side. Elena examined the wound again and seemed satisfied that she'd managed to stem the blood flow. Still keeping pressure on the towels, she nodded to the blankets. Hanna and Rhys carefully spread them over Ceri's prone body.

When she looked up, Hanna noticed that several guests had started to melt away. Whether through fear, either for themselves or of getting involved, she couldn't tell.

And then, a faint wail in the distance. The ambulance was on its way.

The paramedics loaded Ceri into the back of the ambulance on a stretcher. Elena was allowed in too, in case they needed an additional pair of hands en route. Rhys helped Sergio, dazed and still in shock, into the front cabin. Ignazio insisted on taking Hanna, Rhys and Vincenzo to the hospital. They crammed into his convertible, Hanna and Rhys once again squashed in the back, and roared off at breakneck speed after the ambulance. No one spoke, the air charged with emotion.

After a few kilometres, Hanna finally asked, "Where are they taking her? Did they say?"

"To Elena's hospital, the *policlinico* in Palermo." Ignazio had to shout to make himself heard above the ambulance siren. "It's got a first-class *Pronto Soccorso*. She'll be in the best possible hands. The doctors there are used to dealing with this type of wound."

A look of alarm flickered across Rhys' face. *Christ, he must be wondering what sort of place Sicily is*, thought Hanna. She squeezed his hand and attempted to smile, trying to reassure him, but her face froze in the attempt.

Silence resumed as they hurtled down the dark country roads, lit only by the screaming ambulance ahead of them and the twinkling stars above. Hanna shivered despite the clammy, humid night, and slipped her jacket round her shoulders. Rhys sat staring out of the car window into the darkness.

Gradually the roads widened, and streetlights appeared as they approached the coast. The late hour meant there was little traffic for the ambulance to contend with on its mad dash towards the city hospital. Ignazio followed closely behind, but the traffic thickened once they reached the outskirts of Palermo and the ambulance disappeared out of sight.

"*Minchia!*" growled Ignazio, punching the steering wheel in exasperation. "What the hell do we do now?"

Rhys looked puzzled.

"Roughly translated, that means 'fuck'," Hanna murmured in his ear. Rhys nodded.

"Don't worry, I remember which road the hospital is on – Via del Vespro," said Vincenzo, punching the address into the car's sat-nav.

Ignazio glanced at him quizzically.

"Years of police work. Having to deal with victims being

rushed to the hospital for emergency treatment," he explained with a shrug. "The address is etched on my memory."

"*Grazie a Dio* – Thank God for that," muttered Ignazio as he swung the car round in a U-turn in response to the sat-nav's instructions.

After a further 10-15 minutes of weaving through the city's streets, they finally spotted the hospital sign: *Azienda Ospedaliera Universitaria Policlinico Paolo Giaccone.*

"Crikey, that's some name. Who's Paolo Giaccone?" asked Rhys.

"He was a professor and forensic pathologist, killed by the Mafia in the early eighties for finding forensic evidence that linked a particular Mafia family to the massacre of three rival Mafia bosses," said Ignazio, peering out of the window for the *Pronto Soccorso* entrance. "The hospital was renamed in his honour."

A look of horror passed over Rhys' face. "But that was a long time ago. Surely that's all over and done with?"

Ignazio gave Rhys a long, hard look in the rear-view mirror.

"You, of all people should know better than that, after what happened to Hanna and Eva," he said evenly.

"Nearly thirty years ago now, more than three hundred *mafiosi* were jailed and nineteen Mafia bosses given life sentences," Vincenzo said. "But organised crime still exists. It's just regrouped. Now its main activities are drugs, prostitution and people-trafficking."

"And the odd EU agricultural scam," added Ignazio, pulling into a space near the *Pronto Soccorso* entrance.

And now this latest shooting, Hanna thought grimly. Her best friend shot on her wedding day. Had Ceri been the intended victim, or had they been trying to kill Sergio? Either way, it was clear: a deadly message, a warning aimed at shutting down the police investigation and media coverage.

CHAPTER THIRTY-NINE

They found Sergio sitting hunched over on a plastic chair, his head in his hands, a lone figure in the waiting area of the red zone where they treated the most urgent patients.

Hanna slipped an arm around his shoulders and asked gently, "Any news?"

Sergio raised his head slightly, his face streaked with tears, his eyes swollen and red-rimmed. "Nothing as yet. They're working on her. It might be a while before we hear anything. You know what hospitals are like."

"I'm sure they're doing everything they can," said Hanna, trying in vain to reassure him, although her words rang hollow, even to her own ears.

Tears sprang to his eyes and Hanna hugged him tightly to her. She could feel him trembling and cold in her arms. Rhys watched helplessly. He seemed at a loss to know what to do or say, until he signalled that he'd go off in search of coffee with Ignazio. Hanna nodded. A warm drink would do them all good.

Sergio detached himself from Hanna's embrace and wiped the tears from his face with the back of his hands. His clothes were spattered with crimson stains.

An uneasy silence hung over the waiting area. No one had the heart to make conversation. From time to time, a doctor or nurse hurried past. The minutes ticked by.

Then suddenly the quiet was shattered by the harsh ring of Vincenzo's mobile. He snatched it up and answered, moving nearer the entrance to take the call, ignoring a scowl from the receptionist behind the desk. His words faded as he stepped further away.

A few minutes later, he returned, grim-faced. "The gunmen managed to give my boys the slip. The lower terrace area is being treated as a crime scene and is being scoured for evidence. We've started to interview the staff, and the few guests that didn't scarper when it happened. I'm not hopeful we'll find anything useful, but you never know."

He collapsed onto a chair next to Sergio and laid a hand on his son's arm. "*Mi dispiace tanto, figlio mio. È tutta colpa mia.* I'm so sorry, son. It's all my fault."

Sergio placed his hand on top of his father's and said in a shaky voice. "'Course it's not. It's our damn home-grown cancer. We try to stamp it out and look what happens..."

"Like so many times before," said Ignazio bleakly, appearing with Rhys, each carrying a paper tray with their cups of coffee.

Hanna shot him a warning look not to elaborate further. Ignazio fell silent and handed round the coffee. They sat huddled together in silence, clasping their plastic cups, each deep in thought, worrying about Ceri, and how badly injured she might be.

And whether she'd pull through.

Nearly an hour had passed when Elena emerged from a side room, looking exhausted, her hair dishevelled, a plastic apron covering her blood-spattered wedding outfit.

Sergio sprang to his feet. "How's Ceri? What can you tell us?"

Elena gave an almost imperceptible shake of her head. "Not much, I'm afraid. She's been whisked off to Theatre for emergency surgery."

"Should we go and wait there instead?" Rhys asked.

"No, you're better waiting here for now," Elena responded. "Doctor Di Mauro is leading the team looking after her. I'll make him aware that you're here and to let you know as soon as there's any news."

"We really appreciate everything you've done, Elena," said Hanna, clasping the nurse's hands. "We can't thank you enough."

Elena shrugged and gave a faint smile. "It was nothing. Only glad I could help out."

Vincenzo's mobile rang again. He listened, then said, "Sorry, but I'm needed back at the *Questura*. There's been an important development. A car's coming to pick me up. Let me know as soon as you hear anything." He embraced Sergio briefly, then turned abruptly on his heel and left.

Sergio sank back onto his chair, looking drained.

"If you don't mind, I'd like to get Elena home so she can get some sleep," said Ignazio, a tad sheepishly. "She's got a shift tomorrow afternoon."

"Of course. You go ahead," said Hanna. "We'll be in touch once we know what's happening."

"That'll leave you without any transport, though," said Ignazio. "Will that be a problem?"

"Believe me, that's the least of our problems," said Hanna grimly. "We're not going anywhere."

The minor treatment area of *Pronto Soccorso* was busy now, with relatives milling around while staff treated their loved ones, but the red zone, the major area, remained quiet. The noise from the minor area filtered through, but in a strange, muted, other-worldly way that didn't touch the three friends waiting and desperately hoping that their loved one would live. They shifted uncomfortably on the plastic chairs below the glare of the fluorescent lights, the air heavy and humid, the air-conditioning struggling to make much of an impact.

Sergio seemed to be in a trance, moving little and speaking even less. Hanna tried to talk to him, but it was if he'd closed down and couldn't hear her. In the end, she gave up and took it in turns with Rhys to get more coffee and bring back bottles of water. She'd drunk so much coffee that she felt wired but exhausted at the same time. The endless waiting was unbearable.

Eventually Rhys whispered in Hanna's ear, "We should have heard *something* by now. D'you think Doctor Di Mauro's forgotten about us? Should we try and contact him?"

She shook her head. "I don't think that's a good idea. He'll have enough to do without us bothering him. Let's give him a bit more time."

Rhys clamped his mouth shut as if to stop himself saying anything further. The waiting continued.

Shortly after 1.30am, a slim middle-aged man in blue surgical scrubs came down the corridor towards them, his face sombre.

"Good morning, I'm Doctor Di Mauro, the clinical lead in Ceri's care. Which one of you is her husband, Signor Graziano?"

Sergio sat up, immediately alert. "I am."

"Would you like to follow me, please?" the doctor asked, indicating the same side room that Elena had been in.

Sergio followed him mechanically. Hanna and Rhys exchanged glances, tight-lipped. After about fifteen minutes he returned, looking dazed and bewildered, his face ashen.

"What is it, Sergio? Is she going to be okay?" Hanna asked, her impatience getting the better of her.

He slumped into the chair he'd recently vacated. "Fortunately, the bullet seems to have missed any of her vital organs and lodged itself in muscle. They've had to operate to remove it. That seems to have gone well, and they reckon she should make a full recovery.

"But the one thing they couldn't do was save the baby."

CHAPTER FORTY

Hanna's jaw dropped in surprise. "The baby? What baby? I didn't even know she was pregnant!"

Sergio shook his head sadly. "Nor did we. Apparently, she was in the very early stages. Neither of us knew, or even guessed..."

Sobs racked his body and tears began to flood down his cheeks. Hanna took him in her arms and tried to calm him down while Rhys looked on helplessly. After a few minutes she reached into her handbag, pulled out a packet of paper hankies and handed them to Sergio. He wiped his eyes and face and blew his nose loudly, clearly embarrassed at his outburst.

When the sobs and tears had finally subsided, she asked, "Is she still in Theatre?"

"N...no. They've t...transferred her to Intensive Care." Sergio paused and took a long gulp from a bottle of water. "As a precaution, they said. Standard practice. She's lost a lot of blood and is very weak. She needs time to recover."

Hanna's head was swimming with this news. On the one hand she was relieved that Ceri would recover, but on the other she was devastated that her friend's unborn child hadn't survived the ordeal. Regardless of whether Ceri or Sergio had been the intended victim of the shooting, they were both suffering now.

"Is there anything we can do? Can we see her?" she asked, struggling to keep her emotions in check.

Sergio shook his head again. "Doctor Di Mauro says she needs to rest now. Give her body a chance to recuperate. But he did say there could be long-term effects. There's always a risk of PTSD, and not just in the immediate aftermath. Apparently, it can develop weeks, even months, afterwards."

Hanna made no comment. What could she possibly say that would be of any comfort?

"We can ring tomorrow to see how she is and if she's up to visitors," Sergio continued, more composed now.

"I guess we should go and try to get some sleep ourselves," said Rhys. "We can take stock in the morning. Shall we call a cab to take us back to the hotel?"

"No need," said Sergio. "The newspaper's got a crash pad a few blocks away. We can stay there tonight, rather than go back to the hotel," said Sergio. "It's pretty basic but should do the trick."

Rhys nodded in agreement. "Sounds like a good idea. Can we walk there, or do we need to get a taxi?"

"I'd prefer to walk, get some air, if that's alright with you," said Sergio, getting awkwardly to his feet.

"Fine with me," said Hanna, offering him a steadying hand.

"I'll let Dad know the news." Sergio's fingers trembled as he tried to compose a quick text on his mobile phone. "Not about the baby, just that she's out of Theatre," he added in a low murmur.

He waited for a response and listened for a minute or two before turning back to them. "Dad's arranged for an armed police guard to sit outside the entrance to Intensive Care in case the gunmen come back."

The mere thought made Hanna's skin crawl.

"Only a precaution," he added. "It's unlikely but you never know. C'mon, let's go."

He slipped the phone back in his pocket and they weaved their way through the people gathered in the adjacent waiting area, flinching at their noisy conversations. Outside, the road seemed quiet in comparison, with few people around and little traffic at that hour.

Which was just as well, for they would have presented a sorry sight as they made their way along the pavement with shaky steps, their wedding clothes caked in blood. Hanna recalled a Spanish horror film she'd once seen, where the guests at a wedding reception turn into zombies and the bride and groom have to fight their way out to survive. *Things aren't quite that bad*, thought Hanna grimly.

But almost.

"How come your newspaper keeps a flat here?" asked Rhys, as they reached the crumbling apartment building in a rather run-down part of the city.

Sergio shrugged. "It belongs to the editor. Some family inheritance or other that he never got round to selling. Some of my colleagues have used it as a safe house when they've been working on high-profile stories."

For high-profile, read dangerous, thought Hanna, as they wearily climbed the stairs up to the second floor. Sergio produced a bunch of keys from his pocket, selected one and slotted it into the lock. The door opened with a reassuring click.

"All the journalists have keys," he explained, switching on the lights. "You never know when you might need the place."

The apartment was clean and tidy, a faint floral scent in the welcome cool air. They went into the lounge and flopped onto the sofa while Sergio went into the kitchen and rummaged through the cupboards, returning with a bottle of brandy and three glasses. He poured a generous measure into each glass. They knocked them back in silence. Hanna felt empty, as if she didn't even have the energy to talk. Sergio and Rhys probably felt the same.

"The beds are kept made up, ready for occupants. You two take the double, and I'll have one of the singles. See you in the morning." Sergio stood up, swayed slightly, then shuffled off towards the bedrooms. They followed, quickly found the double, shrugged out of their clothes, and collapsed exhausted on the bed, pulling the covers over them.

The last thing Hanna remembered thinking as she closed her eyes was wondering what they'd wear the next morning.

A shaft of sunlight shone through a chink in the heavy wooden shutters. Hanna looked around, puzzled. Slowly, the memories came floating back. There was no sign of Rhys, but she could hear the faint sound of voices. Tossing back the covers, she got up, treading over her bloodstained wedding outfit lying in a crumpled heap at the side of the bed. She threw back the shutters. The morning light dazzled her eyes. Shielding them, she looked out of the window at the street below: a side street, the only noise coming from an occasional passing car or scooter, or the odd jovial exchange of greetings between neighbours.

Turning around, she caught her reflection in the mirror of a heavy old-fashioned wardrobe standing opposite. She grimaced at the traces of dried blood still on her body in several places. She moved towards the wardrobe. The door opened with a creaky protest. Inside was a treasure trove of clean bedding and towels, plus a selection of t-shirts and jeans, and even trainers. She rummaged through and found a faded lemon t-shirt and a pair of black jeans, plus a pair of pale blue pumps half a size too big.

Wrapping herself in a bath sheet, she dived out of the room and padded along the corridor until she found the bathroom. Stepping into the shower, she let the pulsating jets of warm water gradually revive her. She dried herself quickly, pulled on the borrowed clothes, combed her still-damp hair and applied a little mascara and lipstick, all the make-up she had with her. Voices and the smell of coffee drew her to the kitchen. Sergio and Rhys were sitting at the little table deep in conversation, a bag of fresh croissants in front of them.

Pulling out a chair she noticed how haggard Sergio looked, and pale, save for the dark circles under his eyes and the stubble across his face. Rhys looked only marginally better.

"Either of you manage to get any sleep?" Hanna asked.

Rhys nodded. "A little."

Sergio shook his head. "Not much. I kept reliving the dance... those last few moments before...." He shuddered, and Hanna touched his arm in a comforting gesture. "I've already phoned the hospital, but the staff were changing shifts and couldn't tell me anything. They asked me to ring later."

Rhys got up and retrieved the coffee pot and a pan of hot milk from the stove, mixing the contents in a large cup which he handed to Hanna. "Help yourself," he said, pointing to the bag of pastries. "Afterwards we can maybe head up to the hospital in person."

"Seems like a plan." Hanna reached out for a croissant, feeling strangely hungry. "Hope it's okay to borrow some clothes."

"We've all done the same," said Rhys, between munches. It

was only then Hanna noticed he was wearing a worn grey t-shirt that barely stretched across his broad shoulders.

She took a sip of *caffélatte* and glanced at the kitchen clock. Not yet eight. Sergio hunched over the table, drinking his coffee, leaving the croissants untouched. He seemed to have retreated within himself. Hanna shot Rhys a worried glance. A mobile rang, shattering the silence. Sergio snatched his phone off the table and listened attentively to the voice on the other end.

"Okay," he said in conclusion. "Send it over. We'll see if any of us can identify it." He ended the call but continued to stare at the screen without speaking.

"What's going on, Sergio? What's happened?" Hanna shook his arm gently to get his attention.

He turned and looked at her with wild eyes. "It was my dad. The police found something on the track next to the hotel terrace. A cufflink with a distinctive marking. He's sending a photo over to see if we recognise it."

An incoming message alert pinged on his mobile. Sergio opened the image and glanced at it briefly before handing the phone to Hanna and Rhys.

Hanna stared at the screen, a knot forming in the pit of her stomach.

"What is it, Hanna? Do you recognise it?" Rhys prompted.

She opened her mouth to speak but the words stuck in her throat.

The cufflink bore an engraved crest. One she had seen many times before. On every bottle of wine produced by the Cortazzo estate.

Luciano's family crest.

CHAPTER FORTY-ONE

Hanna ran into the bathroom and retched over the basin.

Rhys appeared in the doorway, looking concerned. "Are you okay?"

Hanna nodded. "Just give me a sec." She was far from okay; she felt faint and about to throw up again any minute, but she didn't want any spectators.

"Fine." He turned on his heel and disappeared.

Hanna staggered across the bathroom and kicked the door shut. She turned on the taps and splashed tepid water on her face. The nausea was passing. Grabbing a towel, she dabbed her face and perched on the loo seat, resting her head against the cool tiles as she tried to gather her thoughts and emotions.

The cufflink proved to her, beyond any doubt, that a member of Luciano's family was responsible for shooting Ceri and causing the death of her unborn baby. This time Luciano and his family had gone too far. They couldn't be allowed to get away with it. She felt a burning desire, a compulsion, to help. But what could she do? Her head was spinning as she tried to think of a possible solution.

The door creaked open, and Rhys appeared with a glass of water. She took it gratefully and gulped down the contents.

"Feeling any better?"

"A little."

"You recognised the crest on the cufflink, didn't you? So, whose is it?"

Hanna nodded. "Yes, it's... It's the Cortazzo family crest. Luciano's family. It's on all the wine bottles from their estate."

Rhys looked grim. "Thought as much, given your reaction. C'mon on, we need to tell Sergio."

Hanna rose unsteadily to her feet and followed Rhys back into the kitchen where Sergio was waiting expectantly. She repeated what she'd told Rhys. Sergio's face paled and he swayed as if on the verge of collapse.

"Steady on!" Rhys grabbed him, before turning to Hanna. "You're sure?"

Hanna shot him a withering look. "Of course, I'm sure. I've seen it so many times. Google it if you don't believe me." She slumped into the chair next to Sergio. Rhys remained standing, as if at a loss of what to do or say. Sergio buried his head in his hands and uttered a long groan.

A few minutes passed as they each tried to deal with the situation. A thick cloud of despondency hung over them. No one felt inclined to speak. Hanna could see the despair etched on the two men's faces. It was as if they all realised that they'd reached a tipping point, a point of no return.

Rhys was the first to snap out of it. "Sergio, we need to get back to your dad. He's waiting for an answer. I can do it."

Hanna reached for the phone, grateful for something positive to do. "I'll do it. It's easier for me and he may have more questions."

Vincenzo answered immediately and listened as Hanna explained for the third time about the cufflink. "We also found some tyre tracks at the scene, so at least we've got something to work on now. Any news of Ceri?"

Hanna couldn't quite believe he hadn't already made his own enquiries. "Not yet. We're just about to phone the hospital."

"Let me know when you hear something, okay?"

"We will." Hanna ended the call and turned to the other two.

"What's best, phone or go straight to the hospital?" asked Rhys who had obviously been listening to the call.

"Probably phone first, see how she is and whether she's up to having visitors." Hanna nudged Sergio gently. "Better if you call, as her next of kin. They're unlikely to give out information to anyone else."

Sergio straightened up and took the phone from Hanna, searched for the number, and punched it in. The call was answered quickly but then he seemed to be left hanging on for several minutes, probably while the receptionist went to check on Ceri's condition. Finally, Sergio mumbled a few incomprehensible words and hung up, a grimace on his face.

"Christ, it's so difficult to get information out of these people!" he exploded, hitting the table in frustration. "No news, I'm afraid. The consultant was with her and the receptionist didn't want to interrupt. She asked me to call back later."

Half an hour passed before Sergio tried the hospital again, to be told that his wife would be well enough for them to visit that afternoon but only for a few minutes.

"Well, at least that's something," said Hanna soothingly, wondering why the hospital hadn't commented on her condition. They'd probably find out more once they were there in person.

Sergio remained grim-faced, although his expression had softened slightly. He fell silent, scouring his phone for God knows what.

"I'll make some more coffee." Rhys got up, filled the coffee pot, and put it on the stove.

Desperate for something to do, Hanna left the kitchen and began to gather up their ruined wedding outfits, stuffing them into a carrier bag she found in one of the bedrooms. She left it by the front door, ready to dispose of when they went out. As she returned to the kitchen, the echoey ring of the entry phone resonated through the apartment.

Sergio's initial look of concern turned to relief when he answered it. "My dad. He wants to talk to us."

Moments later, a slightly breathless Vincenzo appeared at the front door. Despite a change of clothes, he looked dishevelled and had dark circles under his eyes as if he'd had little sleep, his expression sombre. Sergio ushered him into the kitchen without a word. Rhys poured him a coffee and set it down on the table.

"I think you should all stay here for a few days," he said, without preamble. "The hotel is closed off as a crime scene. And it's much too dangerous for you to return home to Cefalù yet. I'll get your bags packed and brought here. We'll also need to take statements from you, but we can arrange to do that here. This way we can keep both the apartment and the hospital under surveillance in case of any further trouble."

"What do you mean, further trouble?" Sergio looked hard at his father.

Vincenzo held his gaze. "The gunmen may well come back to finish the job. Or Ceri may not have been their intended target."

CHAPTER FORTY-TWO

"You... you mean, they might have been after one of us?" Hanna asked, incredulously.

Vincenzo shrugged. "It's a possibility. We can't rule anything out at this stage."

"There's something else you should know, *Papà*," said Sergio gravely. "The night before the wedding, I was threatened the night before by three men in the hotel restaurant. They told me to forget the police investigation and the media story into the people-trafficking. Or else."

"Why didn't you tell me this before?" Vincenzo's face was stern. "Did they assault you?"

"No, they didn't lay a finger on me. I told them to go to hell."

"Very wise. Now look what's happened." Vincenzo was more exasperated than cross, as if amazed that his usual streetwise son could be so naïve. "If I'd known, I could have put a closer watch on the church and the hotel. Why didn't you take it more seriously?"

Sergio looked contrite. "I should have. But it's not unusual to get threatened in my line of work. If I told you every time it happens, we'd never talk of anything else."

Vincenzo glared at him. "What's happened has happened," he said gruffly. "We just have to pray that Ceri survives and nothing else occurs. But let me make it clear, I have no intention of dropping the police investigation. It's up to you whether you publish the story or not."

"If I don't, other journalists will run with it."

"Yes, but not in as much depth or with as much passion," responded Vincenzo drily. "For you, it's almost a personal vendetta." Then under his breath, scarcely audible: "As it is for me."

How much sorrow could one family take, thought Hanna? Two deaths at the hands of Luciano or his henchmen. First, Sergio's brother Pino; now, Ceri's unborn baby. Would this harden their resolve, or soften it?

"There's something else you should know," said Sergio, leading his father into the lounge, shutting the door behind them.

The two men were gone some time. All that could be heard was the sound of low voices and the occasional sob. It was unclear whether it came from Sergio or his father.

Hanna looked helplessly at Rhys. "D'you think that either of us could have been the target?"

Rhys looked blank. "You tell me. You know how things work round here, and you were the one married into the mob."

Hanna felt a jolt of anger. "Not knowingly! I would never have married Luciano had I known the truth about the family business. I certainly wouldn't have brought a child into such a world," she said, kicking herself for having been so naïve.

Rhys held his hands up. "Sorry. Bad choice of words. I wouldn't have thought either of us pose much of a risk. We discovered the Welsh connection, but that's all. It's Sergio and his dad who are threatening to expose the trafficking ring and arrest the ringleaders. The gunmen may have shot Ceri by mistake or done it deliberately to warn off Sergio. Who knows?"

They sat in silence, lost in thought. When father and son returned, Vincenzo seemed to have aged ten years. His skin was the colour of ashes and his gait unsteady, so visibly shaken was he by the conversation he'd just had with his son. Hanna presumed Sergio had told him about the baby. Rhys rummaged through the cupboards for the bottle of brandy, poured a couple of generous measures into glasses and handed them to the two men.

Vincenzo downed his drink in one. He set his glass back on the table with a resounding thud and said, "Let me know how you get on at the hospital. I'll send an officer round later to take your statements. In the meantime, if there's anything – anything at all – you remember that might be important, get in touch straight away." With that, he turned on his heel and left without a backward glance, slamming the front door shut behind him.

Hanna flinched at the noise. "When did the hospital say we could visit?" she asked.

"Anytime between two and three this afternoon, but only for a few minutes," Sergio muttered in response.

Hanna glanced at the kitchen clock. "Okay, I'll pop out and get something for lunch."

"I'll come too," said Rhys, getting up.

"No, you stay here with Sergio. I won't be long."

"Hanna, it might not be safe," said Rhys, with a frown.

Hanna went over to the kitchen window and looked out on the street below. Sure enough, she noticed what she suspected: two men sitting at a pavement café, deep in conversation, cigarettes in hand. Two men she recognised from the church the day before. She beckoned Rhys over and pointed out the two men.

"See? Vincenzo's already keeping us under observation. No need to worry about me. I'll be fine. And the *alimentari* is only a stone's throw away."

"Sure?"

"Positive. I'll only be a couple of minutes."

She collected a key from the hook by the front door, picking up the carrier bag full of their ruined clothes on the way out. She dumped it in one of the communal refuse bins at the side of the apartment block before continuing on to the small supermarket further down the street, wondering what on earth she could buy that would stimulate their non-existent appetites.

Ceri looked so frail and vulnerable, lying motionless in the hospital bed, wired up to various monitors, her eyes closed as if asleep. Her face was pinched and pale, a shadow of her former self. Hanna felt a rush of affection for her best friend. What if she didn't pull through? Her insides tightened, and affection was replaced by dread.

As they watched, Ceri's eyelids suddenly flickered. Slowly, she opened her eyes, screwing them up against the harsh light, trying to focus.

Sergio stepped forward, kissed the top of her head and squeezed her shoulder, steering clear of all the wires connecting her to the equipment. "*Amore*," he said softly. "I'm here. How are you feeling?"

Ceri didn't respond. The nurse had warned them that she had been heavily sedated and might not recognise them at first. Sergio continued talking, as if to reassure her it was really him.

"Your brother and Hanna are here too, *tesoro*. D'you see them?"

Ceri stared at them, blankly at first, then with a faint

glimmer of recognition. Several minutes passed before she summoned up the strength to speak.

"Some wedding day," she whispered with a thin smile, her face distorted with the effort.

Sergio looked overjoyed, his face transformed by a beaming smile. "That's my girl!" He looked as if he was going to hug her but then thought better of it, given the amount of equipment she was hooked up to. Her eyes flickered again, closing and opening, until finally they shut completely as she drifted off to sleep. A nurse popped her head around the curtain.

"Did she wake up?" she asked gently, checking the readings on the monitors as she did so.

Sergio gulped and nodded. "Very briefly."

"Don't worry, that's only to be expected, what with the sedation and the trauma. Did she recognise you?"

Sergio nodded again.

"That's a good sign. Better leave her to get some rest now."

The nurse smiled kindly as she led them out of the unit. Turning to Sergio, she added: "Signor Graziano, Doctor Di Mauro would like a word with you before you go. This way, please."

CHAPTER FORTY-THREE

"So, what did the doctor say?" Hanna asked as soon as Sergio appeared from the doctor's office. She had been pacing the corridor outside, thinking all sorts and fearing the worst the longer the meeting lasted.

Sergio looked beaten, his shoulders hunched, his face screwed into a grimace. He flopped onto the nearest plastic chair. Hanna could feel her heart and pulse racing as she waited for his response. He opened his mouth to speak; the words came slowly as if each one caused him pain.

"It's... it's... still..." he began in a shaky voice, "early days. But the surgery went well. Difficult to tell yet if she'll make a full recovery." He gulped, then struggled on. "No damage to any of the major organs. Just the baby..."

He broke out in sobs, covering his face with his hands as the tears started to flow. Hanna flew to his side and flung her arms round him. She had no words. What could she say that would make him feel better? Rhys looked on helplessly. She cradled Sergio in her arms, making soothing noises until he calmed down. A uniformed police officer appeared out of nowhere and asked if he could do anything to help. He was obviously one of the police guard that Vincenzo had arranged for Ceri.

Hanna shook her head and gently helped Sergio to his feet. "Thanks, but we'll be fine. We're going now."

The policeman smiled politely and disappeared down the corridor.

Back at the apartment Sergio lay slumped on the sofa in a catatonic state. His eyes were open, and he stared blankly at the ceiling. All attempts to engage him in conversation or persuade him to eat or drink failed. It was as if his world had ended. Hanna wondered whether he knew more about Ceri's condition than he was admitting to. Eventually she and Rhys left him alone and retreated to the kitchen. They sat at the table, nursing yet another cup of coffee.

"I've never seen him like this," said Hanna. "He's always been so strong, so in control. D'you think it's shock that's causing it?"

"Possibly. It could be his way of coping." Rhys finished off the last of his coffee. "As if getting married wasn't stressful enough. But seeing your new bride getting shot during the first dance, then the awful news about the baby she was carrying... It's the stuff of nightmares."

"D'you think it's just a temporary thing?"

Rhys shrugged. "Who knows? We'll have to wait and see."

Hanna sat back in her chair. The shooting may well have stalled the police investigation into the trafficking ring and any imminent arrests, if not stopped it altogether. Would it still go ahead now, given the risks? And what about the media story? Surely Sergio wouldn't want to pursue it now? Her head throbbed.

A ping from her mobile phone alerted her to a new message from Vincenzo:

> Tried to get hold of Sergio but he's not answering his phone. How's Ceri doing? Marta's taken a turn for the worse. On my way home now. Be in touch later.

She showed Rhys the message. "Strange he didn't even contact his dad after going to see Ceri," she said, her voice anxious. "He doesn't seem to be coping very well. It's as if he's retreated within himself."

"Maybe he feels responsible for everything's that's happened," Rhys replied.

"Could be. Difficult to know what we can do to help."

Rhys shrugged. "Just be here to support him, I guess. See what happens over the next few days."

"We're due to fly home the day after tomorrow, remember," Hanna said with a frown. "We can't leave Eva any longer than that. Which reminds me, I must call and check how she's doing."

She sent a quick text to Vincenzo to tell him what little they knew about Ceri. Then she dialled Nerys' number and waited so long for a response that she was starting to panic. Finally, a breathless Nerys picked up.

"Thank God!" Hanna blurted out. "I was beginning to think something was wrong."

Nerys laughed. "No, everything's fine. I'd left my mobile in the kitchen, and we were just coming in from the studio when I heard it ring. Everything OK?"

"Not really. I'll explain later. How's Eva? How are things with you?"

"We're having a whale of a time, aren't we, poppet?" Nerys sounded happy and carefree.

Hanna could hear Eva giggling in the background and felt a huge surge of relief. "And the cottage?"

"Nothing that we've noticed. Let me put Eva on. She's dying to talk to you!"

"Mummy!"

"Hi, sweet pea. Are you enjoying yourself with Auntie Nerys? How are Bryn and Cosmo?"

"Yes, we're having an awesome time! I've been making pots and painting and helping Auntie Nerys with the animals. Lulu and Eric are amazing. Mummy, can we get an al...capa when you get back?"

She babbled on for several minutes, recounting everything she'd done in the short time they'd been away. It was such a joy hearing her voice, knowing that she, at least, was safe and happy. Eventually, Eva ran out of steam and handed the phone back to Nerys. Hanna briefly explained recent events. She could hear her friend's sharp intake of breath at the end of the line.

"Oh my God! It sounds like something straight out of a film! Will you be okay? Do you need to stay on? It's not a problem if you do."

"Thanks, Nerys. Not too sure what's happening yet. We've got to give statements to the police later today. Sergio's taking the whole thing really badly, and now his mother has fallen ill again. I'll call again tomorrow with an update."

"OK. I'll pass you back to Eva."

Hanna blew several kisses down the phone to her daughter, promising to speak again the following day, and rang off. No sooner had she put the phone back on the table, the entry phone sounded. Rhys got up to answer it.

"It's the police," he announced. He glanced around the door into the lounge. Sergio hadn't moved. "Let's hope Sergio's up to talking to them."

Hanna opened the door to two uniformed police officers, both carrying a suitcase in each hand. They flashed their identity cards and introduced themselves, the older officer taking charge.

"*Buongiorno, signora.* Inspector Graziano asked us to collect your effects from the hotel," said the older officer, indicating the cases. "He'd also like us to take your statements while we're here. Save you from coming down to the *Questura*, in the circumstances. If that's convenient with you, of course."

"Yes, of course," said Hanna, showing them into the kitchen. "I presume you'll want to interview us individually?"

The older officer nodded. "Please. Will that be a problem?"

"My partner doesn't speak much Italian. I can translate for him, or you can interview us together."

"We can interview you together, in that case." The two officers took a seat at the table, the younger officer producing a tablet from a pocket of his uniform.

"Is it okay with you if we record the interviews?" he asked.

"That's fine. Our friend, Sergio – the husband – is still pretty much in shock. I don't know how communicative he will be."

"*Eh, signora, non si preoccupi.* Don't worry," said the older man. "We're well used to dealing with victims of shootings."

I bet you are, thought Hanna grimly.

CHAPTER FORTY-FOUR

It didn't take long to make their statements to the two police officers. After all, there was really very little to tell. The police were particularly interested in the men who'd threatened Sergio in the hotel restaurant the evening before, pressing Hanna to give them a detailed description. She struggled to do so as her back had been turned to them most of the time. Maybe Sergio had been able to be more helpful, although she doubted it in his current state. With Hanna and Rhys, he remained monosyllabic and grim-faced; with the police officers, he was little better. Hanna wondered how long this would last.

Although no-one had any real appetite, for dinner Hanna ordered takeaway pizza from a little place they had passed down the street earlier on their way to the hospital. Sergio ate one piece of his pizza, chewing each mouthful painfully as if he suspected it might be poisoned, washing it down with a bottle of Peroni beer. The beer went down much more easily than the pizza. When he'd drained the last drop, he rose wearily to his feet and announced that he was going to lie down. Hanna glanced at the kitchen clock. It was shortly after ten. Unlikely they'd see much more of him before morning.

Wearily she started to clear away the dishes, when her mobile rang. Vincenzo.

"Thanks for the message about Ceri. Are you going to see her again tomorrow?"

"All being well, if they let us," said Hanna.

"And Sergio? He's still not answering my calls or messages."

"He's pretty unresponsive with us, too. It must be delayed shock. He's taken himself off to bed. How's Marta?"

"I think the shock has affected her, too. She's barely lucid. The doctor's given her a sedative to calm her down. Her sister's coming to look after her while I go to work. I shouldn't really be investigating the shooting as it affects my family, but given the likely link to the trafficking investigation, my boss has agreed to let me stay on."

Hanna wondered again what would happen to the main police investigation now, but she didn't have the energy to discuss it any further that evening. She ended the call, having agreed to speak to Vincenzo again the following day. In response to Rhys' questioning look, she relayed the contents of the conversation.

"We'll have to make a decision tomorrow about what we're doing," he said with a frown. "Our flight is on Tuesday. Whether we're staying or what..."

"It's difficult. We don't know yet if Ceri's going to pull through, and Sergio's in such a state. But we've got Eva to think of, too, and I really don't want to leave her any longer than necessary."

"And I have to get back to work."

Hanna sighed. "Let's see what tomorrow brings and make a decision then."

The following morning, Hanna lay awake for some time, the events of the past forty-eight hours replaying in her head as if an important clue was buried deep in her memory. Next to her, Rhys snored gently. Eventually she got up and padded into the kitchen to make some coffee. Halfway through the first cup, she heard the jets of the shower start up in the bathroom. Shortly afterwards, Sergio appeared, bleary-eyed and morose, his face dark with stubble, his hair wild and unkempt. No sign of him having been near the shower. That must have been Rhys.

She poured another coffee and handed it to him. "Morning. How are you feeling? Did you manage to get much sleep?"

"Not really. I kept getting nightmarish visions about Ceri vanishing." He sank heavily onto a chair and drained his cup. "It feels like being dragged through a hell from which there's no escape."

"That's understandable after everything that's happened," said Hanna sympathetically, refilling his cup.

He fumbled in the pocket of his pyjama bottoms and pulled out his phone. "I'd better check on Ceri, see how she is and whether we can visit." He scrolled through his contacts to find the number for the hospital and dialled. Like the previous time, it rang for several minutes before being answered, then another wait while presumably the receptionist sought an update.

Sergio's features softened slightly as he listened to the response. "*Va bene. Ci vediamo piu tardi, allora.*" Turning to Hanna, he said, "She seems to be doing okay. Better. We can go up there and see her this afternoon. Same time as yesterday."

"You may want to get a shower first. You don't want her to see you looking like that, do you?"

Sergio glanced at his reflection in the kitchen window. "Suppose not," he agreed reluctantly, dragging himself to his feet and heading slowly towards the bathroom as if bereft of energy. Hanna heard the bathroom door open and an exchange between the two men, although she couldn't make out the words. Then, the sound of a door shutting.

A barefoot Rhys appeared in the doorway, a towel wrapped around his lower half, another around his shoulders "Sergio looks terrible. He's going back to bed for a while. Said he didn't get much sleep."

Hanna looked surprised. "Oh, I thought he was going for a shower. Never mind, plenty of time yet. He phoned the hospital, and Ceri seems to be making progress. We can go up there later."

"Well, that's something." He pulled the towel from his shoulders and started rubbing his wet hair. "Any coffee left in the pot?"

Ceri was awake when they visited the intensive care unit that afternoon. She lay on her back, still attached to several monitors and looking frail, but with a little more colour to her cheeks. She brightened when she saw them.

Sergio looked vaguely presentable, having eventually spruced himself up for the visit after some patient coaxing from Hanna. Left to his own devices, she suspected he wouldn't have bothered.

"*Come stai, amore?*" Sergio murmured, kissing her lightly on the top of her head. He settled himself into the hard plastic chair next to the bed, gingerly taking hold of her cannula-free hand in his.

"I'm... I'm doing okay, thanks." The words came out slowly, as if the effort was almost too much.

"Are you in any pain?" Sergio continued.

"Not really," said Ceri, moving her head sideways slightly to indicate all the drips and monitors. "The medics take care of that."

"We've brought you some things," said Hanna, who'd raided Ceri's bag that had been brought from the hotel. "Toiletries, nightie, etcetera."

Ceri smiled weakly. "Thanks."

"We'll leave the two of you to talk for a few minutes," said Hanna, pulling Rhys' sleeve in the direction of the exit. "See you later."

"They need time and space," she explained to Rhys once they were back outside in the corridor, "if they're ever going to get through this. It's bad enough to get shot on your wedding day, but when she finds out that she's lost the baby she didn't even know she was carrying... It doesn't bear thinking about."

"You're right," Rhys agreed, falling into step as she headed for the hospital exit, "As usual."

CHAPTER FORTY-FIVE

Once back at the apartment, Sergio went straight into the lounge and turned on the TV to the local news. A short item on the shooting revealed little, only that the police were pursuing a number of leads. He turned it off, and slumped dejected into an armchair, closing his eyes, as if the hospital visit had sapped him of what little energy he had. Hanna and Rhys left him in peace and retired to the kitchen to talk.

Hanna was feeling happier. She had been relieved to see Ceri looking marginally better, and the news from Dr Di Mauro that they planned to transfer her to a lower-dependency ward the following day filled her with hope. But it would be a long haul to recovery, and God only knew what mental scars would be left. And would the shooting effectively scupper the police investigation and media interest into the trafficking network?

"So, what do you think we should do?" Rhys said, extracting a bottle of beer from the fridge and pouring a glass of chilled white wine for Hanna.

Hanna took a sip and said thoughtfully, "I'm worried about Sergio. I've never seen him like this before. He's doesn't seem to be dealing with what's happened."

"Hardly surprising," said Rhys drily. "It's not every day your bride gets shot on your wedding day and loses the baby she's carrying."

"Yes, I know. But Sergio's usually so... in control, able to deal with anything."

"Different when it's so personal, though. And in such circumstances."

"I guess so. It's been pretty traumatic for everyone." She fell silent, considering the options as she downed her wine. Finally, she said: "Well, I think one of us should return home and one should stay on here, at least for a few days to support Sergio and Ceri. To my mind, it makes more sense for me to stay than you, as I can be of more use. What d'you reckon?"

Rhys mulled her suggestion over for a few moments before responding. "That seems to add up. Will Eva be okay on her own with me, d'you think?"

Hanna smiled. "Of course, she will! That won't be a problem at all. She adores you, you know that. And it won't be for long. Sure you're happy with that?"

Rhys looked thoughtful again. "What about you, though? You don't think it's too risky staying on here on your own?"

"What, with an armed police protection team in tow? Never felt safer!" Hanna made a hollow attempt at a laugh.

A look of concern flitted across Rhys' face. "Yeah, but look what's happened, even with police protection."

"At the wedding, it was merely a precautionary measure. This is hard-core police protection," said Hanna, trying to reassure him.

Rhys didn't look convinced. "I really don't want to leave you on your own..."

"I won't be. I'll be with Sergio. I don't think he should be left on his own. And it's only for a few days, until he gets back on his feet. His father's got enough on his hands, what with the police investigation and Marta being ill. Once Ceri is out of ICU, and starts to recover, I think Sergio'll get a better grip on the situation."

Rhys still looked doubtful. "Well, if you're sure..."

"I'm positive it's the best solution," she said, wrapping her arms around him and kissing him passionately on the lips. "You'll see."

Early that evening Vincenzo sent a text to say he'd drop by on his way home about nine-ish to give them an update. Hanna rustled up a makeshift dinner of pasta with a ready-made pistachio pesto sauce, ingredients she'd bought from the local *alimentari*. No one was really hungry, although the locally-produced sauce was really quite tasty.

Over dinner Hanna and Rhys made various attempts to engage Sergio in conversation, but the most response they got was only ever a handful of words. Eventually they gave up, and a taciturn Sergio became engrossed in scrolling through his phone.

Rhys went off to pack while Hanna cleared away the dishes. Shortly before nine o' clock, the entry phone buzzed and the word *'papavero'* – the Italian word for poppy – could be heard quite distinctly. Vincenzo insisted on using this new codeword so they could be sure any visitors to the apartment were genuine. Overkill, Hanna had thought when he suggested it, but had agreed to humour him, even though the only visitors to the apartment up till then had been him and his police colleagues.

Hanna opened the door of the apartment and watched Vincenzo wearily climb the last few stairs. He smiled as he reached the top, gave her a hug, and handed her a small package wrapped in red paper and tied with gold ribbon.

"What's this?"

"Just some *pasticcini*, little pastries, that might tempt you all to eat a little," he explained. "I was buying some for Marta for the same reason – they're her favourite – and I thought you might like some, too."

"That's very kind. Come on in. Have you eaten?"

He shook his head. "No, not yet, but Marta's sister will have prepared dinner for me so I can't be long."

"A drink, then? A coffee, maybe?"

"Nothing, thanks. If I have any more coffee today, my head will explode."

Hanna smiled and led him into the lounge where Rhys and Sergio were watching the TV news. They both looked up expectantly and Rhys turned the TV off.

"*Ciao, ragazzi,*" he said, lowering himself into an armchair. "I wanted to pop around and check how you're all doing. How's Ceri?"

Sergio started to explain but the words seemed to stick in his throat, and he insisted that Hanna take over.

"Thank God, she's going to be okay," Vincenzo said, crossing himself. "But it's terrible news about the baby. How's she taking it?"

"They've not told her yet, not while her condition was still critical," said Hanna. "The doctor's planning to tell her tomorrow, once they've moved her out of intensive care."

Vincenzo sighed. "It'll come as a dreadful shock. The whole incident is just so horrific." He paused, staring blankly into space as if gathering his thoughts. "Aren't you two flying home soon?"

"We were supposed to be going tomorrow. But I've decided to stay on, and Rhys will go back on his own," Hanna replied, before quickly adding, "If that's OK with you, that is. I don't want to pose an extra risk."

Vincenzo waved his hands in the air dismissively. "No, it's

fine. There's no suggestion at present that you're in any sort of danger. I think it would do Sergio good to have you around, and Ceri will need your support, too, especially when she learns about the baby."

"So, how's the investigation into the shooting going?" Hanna asked.

Vincenzo leaned forward in his chair, an earnest expression on his face. "We need concrete evidence before we approach the Cortazzo family. I don't want to tip them off that we suspect them of any involvement in the shooting until we've got good reason for doing so. Otherwise, they'll simply lawyer up and wriggle out of it. We can't afford to jeopardise the main trafficking investigation."

He paused a minute before continuing. "We checked the wiretap on their phone, but nothing's come up that's related to the shooting. The cufflink we found at the scene has been sent off to Forensics to check for DNA. Oh, and we're still trying to trace the tyre tracks we found near the scene. If we come up with anything that ties directly to any member of the family, we can make a move. But not until then. In the meantime, we're keeping a watch on the family estate and Luciano's apartment in Cefalù. There's been no sign of Luciano at either place up till now."

"And what about the main investigation?" Sergio piped up. "Is it on hold?"

Vincenzo sighed. "*Eh, beh*, it's stalled temporarily while we look into the link with the shooting. We need to make sure there won't be any repercussions."

"Repercussions?" asked Hanna, alarmed.

"*Eh, sì, mia cara.* As I said before, we don't want the shooters coming back for more."

CHAPTER FORTY-SIX

Hanna's mouth went dry. "Do you think any of us could be in danger?"

"Anything is possible," Vincenzo replied. "So far my men haven't spotted anything suspicious, either here at the apartment or at the hospital. The likelihood is that the gunmen have gone to ground. I'd say give it another couple of days before you go back to your own place. It should be safe enough then. In the meantime, it's easier for us to keep an eye on you while you're here and easier for you to visit the hospital with it being so close. Does that sound okay?"

Vincenzo's glance flitted from Hanna to Sergio. "I suppose Hanna will be staying with you while she's here?"

Sergio ran his hands through his hair. "Hadn't really thought about it, but, yes, of course, she's more than welcome. And I could use the company right now."

"That's settled then." The older man got up to leave. "I'll say goodnight. Keep in touch. Oh, and *buon viaggio*, Rhys, for tomorrow." Rhys stood up as he approached, and the two men embraced a little awkwardly.

Sergio showed his father out, and they stayed chatting in the hall for several minutes in low tones. Hanna quickly related the gist of the conversation to Rhys, careful to skip over the possibility that the shooters could still be a threat. If he knew that, he would never agree to leave. She was beginning to wonder if she'd made the right decision. But why should she be a target? Vincenzo seemed to think there was no imminent danger. But why then had he insisted they use a codeword? Nothing seemed to make sense.

"I wonder what will happen with the main investigation now?" Rhys mused.

"Who knows?" Hanna replied. "I got the impression that Vincenzo is keen to prove the link to the shooting, especially if the Cortazzos are directly involved."

"Are you sure you're happy to stay on, on your own?" He searched her face for a response.

Hanna gave what she hoped was a reassuring smile. "Of course. It'll be fine. Just a few days to get Ceri and Sergio through the worst. Then back to normality."

Rhys didn't look wholly convinced. "When did Dr Di Mauro say they'd be moving Ceri out of ICU?"

"Tomorrow afternoon, if I remember correctly. Are you thinking of popping up there before you leave?"

Rhys nodded. "The flight's late afternoon, so I could go over in the morning to say goodbye, if they'll let me."

Hanna took a quick look at her phone: ten past ten. "We can check in the morning. It's a bit late to call now."

They heard the door shut with a soft thud, then Sergio reappeared in the doorway.

"Dad's suggested I go into the office tomorrow to check if everything's still in place with the story and it's ready to go," he said, his reluctance evident. "But all I can think of right now is

Ceri. Nothing else seems to matter. And I need to be there when Dr Di Mauro tells Ceri about the baby."

"Don't worry, Sergio," said Hanna, laying a soothing hand on his arm. "You do as you see fit. Maybe you could do some work from here, without going into the office? As for Ceri, we'll agree a suitable time with Dr Di Mauro tomorrow."

A call to ICU the following morning confirmed that Ceri would be moved out that afternoon and that they could visit that morning. By the time Hanna and Rhys were ready to leave the apartment, Sergio still hadn't put in an appearance. Hanna knocked on his bedroom door. No response. She continued to knock, opening the door slowly. Sergio seemed to be sleeping soundly, cocooned in a lightweight duvet. Perhaps he'd taken a sleeping pill that had knocked him out. As Hanna crept nearer the bed, she could hear him snoring softly. Satisfied that he was okay, she retreated and joined Rhys in the hallway.

"He's still asleep. He must be exhausted; he's barely slept since it happened," she whispered. "Best leave him be. We can always visit Ceri again later if they're both up to it."

Rhys nodded and they left the apartment, descending the stairs to ground level. The morning sun dazzled their eyes as they stepped out into the street, one side half-bathed in light, the other in shadow. By the time they reached the hospital entrance a few blocks away, they'd both worked up a sweat and a thirst. Hanna rummaged in her bag for the bottle of water she'd brought with her and handed it to Rhys.

"Phew! I'll be glad to get back to normal temperatures," he said, taking a massive glug and wiping his forehead with the back of his hand.

Hanna smiled. "You'd get used to the heat if you were here for any length of time. I certainly did."

They continued on through the busy corridors, passing porters wheeling patients in hospital beds, doctors in scrubs and nurses in uniform scurrying to their next shift. As they approached the entrance to ICU, a side door opened, and Dr Di Mauro appeared. He beckoned them into the consulting room, and closed the door, taking a seat behind a small desk and pointing to the spare chairs, invited them to do the same.

"Is Signor Graziano not with you?" he asked, his brows knitted.

"No, why? Has something happened? Is Ceri OK?" asked Hanna anxiously.

"There was a slight issue earlier this morning," the doctor continued. "Ceri was recovering sufficiently to realise that she was haemorrhaging blood from below. She insisted on knowing why. I'm afraid that we've had to tell her about the baby. You can imagine how she's taken it. She's shocked, confused, angry even. I was hoping her husband would have been here. She's going to need support to get through this. Although she's being transferred off ICU, she's still fragile, and this news could derail her whole healing process if handled badly."

Shocked, Hanna translated the conversation for Rhys in a faltering voice. They exchanged glances, both at a loss as to how to respond.

"I... I... I don't think her husband is dealing with the whole incident very well either," stammered Hanna. "I'm staying on for a few more days to support them both."

"That sounds like an excellent idea. Ceri will certainly need all your support." The doctor rose to his feet, his mission clearly accomplished. "She'll probably still be pretty upset. Please do what you can to calm her."

"Of course," said Hanna, passing through the door the doctor held open for them.

"I will remain in charge of her care. Her transfer to Ward 18 will go ahead this afternoon as planned. All future visits will take place there."

Hanna mumbled her thanks and walked in a daze towards the ICU reception desk, Rhys beside her. They gave their names to the receptionist, and a nurse led them to Ceri's bedside. She was sitting up in bed, connected to fewer monitors than before, looking sad and tearful. Hanna went over and gave her a clumsy hug, trying not to dislodge any of the medical equipment. Then Rhys did the same, Ceri clinging to each of them in turn, the occasional sob escaping from her throat.

"You knew, didn't you?" said Ceri, making it sound more like a statement than a question, her voice wavering.

Rhys bowed his head. "The doctor was waiting to tell you once you'd come out of the critical phase. Once you were strong enough..."

"We didn't want you finding out like this," said Hanna softly.

"Never a good time, I guess." Ceri looked around the cubicle. "Isn't Sergio with you?"

"He was fast asleep when we left," Hanna explained. "I think he'd taken something to make him sleep. He hasn't been coping terribly well with everything that's happened."

"That's understandable," Ceri said, laying her head back on the pillow, looking drained. "It's all been such a shock, for everyone."

"We should have been going home today, but I've decided to stay on a bit longer to help out any way I can while you get better," said Hanna.

"But I'm going back this afternoon," said Rhys. "Eva's about to start school and I'm needed at work. It's peak season; I can't let them down. I just came to say goodbye. If there's anything Hanna can't deal with and you need me here, let me know and I'll jump on the next plane back."

Ceri took an intake of breath as if summoning all her strength, then said weakly: "I'm sure... it will... all work out. Let's... let's hope so."

CHAPTER FORTY-SEVEN

As Hanna approached the ward two days later, she passed a young guy dressed in jeans and a tight-fitting white t-shirt sitting in the corridor, scanning through his phone. He looked up as she passed, smiled, and said *"Buongiorno."* He must be the plain-clothes police officer, she thought, as she returned the greeting.

Ceri's bed was empty, and a nurse directed her to the day area. Hanna found Ceri sitting in a wheelchair, dressed in a light floral cover-up over her nightie, chatting in Italian to another patient, a stout middle-aged woman with a florid face. The room was stifling; the late morning sun shone in full force through the window and the air-conditioning rattled as it struggled to cope.

Seeing Hanna approach, Ceri smiled and beckoned her over. "Thought you'd forgotten me!"

"As if!" Hanna planted a kiss on the top of her head and drew up a chair next to her. "How are you doing?" Despite looking pale and drawn, Ceri seemed to be in good spirits.

"Ready to get out of here!" growled Ceri good-naturedly. "I need some decent food and a comfy bed."

Hanna smiled. "All being well, you'll be discharged tomorrow so we'll be able to get you home."

Ceri looked around expectantly. "Where's Sergio?"

"He's back at the apartment with a migraine. Sends his apologies. You've got me as substitute."

The other patient got up and excused herself, shuffling back towards the ward in a pair of worn slippers, leaving the two of them alone.

Ceri looked pensive. "I'm a bit concerned about him actually. He's not been himself since the... the... shooting. Hopefully, he'll come round a bit once I'm home. Has he been going into work at all?"

Hanna shifted uncomfortably. "Not really. A couple of times, maybe, but only for an hour or so. He seems to have taken the whole thing hard. I think he's still struggling to come to terms with what's happened."

Ceri's face darkened. "Aren't we all?" Her tone was bitter. "But life goes on, doesn't it?"

"I guess so." Hanna stared at her friend's hardened expression. Ceri was obviously trying to put on a brave face, but it was far from convincing. God knows how deeply scarred the incident had left her, not only physically but mentally too. No doubt it would take her some time to get over it.

Ceri changed the subject. "And how are you doing? How are Rhys and Eva getting on without you?"

"Oh, they're fine. Eva's been 'helping' Rhys at work, imagine that! She goes back to school next week."

Despite daily video calls, Hanna was worried about being away from Eva for too long. She wanted to support Ceri, but she longed to be home. Rhys seemed to be doing a great job. Being away from him made her realise how much she trusted him and that she really should think about their future as a family rather than being stuck in the past.

"Any plans for going home?"

"Thought I'd stay another couple of days, until you're on your feet again."

Ceri nodded. "I'm really grateful for you staying on, especially with Sergio, the way he is. I was worried he might..." She left the sentence dangling in mid-air.

"I've been talking to him about the future, trying to reassure him and get him in a more positive state of mind, said Hanna. "Not sure how successful it's been, but I'm sure he'll cheer up no end once you're back home."

"And have there been any problems? Any hint that we might still be a target?"

Hanna shook her head. "No, nothing. There's still a police guard on you here at the hospital – I passed him on my way in. And another on the apartment in the city. Vincenzo has arranged for that to continue for a while once we get back to Cefalù. I get the feeling that the danger may have passed, but you never know."

"And are the police getting anywhere with their investigation and in discovering who's behind it?"

"They're still waiting for the results from Forensics on the cufflink found at the scene. The tyre tracks they've traced to a special edition Alfa Romeo SUV. Vincenzo says there are very few about, but the Cortazzo family seem to have one. Regardless of who did the actual shooting, the Cortazzos are definitely involved."

Ceri frowned. "Haven't the police brought anyone in for questioning?"

"They want to be sure of their ground before they do so. They've not managed to track Luciano down yet. He's not at the family estate or at his apartment in Cefalù. The police want to bring the whole family in, but it all needs to tie in with the main investigation. The police reckon they'll only get one chance to arrest the ringleaders and they don't want to blow it."

Ceri sat back in her chair and uttered a deep sigh. She suddenly looked shattered, as if the conversation, or the subject matter, had drained her of energy. Hanna got up.

"C'mon, enough chatter. I don't want to tire you out. Let me wheel you back to bed. Only another night of awful food and then you'll be home."

Ceri gave a wan smile. "At last! I've been dreaming of a big steaming plate of *spaghetti alle vongole*."

"I'm sure I could rustle up some spaghetti with clams on your first night home."

A warmer smile now. "At least that'll be something to look forward to."

At lunchtime the following day Hanna's mobile pinged, alerting her to a new text message. It was from Ceri to say that Dr Di Mauro had given her a final check and had cleared her for discharge. She'd be ready to collect any time after 2pm.

By the time Hanna and Sergio arrived at the hospital to pick her up, it was almost three o'clock. They found her sitting in the day room area, looking bored, with her bag packed beside her.

"Sorry," said Hanna. "We came as soon as we could. Have you been waiting long?"

"They turfed me off the ward at dead-on two o'clock, armed with a lifetime's supply of painkillers." She grinned and rattled a giant paper bag to demonstrate. "Needed the bed for some other poor old soul."

"My fault," Sergio mumbled. "I was working on something. Zhuri, the witness from the refugee centre, is having second thoughts about testifying."

"D'you think someone's got to her?" Ceri asked, as Sergio began to wheel her out of the room.

"It's possible. I've arranged to meet her tomorrow to try and talk her round."

At least Sergio was taking an interest in work again, thought Hanna. He seemed much brighter now that Ceri was on the mend and finally coming home.

"We can't take the wheelchair with us," said Ceri, as they headed for the exit. "Doctor's orders, part of my rehab, I have to start moving around. He's told me to take it easy at first and build it up gradually." She grimaced as the wheelchair bounced over an uneven stretch of floor. "Take it easy! Delicate cargo on board!"

Sergio smiled and slowed down. It was the first time Hanna remembered seeing him smile since the day of the wedding. Hopefully the two newly-weds would start to recuperate together now that life was getting back to normal, Hanna thought, as they helped Ceri into the waiting car.

Hanna carried the tray laden with three dishes heaped high with *spaghetti alle vongole* out onto the balcony where Ceri and Sergio were enjoying the glorious sunset. Ceri clapped her hands together like a little girl when Hanna set a dish of pasta in front of her.

"Ooh, you're such a sweetie, Hanna! Just what the doctor ordered!"

"Tuck in, enjoy!" said Hanna, relieved that Ceri was hungry, a sure sign that she was starting to recover from her ordeal.

"*Buon appetito!*" Sergio's fork was already loaded and poised mid-air.

Hanna topped up their glasses with chilled Grillo wine and

watched as her two friends attacked the food with gusto. The temperature had dipped after the heat of the day, and a slight breeze ruffled their hair.

"It's so good to be home again," said Ceri wistfully between mouthfuls.

Hanna smiled, thinking of her best friend's narrow escape. It was worrying that the police hadn't been able to nail down the gunmen. She could see both Ceri and Sergio starting to relax, and decided she'd have an early night to give them some space.

They had barely finished the last few mouthfuls when Sergio's mobile range. He picked the phone up from the table, glanced at the screen and answered: *"Ciao, Papà, come va?"* Vincenzo's words were inaudible, but from the tone of his voice it was obvious he was agitated. Sergio told his father about the problem with the witness. They chatted for a few more minutes before Sergio hung up.

"Dad's going to join me tomorrow when I meet Zhuri. He's getting really frustrated that Luciano's nowhere to be found. He wants to make a move with the main investigation before the chief suspects begin to disappear too. But he's convinced the Cortazzo family are the main players and he's anxious to pin Luciano down."

Hanna started to clear the plates, thoughts buzzing in her head. Maybe she could help track him down. But how?

CHAPTER FORTY-EIGHT

By morning, Hanna had an outline plan in her mind, as well as dark rings under her eyes from a fitful night's sleep. She felt a frisson of excitement at the prospect of helping the investigation. Not being able to do so before had always niggled away at her. But then she'd been left with little choice; she'd had to protect Eva at all costs.

But now, finally, this was the perfect opportunity to get her revenge and punish Luciano, not only for his duplicity but also for his role in the trafficking network, and possibly in the shooting. The plan wasn't without its risks, but if it went well, she would be free of him once and for all, free to live her life as she pleased, free to face the future.

She needed to talk it through with Sergio and his father and see if they thought the idea might work, and if so, work out a detailed plan. And when better to do it than at that morning's meeting?

After a quick shower, Hanna got dressed and wandered into the kitchen to find Sergio making coffee. No sign of Ceri.

"She's still asleep," said Sergio, as if reading her mind. "Probably making up for the nights she spent in hospital. Thought I'd leave her be."

"Good idea," said Hanna, helping herself to coffee. "There's something I need to run by you. Thought I could discuss it with your dad this morning, after your meeting with Zhuri, if you have no objections."

Sergio's eyebrows raised. "Sounds intriguing. What's on your mind?"

Hanna ran through her idea briefly.

"So, what do you think?" Hanna asked, scanning his face for a reaction.

Sergio regarded her sternly. "It's a madcap idea. I think you're crazy even to think of it."

"But isn't it worth a try? Nothing else seems to be working, and I know your dad's in a hurry to bring the investigation to a head."

Sergio's face softened slightly, and he shrugged. "Who knows? It might just work. Let's see what my dad has to say."

Hanna relaxed and sat back in her chair, her cheeks flushed with anticipation.

Hanna, Sergio and Vincenzo were sitting in the shade at a pavement café overlooking the quay, drinking iced coffee. Their table was set back, well away from the other patrons. According to Sergio, the meeting with Zhuri had gone well and they'd managed to persuade her to go ahead with her testimony. Hanna joined them once Zhuri had left.

As Hanna related her proposal, she was conscious how raw it all was. Maybe she should have spent more time on working out the details. Vincenzo studied Hanna's face as she talked. When she'd finished, he turned his head, distracted for a moment by a flock of gulls squawking out in the bay, following a fishing boat bringing its catch ashore.

Turning back, he finished his coffee, rested both forearms on the table and clasped his hands together in front of him. "Well," he said, "That's one hell of an interesting idea, Hanna, but it's full of flaws and fraught with danger. Amazingly gutsy, though, to even propose such a plan, especially after all you've been through. You'd be putting yourself at considerable risk. You do realise that, don't you?"

Hanna gulped and nodded. "I know, but it could flush him out – and relatively quickly, too, if it works. Otherwise, how else are you going to find him? And how long's it going to take to track him down, especially if he gets wind that you're looking for him as a possible person of interest? You may never find him."

"I agree it's a long shot, but it may be worth considering," said Sergio. "Unless you have any better ideas?"

Vincenzo shook his head. "I wish. Sadly, no. We're at an impasse, or so it seems."

"So, what do you think?" asked Hanna.

"I think, young lady, that we need to work out the details, and that can only be done over lunch," said Vincenzo with a wink, springing out of his chair in a manner that belied his years. "I know just the place," he added, tapping his nose with his forefinger. "C'mon, my treat. *Andiamo*."

Lunch turned out to be a long affair. The restaurant looked nothing special: a small family-run *trattoria* on a backstreet, run by an old classmate of Vincenzo's. The owner greeted them like long-lost friends and led them through the gloomy interior to a rooftop terrace ablaze with sunlight and terracotta pots full of marigolds in vivid shades of yellow and tangerine. It was late by lunch standards, approaching 2pm, and there was only one other couple on the far side of the terrace settling their bill and about to leave.

Vincenzo slapped his friend on the back. "*Perfetto, Bruno. Eh, da mangiare, cosa ci consigli?*"

Bruno gave his recommendations – the dishes of the day – verbally. No written menu was evident. And so began a long afternoon, not only of glorious food but also of working through in painstaking fashion the ins and outs of a plan that would hopefully entrap Luciano.

CHAPTER FORTY-NINE

Back at the apartment, Hanna picked up her mobile and scrolled through her contacts with trembling hands, looking for the number. There it was: for some reason, she had never deleted it, maybe waiting for an opportunity such as this. But if the number had been changed, the plan would fall at its first hurdle. She pressed *Dial* and heard the ring tone, loud and clear. She gulped, her throat suddenly dry, worried she might not have the bottle to see this through after all.

"*Pronto,*" the once-familiar male voice answered.

Hanna switched on the speaker.

"It's... it's... Hanna here. We need to meet. I want a divorce. I'm only here for a few days, so it needs to be as soon as possible." She managed to say the carefully-rehearsed words with a confidence she didn't feel.

Silence. She had obviously caught him by surprise. A few moments passed. She was beginning to wonder if he was still there, when he responded.

"Yes, you're right. We should put an end to things, once and for all." His voice was cold, like that of a stranger. "We need to agree the conditions."

"All I want is custody of Eva. I presume that won't be a problem. I'm not looking for anything in terms of assets." She was trying hard to keep her voice neutral and unemotional.

Another pause.

"Nothing at all?"

"No."

"In that case, things should be straightforward." He obviously couldn't believe his luck. "I'll get my lawyer to draw up the papers in the morning ready for you to sign. We could meet tomorrow afternoon. Is that soon enough?"

"Perfect. I'll bring my lawyer with me. Tell me where."

"I'll send you the details in the morning. Just the two of you, okay? No funny business."

Hanna swallowed hard. "'Course not. I simply want to move on and get the formalities over and done with. What time?"

"How about half past two?"

"That's fine. See you then."

"*A domani, allora.*"

The line went dead.

Hanna dropped the mobile on the table, conscious of her heart thudding. "How did I do?" she asked, her voice reduced to a rasp.

"Amazingly well," said Ceri, placing her hand over Hanna's with a reassuring smile.

"Absolutely," Sergio agreed, an incredulous expression on his face.

"Better than we could ever have hoped for, *cara,*" Vincenzo added. "Looks like he's swallowed the bait. Now we just have to make sure he doesn't pull any tricks and slip through the net."

Hanna glanced at her phone again: 11.07. Still no message. *Perhaps he's changed his mind*, she thought. Sergio looked up from his laptop.

"Still nothing?" he asked.

Hanna shook her throbbing head. Her clothes clung to her clammy body. She slipped the phone back into her pocket and went out onto the small balcony to get some air. It was no better there, not a breath of wind. Dark storm clouds gathered in the distance.

She paced up and down, full of nervous energy, unsure whether she wanted the meeting to go ahead or not. It could be the perfect snare – one that offered her release from all formal shackles to the man she had once loved without question, and at the same time payback for his deceit and betrayal. Vincenzo had promised that his men wouldn't intervene immediately, so there could be no direct link back to her. She would be free, and also free from fear of any future reprisals.

Her phone suddenly vibrated. She snatched it from her pocket and stared at the screen. Luciano. No address, only a set of GPS co-ordinates that she didn't recognise.

"He's made contact!" she yelled, thrusting the phone in front of Sergio's face. He frowned, made a note of the GPS co-ordinates, and opened Google Maps on his laptop. A puzzled expression appeared on his face.

"Well, it's somewhere up in the Madonian Mountains, but there aren't any buildings marked in the vicinity. I can't imagine that he'd arrange a meeting of this sort out in the open. Unless he suspects it's a trap – or he's trying to lure you into one."

Hanna felt a buzz of alarm. What if, despite the wiretap conversation, Luciano did still think she was the one who'd turned him in? This might be his chance to turn the tables on her. Vincenzo had warned her that she could be putting herself at risk. What if he was right? Nothing – but nothing – could be taken at face value where Luciano was concerned. She should know that.

"Good job then that there will be police back-up in case of any trouble," she said, feeling less confident than ever about the meeting.

Sergio glanced at his watch, his face grim. "We don't have a lot of time. Acknowledge the message and confirm you'll be there. We'll talk it through when Dad gets here."

Vincenzo lifted his varifocals, lodged them on his forehead and peered closely at the map on the screen.

"I'm not that familiar with the area," he concluded nonchalantly, "but don't assume that there isn't a building there. The whole area is notoriously badly mapped, even the digital version. I'm not sure why that is. Maybe it's in certain people's interests to keep it that way. But you may find that there's a building there even if there's no sign of one here. Whether there is or there isn't, we'll be there to protect you if things go pear-shaped." He must have sensed her anxiety. "And no, we'll only intervene if we have to. If you or Roberto are in any danger."

The Roberto in question was sitting on the edge of the sofa, dressed in a tailored light grey suit, legs akimbo, polishing off his second *espresso*. Tall, with an athletic frame and fair hair, he bore little resemblance to the stereotypical Sicilian. But, Vincenzo explained, Sicilian he was, with generations-old French roots which probably accounted for his physique. Handsome and in his forties, he had studied and practised as a lawyer before changing direction a few years ago and heading into the police, where he'd made an immediate impression. He had quickly risen through the ranks to become Vincenzo's trusted lieutenant. Vincenzo had chosen him specially for this task; he'd easily be able to spot any potential problems with the divorce papers that Luciano's lawyer had prepared.

Roberto had shaken Hanna's hand warmly on arrival, murmured a few niceties but had said very little else. However, Hanna noticed his eyes darting between them, listening intently to all that was said. *This man is no fool*, she thought, and felt reassured by his presence.

Vincenzo stood up. "Right," he said. "We'd better make a move. You don't want to be late and give Luciano cause for concern. You and Roberto go on ahead, and we'll follow on. Forget about us, just go ahead with the meeting as planned. We'll monitor the situation for any problems. Keep an eye on your phone for messages. And no, we won't intervene unless we have to."

Hanna nodded. Now that it was time to act, her legs had suddenly turned to jelly. Roberto flashed her a smile, his eyes a disconcerting ice blue that seemed more canine or lupine than human. Despite her faith in Vincenzo's choice of colleague, her body reacted with an involuntary shudder.

Vincenzo placed his hand on Sergio's shoulder. "You, *figlio mio*, are to stay here with Ceri, *capisci?*"

Sergio opened his mouth as if about to argue.

His father smiled sadly. "I've already lost one son. I can't risk losing another."

CHAPTER FIFTY

Hanna climbed into the passenger seat of Roberto's car, a metallic red Seat Arona SUV, parked a few streets away. It had been standing in full sun and the inside of the car was like a furnace, the fabric of the seats hot to the touch.

Roberto took off his suit jacket and threw it in the back before getting in next to her. He started up the engine and switched the air-con up high, before punching the GPS co-ordinates of the meeting place into the sat-nav.

"Try not to worry too much," the lawyer-turned-policeman said, giving her a brief sideways glance before pulling away from the kerb out into the narrow street. "With any luck, you'll get your divorce and see Luciano brought to justice in one fell swoop."

Hanna remembered she had hoped for justice before with Luciano's previous arrest, but, somehow, he'd managed to avoid serving his full sentence. And the idea she needed luck on her side filled her with gloom, although, she had to admit, a bit of luck would come in handy.

The thought of seeing Luciano again filled Hanna with dread. But, she reminded herself, this wasn't solely about her;

she was determined this time to help put an end to the trafficking that brought misery to so many migrants.

The car cooled rapidly as Roberto navigated his way expertly out of town, ignoring the sat-nav that insisted he go a different route. He laughed when, for the umpteenth time the voice demanded he do a U-turn and follow the recommended route.

"We'll need it in the mountains, but here, in Cefalù, I know my way round better than any sat-nav," he explained with a grin. "This is where I was brought up. I know these streets like the back of my hand, even the one-way system."

Hanna felt herself begin to relax a little as he chattered on about how much Cefalù had changed over the years. From a humble fishing port, it had become a popular destination for tourists in the summer months.

"In fact," he said, "the same is true of much of Sicily. Once a destination for the intrepid, now the darling of the package holidaymaker, especially those on cruises." He screwed his face into a grimace. "They're the worst. They turn the place into a theme park in the summer. I much prefer the Sicily of old, of my youth."

Hanna had to laugh despite herself and the situation. "To hear you talk, anyone'd think you're an old man."

Roberto smiled. "I have some old-fashioned views. My wife would disagree. She works as a tour guide, so for her, the more tourists who come here, the better. She's originally from Rome so is well used to the invading hordes. But me, I like the quiet life."

His words conjured up brief memories of Hanna's own experience of working as a tour guide in the days when Sicily was still an unusual destination. But she kept them to herself and resumed the conversation.

"Is that why you moved into the police?" she couldn't resist asking.

Roberto's face became more serious. "Law, police, it's all for the same purpose: to liberate the island from those who want to manipulate it for their own ends. And release the grip that these people have on the way of life here." His face took on a grim expression. "And it's become our most famous export. Unfortunately."

He fell silent as he continued to drive, now following the sat-nav's instructions and glancing every so often at the map on the screen.

"Not far now," he said, "Maybe another twenty minutes, half an hour or so. Shall we go through the plan again?"

Hanna nodded. For the next few minutes, they ran through everything they had discussed, with Roberto emphasising the key outcomes of the meeting. Hanna tried hard to concentrate and commit it all to memory.

"Don't worry if you forget anything," said Roberto who must have sensed her concern. "I'll be by your side to prompt you."

Hanna reached into her bag and took a long swig from the small bottle of water she extracted from within. It did little to quench her thirst, the water being lukewarm and tasting slightly metallic. She looked out of the window. The narrow winding road seemed vaguely familiar, as did the chestnut and cork oak forests they were driving through. Hanna felt a flutter of recognition in her stomach, and a feeling of *déjà-vu* crept over her.

"What is it, Hanna?" asked Roberto, as if sensing her change of mood.

"I'm not sure... How far away are we now?"

"Ten minutes maybe. Do you recognise where we are?"

Hanna peered at the map displayed on the sat-nav, adjusting the controls to zoom in and out.

"It can't be... can it?" Hanna shifted her gaze from their surroundings to the map and back again, trying to get her bearings and find a landmark she might remember. As she looked out of the window, she spotted a small structure by the side of the road. "Roberto, can you pull up a minute?"

"Sure," he said, braking and bringing the car to a standstill at the side of the road. "What is it?"

"I need to check something. Won't be a sec." Hanna slid out of her seat and approached the roadside shrine, sure now of what she would find. She read the inscription quickly – a nineteen-year-old who'd been killed in a road accident – and returned to the car.

"Christ, how stupid of me not to fathom it out before! I *do* know this area; I simply didn't recognise it from the GPS co-ordinates he gave us. No wonder he didn't give us the address. If I'm not mistaken, we're going to the house we lived in when Eva was a baby."

Why hadn't Luciano told her? Could it be a trap? But what would he have to gain? The upper hand, as usual: the meeting would take place on his terms, on his territory, even if she'd instigated it. He'd be the one in control. For her, the location would bring memories flooding back, not only of the early days of their marriage when Eva was a baby, but also of the kidnapping. She'd be at a definite disadvantage.

Next to her, Roberto was jabbering away on the hands-free phone to Vincenzo, in quick-fire almost impenetrable dialect that Hanna struggled to understand.

The terrain became more and more familiar as they drew nearer to their destination. Little had changed. The countryside altered only with the seasons; buildings were few, mostly agricultural in nature, shelters for the animals and such-like; and there at the crossroads leading up to the house, a ramshackle hall used for occasional church services by the itinerant parish priest.

Roberto took the single-track road that climbed steeply from the junction. Hanna felt beads of sweat break out across her forehead. She reached again for the bottle of water and drained the remains. The house should appear immediately after the next sharp bend. But instead, an ominous high fence swung into view. It appeared to surround the property, only interrupted by a set of electronic gates that revealed nothing of the house and gardens within.

Hanna's hand flew involuntarily to her mouth in shock. "Oh, my God, what's he done? He's turned the place into a fortress."

"It wasn't like this before?" Roberto asked.

She shook her head. "No, there was no fence. I didn't think that was allowed in the national park."

"It's not," said Roberto grim-faced, stopping the car a short distance before the electronic gates. "Obviously Luciano acts as if he has special privileges."

Hanna's face fell. This didn't bode well. "He's always been arrogant. Thinks he's untouchable. Probably more so, since wriggling out of a long prison sentence."

Roberto turned to her. "Will you be okay to see this through?" he asked, with a look of concern.

"I'll have to be," she replied through gritted teeth. "Come on, let's get this over with."

CHAPTER FIFTY-ONE

Roberto drove up to the gates and slipped out of the driving seat. As he announced their arrival over the entry system's intercom, a camera blinked, capturing his image. *Designed to deter any unwelcome visitors,* Hanna thought with a shiver.

He got back in the car and waited a few moments. The gates slid open slowly, allowing them to pass through. Hanna half-expected the house to have been transformed, but the exterior was just as she remembered it. Built of warm honey-coloured stone, with a heavy oak front door, wooden shutters framing the windows, surrounded by a garden ablaze with colour, it oozed the same rustic charm as before. But any charm quickly vanished as the memory of having been abducted by Luciano's men came flooding back. That was the last time she'd been here.

Nevertheless, she felt slightly reassured that the meeting would be on familiar ground. But her pulse quickened, and her stomach felt queasy at the prospect of confronting Luciano in the flesh.

Roberto pulled up in front of the house alongside a silver Mercedes C class cabriolet with the roof down. *Probably the lawyer's,* she thought. Roberto turned to her. "Ready?" he asked.

She took a deep breath. "As ready as I'll ever be. Let's go before I change my mind."

He patted her hand and smiled. She opened the car door and got out. As they approached the house, the front door swung open and a stern-looking elder-statesman-like figure appeared, dressed in a three-piece suit despite the heat, with a pair of half-moon glasses perched on the end of his nose.

"*Gaspare Benedetto, l'avvocato di Signor Cortazzo,*" he introduced himself, shaking their hands in turn, po-faced and unsmiling. "Please come in."

He led the way to a room at the back of the house which Hanna remembered as being a playroom when Eva was little. A massive glass and chrome desk now dominated the room, behind which a bookcase filled the entire wall. In its new guise as an office, it was almost completely unrecognisable apart from the French windows that stood open leading out onto a patio area in the garden.

The lawyer indicated a pair of matching cream leather sofas positioned around a glass coffee table. "Please sit down. Signor Cortazzo will join us shortly." Hanna and Roberto took a seat next to each other, the lawyer perching on the edge of the other sofa.

"Can I offer you coffee, or tea if you prefer?" he asked.

Hanna was about to refuse when Roberto replied, "Coffee, thank you."

"Same for me, too, please," she relented.

"If you'll excuse me for a minute..." He rose and disappeared, quickly returning and resuming his place on the sofa.

"The paperwork is all ready for you to sign. That is, if nothing has changed since your conversation with my client yesterday?"

Hanna steeled herself to respond. "No, nothing has

changed. My only stipulation is that permanent custody of our daughter, Eva, should remain with me. I have no interest in any other assets or financial support of any sort."

Avvocato Benedetto raised an eyebrow as if to acknowledge the rarity of such an occurrence. "So I understand from my client, who has instructed me to prepare the paperwork on this basis. I trust you will find everything in order."

Despite his words, he made no move to show them the documents; he seemed to be waiting for Luciano. A few minutes passed with no further conversation, the silence between them hanging heavy in the sultry air. Then the door slowly opened and a pretty young girl, who looked no older than seventeen, entered the room carrying a tray which she set down on the glass table.

"*Grazie*, Silvana," the lawyer said, dismissing her and handing them tiny cups of *espresso*.

More silence as they sipped their coffee, waiting for Luciano to arrive. Roberto consulted his watch in a deliberate gesture as if to provoke a reaction.

The other lawyer shrugged. "He won't be long." No apology.

The atmosphere in the room was decidedly frosty despite the searing summer heat. Frosty and claustrophobic. All this waiting was making Hanna nervous. Beads of sweat broke out across her forehead. The only sound was the loud ticking of a clock somewhere in the room.

Roberto opened his mouth and was about to speak when Luciano swept into the room, and with a cursory glance at the three of them, he took a seat in the soft leather chair behind the desk. A cold shiver crept through Hanna's body. Despite this, she couldn't help stealing a surreptitious glance at the man she had once loved so unconditionally. He looked much the same as she remembered, except for a little greying at the temples. Still a handsome brute of a man. But still a brute.

Luciano eyed them dispassionately. Dispensing with any greeting or other niceties, he said coldly, "Let's get this concluded. *Avvocato* Benedetto, please hand out copies of the document so we can all check that we're in agreement with the terms and that nothing has been overlooked."

With a slight deferential bow of his head, the lawyer got up and retrieved the copies from the desk, handing one to each of them. Hanna stared at hers, trying hard to concentrate, but found the Italian legal terminology difficult to follow. She was conscious of Luciano's steely gaze.

"Perhaps we could have a minute or two on our own to study this and talk it over between ourselves?" Roberto asked.

"You can go out into the garden if you like," said Luciano. "We'll wait here."

"*Grazie*," said Roberto, rising from the sofa. "We won't be long."

He extended a steadying arm to Hanna as she rose, feeling slightly shaky, and led the way to the table and chairs outside on the patio.

"We should be okay to talk here. We're far enough away to be out of earshot. But we need to keep our voices low," said Roberto. "Let me read the document through first, then we can discuss it."

Hanna nodded in agreement. "I'll try and do the same, but I'm struggling a bit with the legal jargon. You may have to translate some of it for me."

"No problem," he replied. "It's important that we get this right. There won't be a second chance."

"No pressure, then," she muttered, turning back to the document, trying to ignore Luciano, whose gaze, she was convinced, was still fixed on her even from within the confines of his office.

"Everything seems to be in order," said Roberto when they returned inside. "I note that there is no mention of a visitation order for the daughter."

"My client has no interest in seeing his daughter," said *Avvocato* Benedetto, his mouth twisted into more of a snarl than a smile, his lips parting to reveal a set of unusually white teeth. He reminded Hanna of a shark.

"Ever?" asked Roberto.

"Ever," the older man confirmed.

"Then there needs to be a clause to clarify this."

"Let us agree the wording then so it can be added. We can still conclude everything today. Does the rest of the document seem satisfactory?" The lawyer glowered at them, as if expecting a further challenge.

Roberto looked at Hanna. They had already agreed there were no other areas of contention. Hanna nodded, shocked that Luciano still wanted no contact with his daughter, but relieved too.

"Yes, we are happy to sign once the visitation issue has been addressed," he said.

Luciano rose from his throne behind the desk. "*Prego, Avvocato* Benedetto, please use my PC to make the necessary amendments."

Another obsequious nod of the head from the lawyer as they swapped places. He began to tap on the keyboard, added in the missing clause, and printed copies for them all to approve.

Luciano was the first to speak. "That's fine by me."

"And you two, are you happy now?" the lawyer asked with a sneer.

Hanna and Roberto exchanged glances. "Yes, we are," said Roberto.

"In that case, all that remains is for both parties to sign the document. I'll call Silvana to act as witness," said the lawyer, rising from his chair to summon the girl.

"Excellent work, *Avvocato*," said Luciano with a frosty smile. "After the signing, each party will be free to go their separate ways."

Hanna's heart skipped a beat. Somehow, he made this sound like a threat rather than the conclusion she had been hoping for.

Luciano turned to Hanna and fixed her with a penetrating stare. "By the way, I heard about Ceri on the news. What a terrible thing to happen. And on her wedding day, too. Please send her my best wishes."

CHAPTER FIFTY-TWO

Hanna couldn't believe her ears. What a callous bastard! She gazed at Luciano coldly, not trusting herself to respond. It was all she could do to stop herself from blurting out that the police knew he was behind it. Instead, she remained tight-lipped, reassuring herself that if everything went to plan, he'd find that out soon enough. She stood up, quickly followed by Roberto. *Avvocato* Benedetto showed them out.

The front door of the villa closed behind them with a thud. They hurried back to the car, the precious divorce document clutched tightly in the lawyer's grip. Roberto swung the car towards the electronic gates which parted slowly as they approached.

The confrontation with Luciano had left Hanna with a throbbing head. Although the meeting had gone without a hitch, for her it had still been an ordeal. But now, hopefully, this period of her life was at last behind her, and they would never have to meet again.

Back on the road, she took in a series of deep breaths, trying to fight back the waves of nausea that threatened to engulf her. She ended up in a fit of coughing and spluttering. Roberto pulled over, a look of concern on his face. He reached into the glovebox and handed her a bottle of water.

"Here, take a sip," he said. "Slowly does it, you don't want to choke."

Hanna did as she was told, and the coughing gradually eased. She opened the car door and swivelled sideways, splashing her face with the remaining water.

"Feeling better?" Roberto asked gently.

Hanna nodded. "Yes, thanks. Sorry for reacting like that."

"You don't have to apologise." He started up the car again and manoeuvred it back on the road with one hand, adjusting the air-con with the other.

Hanna relaxed back into the passenger seat and closed her eyes. She was coming round now, almost back to normal. When she opened them again, she realised that they must have come some way.

"Did I doze off?" she asked, embarrassed.

Roberto turned to her with a smile. "Only for a few minutes. At least, it's all over now. Mission accomplished. Stage One, at least."

"Stage One?"

"As far as the police investigation is concerned. We've managed to track Luciano down. Now, we need to step in and arrest him before he gets wind that we're ready to detain him. We don't want him disappearing on us."

Hanna swallowed, her throat suddenly like sandpaper. "How quickly do you reckon you'll be able to act?"

"Just as soon as we can. We need to make sure we have good reason to question him and obtain a warrant to search this, and any of his other houses, for further evidence of his involvement in the shooting and/or trafficking. We can't afford to take him in for questioning and then not have enough evidence to make any charges stick. And all the arrests of the other traffickers in the network need to be done simultaneously. This time, we mean business."

His face grew increasingly serious as he talked. "I'll let Vincenzo know we're out of there and that everything went okay," he said, searching the touch screen on the dashboard for the number.

As the two policemen engaged in conversation, Hanna gazed out of the window and tried to make sense of her jumbled thoughts and emotions. Ideally, she would have liked to get on the next plane home and put as much distance between her and this damn island as possible. But her best friend was still here and recovering from a gunshot wound. Whether she was the intended victim or not, no way could Hanna turn her back on Ceri and leave. Ceri was like the sister she'd never had. And until Luciano was in custody, the police might still need her help.

She tried to relax but could feel knots forming in her stomach and her shoulders tense. Suddenly, she became aware of the heavy silence in the car.

"You okay, Hanna?" Roberto asked with a flicker of concern. "You seem miles away."

If only, she thought. "No, I'm fine. Still a little shaky, I guess." She forced a wan smile.

"Understandable. Vincenzo reckons we should be in a position to make our move in the next few days, all being well."

"So soon?"

Roberto nodded. "He needs to confirm that everything's co-ordinated with all the police forces involved and that Sergio's ready with the media story. But otherwise..." He left the sentence dangling in mid-air.

Realising she might be able to return home sooner than she thought sent a warm glow of joy coursing through her body. Back to Eva, her amazing little girl, and Rhys, her fabulous partner, both of whom she was missing so much. Back to some semblance of normality.

Roberto was taking the bends along the winding road that led back to the coast at his usual speed. Feeling increasingly nauseous, Hanna was on the verge of asking him to slow down when he abruptly pulled into a layby where there was a makeshift bar.

He turned to her and grinned. "I thought you could do with a break."

"Too right," she muttered, flinging open the car door and stepping out into the merciless afternoon sun.

She immediately understood the reason for the bar – no more than a small trailer and a few tacky plastic chairs – being there. From the layby, there was a clear view over the sweeping bay of Cefalù and its rocky promontory.

"Wow," she said, "that view's simply stunning."

"Isn't it just? We're lucky to have the place to ourselves. It's usually busy with tourists on their way up to the nearby Gibilmanna sanctuary." He steered her towards the bar where he ordered two fresh lemonades. "Local speciality," he explained.

The stocky vendor proceeded to fill two tall glasses with cloudy lemonade and chunks of fresh lemon and ice from an enormous jug. He set them down on the counter of the trailer with a smile. Roberto grabbed the drinks and headed for a nearby table. Hanna took a seat, grateful for the shade provided by a pair of lofty umbrella pines and the gentle breeze that rustled through their boughs. She took a massive gulp of lemonade. Its icy sharpness was like a shot to the system.

Roberto was watching her reaction. "Better?"

Hanna nodded. "These roads…" she gesticulated with her hand.

"Yeah, I know. They take some getting used to. Fabulous view up here, though. And it's slightly cooler than down on the coast."

They sipped their drinks, taking in the view, enjoying a brief moment of calm. But it wasn't long before Hanna's thoughts returned to the present.

"So, what happens now? With the divorce, I mean?" she asked.

Roberto stretched his legs out in front of him. "Well, I'll give the papers a final once-over to make sure nothing is missing. Then I'll need to file them with the *Commune* so they can be registered and made legal and binding. We can't rely on Luciano's lawyer seeing it through to the end. Drawing up the paperwork, getting it agreed and signed off may have all been a charade for them."

Hanna felt a prick of alarm. "But it should all go through okay, though?"

Roberto shrugged. "Yes, don't worry. The circumstances are quite unusual, in that it's a no-quibble divorce with no division of assets, but I'm not expecting any problems."

Hanna stared out towards the horizon and the blurred shape of a passing ship. She felt as if a weight was about to be lifted from her shoulders.

Roberto drained his glass and stood up. "*Andiamo.* We'd better make tracks."

He rummaged in his pocket and drew out some crumpled notes and a handful of coins, leaving a selection on the table. Hanna finished her drink and followed him back to the car. They re-joined the road down to the coast, Roberto driving at a slower pace than before. Despite the continuing bends, they were back at the apartment in less than half an hour.

But as Hanna let herself in through the front door, Roberto in her wake, she could sense something was wrong. They found Sergio and Ceri sitting in silence in the kitchen staring at the screen of Sergio's mobile phone, the tension between them almost palpable.

"What's wrong? Has something happened?" asked Hanna anxiously.

Ceri looked up, her face puffy and drained of colour, her eyes red-rimmed. "I don't ever want to get one of those messages again," she said, passing Hanna the phone with trembling hands.

Hanna stared at the screen, feeling her blood turn to ice as she read the message:

> Heed the warning. Next time, you won't be so lucky.

CHAPTER FIFTY-THREE

Roberto snatched the phone from Hanna and quickly read the message, his face clouding over, before handing it back. He delved in his trouser pocket for his own mobile, searched for the number he wanted, dialled, then turned and walked out of the kitchen, waiting for a response.

Hanna sank onto a chair next to Ceri, reaching for her hand. "Are you okay?"

Ceri nodded, still visibly upset, her hands still trembling. The sound of Roberto's voice drifted through from the hallway. He was speaking to someone in hushed tones.

"It came about ten minutes ago," said Sergio, his face pale. "Looks as though the whole shooting incident was deliberately planned. Judging by that message, we could all still be in danger."

With a whimper, Ceri pushed back her chair and hurried off as best as she could. Sounds of retching came from the direction of the bathroom. Not exactly tactful, thought Hanna, giving Sergio a dirty look.

"Sorry, I shouldn't have said that," he said. "I don't want to make the situation any worse than it already is, but we all need to understand the score here..." He ran his hands through his hair, his expression a mixture of anger and bewilderment.

Hanna sighed. "You're probably right. It's just that—"

"Anyway, how did your meeting go?" Sergio interrupted her, as if he'd only just remembered where she'd been. "Any problems? Did Luciano sign the divorce papers?"

"Yes, turned out the meeting was at our old house in the Madonie. The whole thing was a bit of a nightmare for me, as you can imagine..."

Roberto hurried back into the kitchen, grim-faced. "That was Vincenzo. One of his team has picked up a suggestion from the wiretap that Luciano may be leaving the country soon. The message was in code, so it's not clear exactly when, but Vincenzo's determined to nab him before he gets the chance to scarper. If he's going to be arrested at home, we may need your help, Hanna, with the layout of the house, if that's OK?"

"No problem," said Hanna, with a shiver of anticipation. "Happy to help any way I can."

"What about media coverage?" asked Sergio, now fully alert.

Roberto looked thoughtful for a moment. "I think we may need to keep Luciano's arrest under wraps for now, at least until we're ready to make the other arrests. We don't want to tip off his associates."

"That's fine. We're ready to run the story whenever you are," said Sergio.

"Good, we'll keep you posted. Meanwhile, Vincenzo said he'll strengthen the watch on the apartment in case anyone tries to make a move, after that last message. They'll be monitoring Luciano's house, too. And don't worry, Hanna, I won't forget to file the divorce papers."

Hanna smiled. "Thanks, Roberto. And for all your support today."

Roberto shrugged. "*Figurati! Ci mancherebbe altro.* It was nothing; all in a day's work. We just need to make sure that Luciano doesn't give us the slip now." He dug his car keys out from his trouser pocket. "I'd better get back to the *Questura*. Vincenzo's holding a council of war to finalise the plans."

Hanna busied herself in the kitchen throwing together a makeshift meal of pasta with a jar of ready-made *porcini* mushroom sauce. Ceri had gone for a lie-down and Sergio was working on his laptop in the lounge. As the sauce heated up and the garlicky aroma filled the air, she suddenly felt a pang of hunger and hunted through the cupboards and fridge to see what else they had. Some *prosciutto* and Pecorino cheese, a bit of salad and some fresh bread that Ceri or Sergio must have picked up earlier. That would have to do. As she prepared the food, she tried to brush aside all thoughts of Luciano's impending arrest, but to no avail. She couldn't help but wonder how it would all turn out.

A sudden clap of thunder made her jump, sending the wooden spoon she was using to stir the pasta sauce crashing to the floor, smearing the tiles with muddy brown spatters.

"Damn," she muttered, bending down to pick up the spoon. As she straightened, a gust of wind sent the kitchen window crashing against her head. She staggered and almost fell, managing to catch the window before it hit the wall. Another crack of thunder sent her reeling as she struggled to close the window against the wind. A flash of lightning lit up the night sky. The first drops of rain began to fall, gathering in pace until they drummed loudly against the window, turning the street below into a deluge. Hanna watched as the storm increased in ferocity, mesmerised by its energy.

"*Mannaggia,* Hanna, aren't you watching these damn

pans?" Sergio rushed into the kitchen, grabbed the pasta pan from the stove with one hand and turned off the heat under the sauce with the other.

Hanna turned around and flushed. "Sorry, the storm distracted me."

"No worries, I think we caught it in time," said Sergio, testing the pasta and inspecting the sauce. He drained the pasta in the sink, added a little of the water to the sauce and put it back on the hob. "D'you want to finish off and I'll tell Ceri that it's ready?"

"I'm here now. Don't know what came over me..." Hanna rubbed her head where the window had caught her. It was sore, but no more than that. Sergio disappeared and Hanna returned the drained pasta to the pan, added the *porcini* sauce and shavings of Pecorino cheese, mixing it all together ready to serve.

Ceri and Sergio reappeared as she was putting the steaming bowls on the table.

"Mmm, that smells good," said Ceri, slipping into a chair.

"Feeling better?" Hanna asked, sitting down next to her, noticing that some colour had returned to her cheeks.

"Much. I actually feel hungry now."

"Well, you're bound to be," said Sergio, attacking his pasta with a fork. "You've got an empty stomach."

"Thanks for pointing that out, *caro*," said Ceri, with a faint smile.

"Hope it's OK. It was all I could find in the cupboard," said Hanna.

"Yeah, we need to go shopping tomorrow if we don't want to starve," said Ceri.

"It's actually really good," said Sergio, washing down his first mouthful with a sip of white wine.

Hanna had to agree. Ready-made food in Wales never

tasted this good, she thought. One of the few things she missed about Sicily. She tucked in with gusto, relishing the food even if the pasta was a little overdone. The three of them continued to eat in silence for several minutes as the storm raged outside, punctuating the meal with flashes of lightning quickly followed by loud claps of thunder, masking any attempts at further conversation. It was only as they were finishing the last few mouthfuls that it started to wane.

Ceri got up to clear the dishes, much more animated now. "So, how did you get on?" she asked, turning to Hanna.

Hanna did a quick recap of the meeting for her benefit.

"Christ, that sounds almost civilised," said Ceri when she'd finished. "Almost too easy. Was Roberto satisfied that it was all above-board?"

"Yes, he didn't raise any issues apart from the missing clause about custody," Hanna replied. Seeds of doubt were beginning to creep into her consciousness. She had accepted the meeting at face value and Roberto had given her no cause to think otherwise.

Ceri and Sergio exchanged glances.

"Am I missing something?" Hanna asked, her voice starting to crack.

"What's happening with the divorce papers?" Sergio asked.

"Roberto's going to double-check them before filing them with the *Commune*," Hanna replied with a frown. "I'll be notified when it becomes final."

Sergio tore off a chunk of bread and used it to pick up a slice of ham and some cheese. "Considering it's Luciano you're dealing with, it seems to have gone reasonably well," he said.

"So, a result!" said Ceri. "You're free of him, at last."

"Let's hope so," said Hanna, grimly, worried now whether or not the divorce really would go through and if the marriage was well and truly over.

A text alert pinged. Sergio pulled his mobile from his shirt pocket and stared at the screen. "It's Dad. He wants to know if he can come round and pick your brains about the layout of Luciano's house."

"When?" asked Hanna.

"Now, tonight."

She glanced at the clock on the kitchen wall. It was almost 9pm.

"I suppose so," Hanna replied, surprised at the police's quick response.

"It has to be tonight," said Sergio, his fingers already texting a response. "The police are planning a dawn raid to arrest him tomorrow."

CHAPTER FIFTY-FOUR

Hanna slumped back in her chair, overcome by a sudden wave of fatigue. Given the choice, she'd have taken herself straight off to bed. It had been quite a day, but it wasn't over yet. She gritted her teeth; she needed to see this through.

Sergio looked at her closely. "Are you sure you're up to it? You look dead beat. Not surprising really; you've had a pretty traumatic day. Maybe a coffee would help?"

"Yes, thanks, that would be good," said Hanna, stifling a yawn. She watched as he rose from the table and filled the coffee pot, trying to gather her thoughts in preparation for the meeting. She felt that if she didn't keep going, she'd fall asleep right there at the table. "I need some paper."

"Sure, I'll get you some," said Ceri. She left the kitchen, reappearing a few minutes later clutching several sheets of A4 paper and a bundle of pens and pencils. She laid them on the table, removing the remaining plates to make some room. "Will that be enough?"

"More than," said Hanna. Sergio set down a small cup of coffee in front of her. "I want to get a head start and map out

288

what I remember of the house before I nod off," she added by way of explanation.

"Sounds like a good idea," said Sergio. "Ceri and I'll go into the lounge and leave you to it. Dad should be here in about half an hour or so."

"Perfect," said Hanna. Once they'd disappeared, she got up and switched on the radio, tuning it to an easy-listening music channel with the volume down low. Returning to the table, she picked up a pencil and a sheet of paper and set to work.

By the time Vincenzo arrived at the apartment with one of his team in tow, Hanna had sketched out a floor plan of the house and the designation of the rooms as she remembered them, plus a plan of the outbuildings and the gardens. The sketches were spread out over the kitchen table on six sheets of paper.

"*Ammazza!*" said Vincenzo, his eyes widening with delight. "This is wonderful, exactly what we need. Now, *mia cara,* talk me through it, with special emphasis on all the entrances and exits and any security arrangements you noticed on your visit. We need to make sure he doesn't get away this time."

Vincenzo bombarded Hanna with questions for more than an hour. Fatigue was taking over now, and Hanna could barely think straight any more. Finally, Vincenzo sat back in his chair and beamed.

"Hanna, you've been an absolute marvel! I can't thank you enough." He picked up his cup to finish the latest in a long line of coffees. "But before I go, I have one last favour to ask of you."

Hanna frowned. His interrogation had left her feeling drained, mentally and physically. "What's that?"

"Tomorrow, when we go to arrest Luciano, could you and

Sergio ride along as well in a back-up car in case we need anything else?"

As if on cue, Sergio came into the kitchen. He looked at his father quizzically; he'd obviously overheard the last part of the conversation. "Such as?" he asked.

"Well, Hanna knows the layout of the area, and we may need you to document and photograph the event, even if it's just for the record and we decide not to use the material publicly."

Sergio raised an eyebrow. "Why me? Is there no one on the team who could do that?"

"I'd rather you do it. I need someone I can trust, and that way, we're covered should we need it for the media story," explained Vincenzo. "Would you both be up for that? I can send a car over to pick you up, but it'll be an early start, I'm afraid."

"How early is early?" Hanna glanced at the kitchen clock. Almost 11pm already.

"About 5am?" Vincenzo said with an apologetic look. "I don't want to leave it any later..."

She looked over at Sergio. His response was evident; he looked more animated than he had in days, his face full of puppy-dog enthusiasm. She couldn't refuse; this might be their last chance to bring Luciano to justice. At least she'd be able to get a few hours' sleep.

"OK," she said wearily, "but on one condition: that I stay in the background."

"That's the idea," Vincenzo confirmed with a nod. "Not so for you, son."

"Count me in," Sergio said, in a voice brimming with excitement.

Vincenzo rose to his feet. "Great, thanks for that. I need to get back and brief the boys. Not much sleep for me tonight. Let's hope it'll all be worth it."

Hanna fumbled around on the bedside table to turn off the alarm on her mobile. She squinted at the screen: 4.30am. It was a long time since she'd been up this early. Switching on the bedside lamp, she swung her legs out of bed and padded along the corridor to the bathroom. A faint murmur of voices came from the other bedroom. She bent over the basin as a sudden rush of nausea caused her to vomit. Grabbing the basin to steady herself, she quickly splashed her face with water and brushed her teeth. Returning to her room, she pulled on a pair of jeans, a t-shirt and a warm sweatshirt, passed a brush through her hair, and squeezed her feet into a pair of Converse trainers. She threw her phone in her bag and headed for the kitchen.

Sergio was already dressed and sitting at the table, thumbing through his phone, a large cup of *caffelatte* in front of him. Ceri, still in her dressing gown, turned from the stove and pressed another cup into Hanna's hands. "You'll be needing this," she said. "Something to eat?"

"No, thanks. A coffee will do me."

Sergio turned and looked up. "Morning, Hanna. Manage to get some sleep?"

"Amazingly, yes. How about you?"

"Me? I'm good. Never needed much sleep."

He certainly looked and sounded alert, more than Hanna did. She took a gulp of coffee, immediately regretting it as the heat scalded her tongue.

"The car should be here to pick us up in about five minutes."

"Fine. Just enough time to finish my coffee."

Sure enough, the doorbell rang shortly afterwards, and they hurried down the stairs to the front door of the building where Roberto was waiting. An unmarked 4x4 was parked in the middle of the street, with the engine running. Hanna and Sergio climbed into the back seat and Roberto introduced the driver, a young police officer by the name of Massimo, dressed in casual clothes. Massimo took off at speed.

"The rest of the party has gone on ahead," Roberto explained. "We'll catch up with them once we get nearer the house, but we'll stay in contact with them by radio throughout."

The police radio crackled, and a disembodied voice muttered something indecipherable to Hanna's ears. They sped through the town, few people and traffic around at this hour apart from the street cleaners. Dawn was still some way off and the streets were enveloped in darkness.

Massimo fiddled with the controls and Hanna felt a blast of hot air. She soon began to feel drowsy as the heat filled the back seat. The next thing she knew, the car was stationary. Her head had fallen onto Sergio's shoulder. "Sorry," she muttered, moving away. "I must have dropped off."

"Don't worry, you haven't missed anything." Sergio grinned at her. "We've only just arrived."

In the first glimmer of sunrise, Hanna could see that they were parked in a small clearing surrounded by trees. The police radio sprang into life, with Vincenzo barking out orders to his men in an urgent tone, punctuated by short bursts of other voices confirming their positions.

Hanna was fully alert now; she detected a heightened sense of anticipation emanating from the two police officers in the front of the car.

"This is it!" said Roberto. "We're about to make our move."

CHAPTER FIFTY-FIVE

"How far away are we from the house?" Hanna asked as the radio fell silent.

"Only a couple of kilometres," said Roberto. "Close enough to be of any assistance if need be."

"So, what's the plan?" asked Sergio, leaning forward over the front seat.

"A team of men is scaling the perimeter fence as we speak. The drone we sent up to recce the place didn't find any evidence of the fence being alarmed. There are guard dogs, however, but we can easily take care of them," Roberto said.

"How?" Hanna asked, fearing the worst.

"Don't worry, we'll just drug them," said Roberto, as if sensing her uneasiness. "No lasting harm, they'll be fine. But we need them out of the way." He paused. "Once our men are in the grounds, Vincenzo will present himself at the gates with the arrest warrant. If he gains entry and Luciano gives himself up, then fine. If not, the team will storm the house and make the arrest."

"What if he resists arrest?" Hanna asked. "What happens then?"

"Well, we'll have to..." Roberto was interrupted by the radio sputtering back into life. Different voices confirming their positions: the police team all in place now, ready. Then came Vincenzo's voice announcing he was approaching the gates. Static masking distant voices. A whispered confirmation that the gates were opening. More static.

Several minutes passed in silence. Then, suddenly, all hell let loose. Pandemonium. Police officers yelling to announce their presence. Dogs barking. Luciano's name being called. Demands for him to give himself up. The sound of breaking glass. Heavy boots thundering through the house. Furniture shifting, toppling over. Glass shattering. A volley of shots being fired.

Hanna flinched, fearful for what was happening but glad to be well away from the conflict.

The yelling and screaming of Luciano's name continued for a while, gradually decreasing in volume, replaced by whispered conversations, the words inaudible, before ceasing altogether. A long silence followed.

"What the hell's going on?" Roberto muttered impatiently, staring at the police radio as if willing it into a response.

Eventually, a single voice, clear and distinct, grim in tone, rang out: Vincenzo. "Roberto, we've got a problem. Luciano answered the initial call and let me in through the gates. But by the time we got to the house, he'd made himself scarce. We've searched every room and all the outbuildings but there's no sign of him. He's completely disappeared, God knows where. He can't have disappeared into thin air. Can you ask Hanna to rack her brains to think where he might have gone?"

Roberto turned to Hanna with a questioning look. Her body tensed. It felt as if the success of the operation now depended on her. Too much pressure. "Give me a minute or two to think," she said, the words almost sticking in her throat, barely able to breathe, her head spinning. "I need some air, some space." She opened the car door and slid out. "I won't be long."

The sky was gradually lightening now as daybreak approached. The surrounding trees loomed menacingly over her. She took a few tentative steps, guided by the torch on her mobile, walking away from the unmarked police vehicle and three pairs of expectant eyes. She had to think logically. Where could Luciano be if the police had conducted a thorough search of the house, grounds and outbuildings and not found him? Somewhere out of sight, somewhere she'd not mentioned to Vincenzo. Her mind went blank. She kept walking slowly, trying to focus on the uneven ground but failing to see a fallen tree branch that sent her tumbling to her knees. Picking herself up, she suddenly had a brainwave and rushed back to the car.

"I think I know where Luciano might be," she said in an excited voice as she clambered back into the 4x4.

Roberto babbled into the police radio while Massimo accelerated out of the clearing, churning up a handful of stones that thudded against the bodywork. The momentum almost threw Hanna into Sergio's lap. She righted herself to find Sergio staring at her, looking unconvinced.

"It's still a bit of a long shot, Hanna. You might not be able to remember exactly where it leads to, or the way out may have grown over," he said.

"But it's worth checking out, isn't it? And no-one else's got any better ideas," she responded, more certain than ever they would find Luciano there.

Long before she'd found out about his Mafia connections, she recalled him joking once that this would be his escape route if ever the *Guardia di Finanza,* the financial police, came calling. She'd wondered at the time why they might have reason to call, thinking of some obscure tax law violation, not realising the true extent of their remit.

"Vincenzo will leave some of his men at the house and the rest will follow us," said Roberto. "How far away is it, do you reckon?"

"No more than a couple of kilometres, if we can find it okay," Hanna replied.

They were approaching a junction with a small triangular island in the middle of the road and two possible exits.

"Which way now?" asked Roberto.

She peered out of the car window, unsure for a moment. Then she spotted a dark shape standing back from the road which she recognised as the remains of an old thatched shepherd's hut, the roof almost completely caved in.

"Turn left," she said in a firm voice. "If I remember correctly, the road should climb steeply in a series of bends until we reach a track on the right that leads through the woods. We'll have to park up and go the rest of the way on foot, but it's not far from there."

Massimo was exhibiting signs of being a promising rally driver. He threw the 4x4 round the steep bends at incredible speed. They overshot the track and had to reverse, which he did at breakneck speed. Hanna was feeling sick again and was relieved when the car came to a stop.

Roberto was listening to the police radio through an earpiece now. "Vincenzo and the other men aren't far behind. Let's wait for them before we make a move."

Sergio and Massimo nodded, while Hanna concentrated on the woods, trying to get her bearings. She was fairly confident they were on the right track, but the half-light made it difficult to be certain.

Outside, the morning air was cool and still, the only sound the chirping of birds enthusiastically welcoming the new day.

The first shafts of light crept stealthily through the trees, creating long shadows like assassins lurking in wait. Hanna tried to shrug off the thought.

After a few minutes, they heard the rumble of vehicles approaching. Three police jeeps came into view and drew to a halt alongside their 4x4. Vincenzo and a dozen or so armed men jumped out, along with three police dogs. The dogs were a shaggy, long-haired breed that Hanna didn't recognise. They were clearly excited and eager to get going, but stayed strangely silent. She wondered if they'd been specially trained that way.

"You sure we're in the right place, Hanna?" Vincenzo asked.

Hanna nodded. "Absolutely."

"OK, we're in your hands, then. Lead the way."

Vincenzo signalled to his men and passed her a powerful flashlight. Its beam quickly picked up a narrow track that disappeared through the undergrowth. Hanna set off, the dog handlers spread out by her side, the others following behind. Brambles clawed at her jeans as she passed, and partially-hidden boulders caused her to stumble. She pressed on, the others in close pursuit, scouring the undergrowth, praying the marker would still be there. Ten minutes or so later, it appeared in the beam of the flashlight, set back from the track: a small wooden cross, covered in pale green lichen, barely visible. Hanna felt a little bubble of joy.

She pushed her way through the tangle of low spiny bushes behind the cross, trying to ignore the stinging cuts from their thorns. She emerged in a small clearing and shone the flashlight along the ground.

"We're here!" she yelled triumphantly. "We've found it!"

CHAPTER FIFTY-SIX

Vincenzo crashed through the bushes after her and peered into the gloom. "What is it? I can't see anything."

Hanna trained her flashlight along the ground. "There, you can't miss it."

The beam of light shone on a heavy wooden trapdoor, partially covered with leaves.

"It's the entrance to a narrow passageway that eventually leads to the cellars under the house," she said, breathing heavily after the short dash through the woods. "I'd completely forgotten about it until you pressed me."

"We searched the cellars, but didn't find any passageway," said Vincenzo.

"It's well hidden. Not quite sure what it was used for. Probably something secretive."

Hanna remembered the time Luciano had once taken her down the passageway and pointed out the marker at the far side. He'd made that joke about it making a good escape route someday. She'd laughed at the time, thinking he meant an escape from her. How naïve she'd been.

Suddenly, one of the dogs bounded forward, ears alert,

dragging his handler in tow. The other two dogs followed, springing ahead, noses to the ground. In the distance, a dark silhouette could be seen veering through the trees.

"Stay here with the girl," Vincenzo barked at a couple of his men, ordering the rest to follow him. Sergio made to follow his father. "You, too." Sergio made a face, but complied.

Hanna watched as Vincenzo set off with the others, thrashing through the undergrowth in the wake of the dog handlers. The police dogs were barking now, baying hounds hunting their prey. As they gained on the fleeing figure, she recognised Vincenzo's voice shouting, "*Fermati!* Stop right there, or we'll let the dogs loose!"

The figure seemed to pause momentarily before picking up pace and disappearing from sight.

More shouting, the voices increasingly frantic, the words muffled now as the police pressed forward in pursuit of the fugitive. A single shot rang out, echoing through the trees. Hanna flinched. Sergio leapt forward, shaking off the police officers who tried to restrain him, and headed in the direction of the shot. Hanna, filled with a nervous energy, couldn't resist following him.

Then came a volley of shots, followed by more yelling, and a series of single shots in quick succession. After that, a blanket of eerie silence descended.

Hanna panted as she tried to keep up with Sergio, struggling through the dense undergrowth. The woods remained gloomy, even in daylight. Almost hostile, threatening to close in on her. Despite a sense of rising panic, she forced herself to concentrate on the silhouette ahead. Nearly there now.

An anguished howl pierced the air. Across an unexpected clearing, Sergio had come to a halt, his back towards her. She dashed to his side and followed his gaze. A lone figure was slumped against a tree trunk, head drooping onto his chest, eyes closed, one hand clutching his left shoulder. Blood oozed through his fingers, spreading a dark stain across his white shirt. An image of a wounded Ceri flashed through her mind.

"*Porca miseria!*" Sergio cried, his face ashen. "Christ, Dad, what happened? Speak to me!"

Vincenzo's eyelids fluttered open for a second before closing again.

Hanna felt something cold and metallic press into the small of her back. An arm locked around her neck, followed by a hand clamping over her mouth. Next thing she knew she was being dragged backwards away from the clearing into the trees. She heard Sergio shout out in alarm, the sound muffled as if from far away.

Suddenly, her captor relinquished his grip and she felt herself falling. She hit the ground with a soft thud, and everything went black.

Hanna opened her eyes to find two blurry figures confronting each other, their voices raised, but their words remaining indistinct. She felt muzzy, as if she'd taken a blow to the head. Maybe she had. The figures slowly came into focus: Sergio and Luciano. No sign of the others.

"Call them off. Now!" shouted Luciano.

"I can't do that," said Sergio. "I'm only a journalist. I have no power over the police."

"You saw what happened to your wife, and now your father," said Luciano with a sneer, grabbing Hanna by the arm and forcing her to her feet. "Do you want something similar for my soon-to-be ex-wife, too?"

Sergio looked shocked. "Leave Hanna alone. She's got nothing to do with any of this."

"Oh, no? Sheer coincidence, is it, that you managed to find me out here in the middle of nowhere?"

Hanna whimpered and winced at Luciano's tight grip.

"The police tracked you down..." Sergio's voice faltered.

"D'you mean the same police that didn't even know I was living out here? Do me a favour!" Luciano cackled.

"I... err..." Sergio failed to find a suitable response.

Hanna wriggled and tried to break free of Luciano's grasp. He clutched her by the hair and yanked her towards him, fumbling in his jacket pocket with his free hand as he did so. Hanna raked his chest with her nails and aimed a knee in the direction of his groin. Luciano yelled out in pain as she made contact, loosening his grip long enough for her, summoning all her strength, to push him away as hard as she could. The move must have surprised Luciano and he stumbled backwards, toppling over to land face down in a pool of water. He stayed there, unmoving. Sergio shouted a word of warning. Ignoring him, Hanna approached Luciano cautiously, watching for any sudden movement. Keeping her distance, she could see blood seeping from a wound on the side of his head.

Sergio pushed past her and felt for a pulse. "He's still alive, but his pulse is weak. I'll call an ambulance."

Hanna glanced at Luciano's prone body. A thought struck her: how easy it would be to leave him lying there face down in the water, unable to breathe. That would be a sure way to get rid of him for good. But was she capable? Did she have it in her to bring about the death of Eva's father?

CHAPTER FIFTY-SEVEN

Tempting though it was to let him perish, Hanna just couldn't do it. How could she kill the father of her daughter, much as she hated him and everything he stood for? She'd never be able to live with herself if she did.

"Maybe we should leave the bastard to die," said Sergio, catching her eye.

Hanna shivered. "I'd had the same thought myself. But that would make us as bad as him. I don't think either of us would be capable of doing it."

Sergio sighed. "I suppose you're right. C'mon, then, give me a hand with him."

Hanna nodded and together they gently rolled Luciano's inert body onto his back. His eyes were closed. He looked peaceful. Harmless, even.

A rustling noise sounded in the trees. Two of the dogs sprang through the bushes, noses to the ground, and hurtled across to Luciano's body. They circled it, sniffing suspiciously until their handlers appeared.

"He's concussed," Sergio explained in answer to their unspoken question. "My dad's back there, wounded. The paramedics are on their way. Keep an eye on this guy while I go and check on my dad."

The dog handlers nodded in agreement and tethered the dogs before handcuffing Luciano. Concussed or not, they weren't taking any chances.

One of the paramedics, a short, stocky guy in his thirties carrying a medical kit, moved Sergio gently aside.

"*Signore*, don't worry. Let us do our job." He bent over and prised the blood-soaked cloth from Vincenzo's hand to examine the wound. Opening his medical kit, he got to work.

Vincenzo groaned and opened his eyes. He made a brave attempt at a smile when he saw his son, and tried to talk. The paramedic dissuaded him in no uncertain terms. Sergio and Hanna stood by, watching helplessly.

"He *will* be okay, won't he?" Sergio asked.

The paramedic turned his head. "He's been lucky. It's just a flesh wound. Looks worse than it is. He'll be fine once we stem the bleeding."

Sergio exhaled loudly. "Thank God for that."

"But he'll need to be hospitalised." The paramedic called over his colleague and they lifted Vincenzo carefully onto a stretcher. "You're his son, right?" Sergio nodded. "You can come with him in the ambulance."

Sergio's face brightened and he made to follow them. He looked back at Hanna and mouthed, "Will you be okay?"

She made a shooing gesture with her hands. "Course I will. Go!"

They moved off slowly through the trees, leaving Hanna alone with the unknown police officers. The second paramedic crew had gone to attend to Luciano. The men all looked deflated now that the chase was over. Hanna wondered idly how often they were involved in such ventures.

The oldest officer approached her. "We're returning to our jeeps now," he said.

"Fine, I'll come with you."

The officer nodded and indicated to the rest of the men that they were making a move. Hanna trudged after them, feeling exhausted now, her energy depleted.

A tired-looking Roberto was leaning on the car, waiting for her to return. His face brightened when she appeared. He laid his hand on her shoulder.

"Mission accomplished," he said with a weary smile. "And it's all down to you. If you hadn't remembered that old passageway out of the house, Luciano would have got away, and we might never have caught him."

Hanna felt a strange prickle down her spine.

"Just glad I could be of help," she mumbled, with a swell of pride.

Game over. She'd done it.

CHAPTER FIFTY-EIGHT

Hanna gazed out over the terracotta rooftops from the kitchen window of the Cefalù apartment, her mobile pressed to her ear.

"When are you coming home, Mummy? I miss you. You've been gone aaaages..."

Her heart ached at hearing her daughter's voice, so clear that Eva could have been in the same room. Tears sprang to her eyes.

"Won't be long now, sweetheart. Only a few more days..." How she longed to get back to her, back home, back to Rhys.

"Can we get an alcapa? Daddy said he'd talk to you about it when you got home."

"Did he now? Well, we'll see when I get back. Gotta go now. Love you."

"Love you too, Mummy!"

Hanna smiled sadly and put the phone down with a sigh. *It will all be over soon,* she told herself. Back to normality. She felt restless, despite her initial elation following Luciano's arrest. There was no real reason for her to remain here now that she'd helped the police track him down, but she felt duty-bound to stay on for a few more days until the police made all their arrests. She was helping Sergio's sister, Lina, take care of Marta while Vincenzo was recovering in hospital. Ceri was making good physical progress, but she had been left badly shaken by the shooting.

Roberto had taken over the police investigation from Vincenzo and was finalising the arrangements for arresting the traffickers. Sergio was rarely home, busy preparing the media coverage for the forthcoming arrests.

Luciano, according to Roberto, was under police guard in a different hospital from Vincenzo. He had undergone a brain scan as a precautionary measure, and would need plastic surgery on his leg where it had been mauled by a police dog. But doctors predicted he would recover and be fit enough to stand trial.

Her phone rang, interrupting her thoughts. She picked it up to hear a familiar voice.

"Hanna, it's Roberto. *Come stai?*" Without waiting for a response, he ploughed on at breakneck speed. "I've only got a minute. Just wanted to give you a quick update. First: your divorce is going through, and everything should be concluded in the next few days. Second: it turns out the fingerprint on the cufflink isn't Luciano's after all; it's his brother Giulio's. And we know from his phone records that Giulio was the one who sent that threatening text to Ceri and Sergio." He paused for breath. "And finally, the arrests are all set for Friday, both here and in Wales. Thought you'd want to know."

Hanna was momentarily lost for words. It seemed incredible that everything was finally coming to a head. "That's great news, Roberto. Thanks for letting me know. And thanks again for all your help."

"It was nothing..." Someone shouted his name. "Gotta go, I'm afraid. Speak soon. *Ciao.*"

Hanna sank onto the nearest chair, her head churning as she

tried to make sense of it, her body trembling. She wouldn't be needed any more; she could now make plans to return home.

So, it looked as if Luciano hadn't been responsible for shooting Ceri after all. Not directly, but he'd probably had a hand in organising it. The arrests would hopefully end in prosecution, and long prison sentences that would bring an end to the odious trafficking, particularly that of underage girls forced into prostitution.

And for her? The divorce meant she was finally free to move on. A buzz of sheer joy ran through her body at the prospect: a new beginning, free of fears from the past.

"So much has happened, hasn't it?" Ceri said as she sipped her iced coffee.

Hanna nodded, and moved her chair under the parasol to avoid the glare of the late afternoon sun. They were sitting on the terrace of a small café overlooking the bay. Small fishing boats lay abandoned on the sandy beach, the sea glimmering in the sunlight. Children played in the shallows, watched by anxious mothers.

"Since we first met, I mean. In our tour guide days," Ceri continued. "We're not the same people we were then."

"Guess not," Hanna agreed. "We didn't have a care in the world in those days. "This place has changed us both."

"You make us sound like two old biddies!" Ceri replied, giving Hanna a playful punch in the ribs.

Hanna smiled. "We've grown up. Learned not to take things at face value."

"That's for sure." Ceri frowned as she contemplated the bay.

"You've got something on your mind, haven't you?" Hanna asked. "I can tell. C'mon, tell me."

Ceri hesitated, playing with the straw in her coffee. "Well, Sergio and I have been discussing the future. We were both pretty cut up by what happened after the wedding. So was Vincenzo. He's decided to retire from the police, get out of Palermo, find a place by the sea somewhere and spend some time with Marta while he can."

Hanna raised her eyebrows in surprise. "Really?" She sensed there was more to come.

Ceri shrugged. "As for Sergio and me, we can't live our lives permanently looking over our shoulders. And we can't jeopardise our chance of having a family."

This was sounding familiar. Hanna looked at her expectantly.

"So, we've decided to move away and go to the mainland. Sergio has accepted that job offer in Rome. It'll be better for his career, but more importantly it'll be better for us." Ceri paused, as if unsure how Hanna would take the news.

Hanna sprang out of her chair and wrapped both arms around her friend and hugged her tightly. "That's amazing! I'm so pleased for you both!"

Ceri grimaced. "Hey, watch out for my stitches!"

"Sorry, I forgot," said Hanna, withdrawing slightly.

"Yeah, I think it's the right decision," Ceri said, wriggling out of the embrace, looking a little embarrassed. "You saw yourself how badly Sergio reacted to the shooting and losing the baby. Then, when his dad announced his decision to retire, it was as if the last obstacle had been removed. Without being so involved with the police, Sergio'll no longer be a potential target. And Rome's not a million miles away from Sicily; we can always come over and visit Vincenzo and Marta."

"Fabulous! And we'll have somewhere to stay when we come to Rome!" Hanna teased.

"Yeah, a ready-made holiday home!" Ceri gave a wry smile and slowly shifted back in her chair.

"How soon will it be before you can make the move?" Hanna asked.

"Just need to get the trafficking story out of the way. You know how these media stories can drag on, with different angles and so on," Ceri replied. "Maybe a couple of weeks? I should be fully recovered by then. They've got a rental apartment waiting for us, apparently."

Hanna looked out to sea. She could just make out the blurred shape of a ferry on the horizon. "I'll have no reason to come back here once you two are in Rome. I'll miss all this when I go back to Wales," she said, a touch wistfully, gesturing with her hands, "but not necessarily for all the right reasons..."

CHAPTER FIFTY-NINE

The early afternoon flight was half–empty, and Hanna had the row of seats to herself. She watched through the window as the plane taxied down the runway and soared effortlessly into a perfect azure sky. The sea below glimmered enticingly in the sun and the mountains rose majestically behind Palermo. A stunning view. Shame the island had such a rotten pervasive core. She felt relieved to be leaving it all behind.

She sighed and settled back in her seat, unfurling the morning edition of *La Gazzetta della Sicilia*. Sergio's exclusive was splashed across the whole front page of the broadsheet, accompanied by several photographs of the arrests.

POLICE BUST MAJOR PEOPLE TRAFFICKING RING, the headline screamed.

Police in Sicily have arrested 54 people, including several alleged mafiosi, in a number of dawn raids, believed to be one of the largest drives against people-trafficking on the island. The arrests are the result of a wide-scale investigation involving several European countries. Further arrests are understood to have been made in Britain, Germany, France and Sweden.

Two Mafia clans are believed to be at the centre of the smuggling network: the Cortazzo and the Mancuso families. The two clans, once in violent conflict, are believed to have ended their turf wars and traditional activities to form a trafficking ring in collaboration with a Nigerian gang based in Palermo. The operation is described by the police as being 'extremely lucrative'.

Most migrants and asylum seekers arrive in Sicily by sea, taking the dangerous route across the Mediterranean from Tunisia and Libya, often arranged by unscrupulous people-smugglers. Many migrants travel without papers and make the crossing in appalling conditions in overcrowded and unseaworthy boats, paying an average of 440 euros for the privilege. Lifejackets and fake documents may be available at extra cost.

Almost 25,000 migrants arrived in Sicily in this way last year – of those, nearly 2,300 were reported as dead or missing at sea. On arrival, many of the women are forced into the sex trade, while some of the men are coerced into low-level crime and drug-dealing.

Before she could read any more, she experienced an overwhelming feeling of nausea. She rose unsteadily to her feet and made a dash for the toilet, only just making it in time to retch over the basin. Her reflection stared back in the mirror, and she realised with a shock how wan and bleary-eyed she looked. *Stress,* she thought, *or was it something more?* Several times that week she had felt like this. She wondered if she might have some underlying condition. *Don't be silly,* she admonished herself, *you're worrying unnecessarily. It'll be nothing.*

She rinsed her mouth, splashed cold water on her face, dried it with a paper towel and staggered back to her seat. She picked up the newspaper and continued reading:

Although the number of migrants is reported to be lower than in previous years, profits are kept high due to the increasing demand for minors. Girls as young as twelve or thirteen have been found working the streets of Palermo and other Italian and European cities.

Among those arrested in the raids by members of the paramilitary carabinieri and Guardia di Finanza financial police were the heads of the two clans, the leader of the Nigerian gang, and several public officials, including a local MP, a mayor, and the director of one of the island's largest migrant reception centres.

The network is believed to be the largest trafficking ring on the island, and the arrests will effectively bring its nefarious activities to an end.

"We are determined to stamp out this insidious traffic on our island once and for all," said Paolo Randazzo, head of the Palermo police flying squad. "We will be seeking maximum prison sentences for all those convicted."

Hanna leaned back in her seat, her heart pounding, thinking back to her last conversation with Vincenzo. He'd just been discharged home from hospital, and Hanna had popped round to say goodbye. He too had assured her that the prosecutors would be looking for maximum sentences.

"This will be a high-profile trial case," he'd said, clasping her hands in his. "The first time we've been able to bust a people-trafficking ring at this level. The prosecutors want to send a clear message to other traffickers that Sicily isn't a free-for-all, and the police will crack down and make offenders pay. The eyes of Europe are upon us with this case. We don't want to make a *brutta figura* – show ourselves up in a bad light.

"You'll see, *mia cara*. This time, they'll lock up the Cortazzos and throw away the key."

"I certainly hope so," Hanna had replied with a smile. She wanted to be convinced, but yet...

Pull yourself together, she told herself. *Time to put the past behind you and move on. Time for a new beginning. Release at last.*

Her hand flew to her mouth as she realised what might be making her feel nauseous.

Oh my God, if only...

That would be simply perfect, she thought, a warm, fuzzy feeling spreading through her body.

ACKNOWLEDGEMENTS

My thanks to the Bloodhound team for all their help and support in republishing this novel.

A special thank-you to everyone who provided invaluable feedback as the book began to take shape and on completion which helped me to polish it into the final version. Of note, Alice Umbarak from Stockport Writers and Sue Barnard, Jo Fenton, Louise Jones, and Pauline Barnett from Manchester Scribes. Louise has a forensic eye for detail and is always ready with helpful advice when she feels something isn't working.

I mustn't forget to mention Lexi, my cat, who has deleted many a paragraph, waltzing across the keyboard trying to attract my attention. Those paragraphs obviously didn't meet her exacting standards.

And lastly, I would like to say how wonderful it has been to see how the writing community has continued to support and encourage each other during this difficult period of enforced isolation.

ABOUT THE AUTHOR

Karen Moore discovered a love of writing after many years spent on the road travelling throughout Europe, North America, and Canada as a tour guide. Tired of living out of a suitcase, she moved on to pursue a career in PR and marketing, working in sectors as diverse as travel, finance, and health.

Italy and all things Italian remain a constant source of inspiration for her writing, as does her fascination with the darker side of human nature and how ordinary people react to challenging situations.

Her first two novels, *Torn* and *Release*, are tales of intrigue and betrayal set in Sicily and North Wales. Both are Amazon bestsellers. A third novel is on the way.

Karen has lived in Italy and France and is currently based in Cheshire, England.

A NOTE FROM THE PUBLISHER

Thank you for reading this book. If you enjoyed it please do consider leaving a review on Amazon to help others find it too.

We hate typos. All of our books have been rigorously edited and proofread, but sometimes mistakes do slip through. If you have spotted a typo, please do let us know and we can get it amended within hours.

info@bloodhoundbooks.com

www.ingramcontent.com/pod-product-compliance
Lightning Source LLC
Chambersburg PA
CBHW031321210726
48287CB00005B/1636